THE

CARIBBEAN

EVENING

EDWIN (EDDIE) ELFORD is a retired police sergeant who, as a rookie, found himself in the East End of London close to the famous Petticoat Lane. After service at several stations in the Metropolis, he had the chance to be an Instructor at Peel House and at Hendon. On leaving the Force, he became a teacher, then one of the managers of a leisure centre and, finally, spent 12 years in management in the Ministry of Defence.

By the same author:

'Confession', a novel

'They can't box at Oxford', a short story

THE

CARIBBEAN

EVENING

Edwin Elford

Published in Great Britain by Edwin Elford

Printed and bound by Lulu

ISBN 978-0-9559770-1-5

My thanks to Richard Ellington, Stuart Maclure and Richard Brown for their help and Philip Maltman for the cover design.

CHAPTER ONE

A piece of dried leaf, disturbed by the movement of air, spiralled very slowly downwards, twisting and turning as if reluctant to complete its journey.

After a seemingly endless passage of time, it finally reached the surface of the water below, sending out circles which slowly increased in size but diminished in density.

Suddenly, the edge of the circle on one side altered dramatically as it traced the outline of something floating in the water.

It was the body of a man.

He was floating incongruously face downwards, arms outstretched, hands hanging loosely and rising up and down gently with the movement of the water, in the shallow part of the Parkdale Leisure Centre pool, at a point where it reduced in depth until it resembled a sea shore.

He was dressed in grey trousers and a blue check shirt, which was open down the front and floated out behind. His blonde hair drifted lazily around the head like a sea anemone and seemed to be matted in places, as if blood from wounds had congealed and then partly washed away. The right ear flapped loosely. Occasionally a faint red stain would issue from the dark open wound, where once the ear had been fully attached. Other lacerations could be seen on the side of the face and neck and the thumb of the right hand drifted crazily beside the fingers.

******

Two elderly cleaners, named Ada and Betty, were approaching the Leisure Centre on this bright, sunny Saturday morning, oblivious of what lay ahead. They were both hardworking cockneys who could be replied upon to get a laugh out of any situation. They were chatting about their families and what they had seen on the telly the previous night.

'Ade, did you see the Two Ronnies last night?'

'Yes...weren't they good? That little one makes me laugh.'

'Me too, but the fat one is the clever one. I read

somewhere that he writes some of those scenes himself.'

'I didn't know that, but they were a good laugh. The scene about the Os and the 'ose in the 'ardware shop creases me up.'

'Me too. You got the keys, Ade?'

Ada was searching for them in her enormous handbag.

'I wonder you can find anything in that bag of yours' Betty chided, waiting patiently, her thoughts turned to the job ahead, which could take longer than usual after the big Caribbean Evening the previous night.

They made their way past the large glass doors to the entrance at the back of the Centre which led to the swimming pool area.

Ada, having found the keys, said in a puzzled voice 'That's funny, Betty, it ain't locked. Who was Duty Manager last night?'

'Dave Fisher. I'll bet he was pissed again' replied Ada, scornfully. It wasn't the first time that they had found the Centre open, and always after Fisher, the Deputy Manager, had been on duty.

'Put the kettle on, Ade' said Betty, as they automatically slipped into their overalls and changed their outdoor shoes. The customary cup of char would have to be brewed before any work began.

Betty made her way to the control panel and switched on all the swimming pool lights. The sudden brightness made her blink as she looked over towards the side of the pool which she knew would require special cleaning. This area of the poolside was covered with a green waterproof carpet and it was here that the dancers from the night before had enjoyed themselves.

'It doesn't look too bad' she thought to herself and turned to go back to the staff room for her tea.

Suddenly she froze.

She had seen the body.

'Ada' she screamed, in a voice which brought Ada scuttling out of the little room faster than she had moved for years.

'What's up Bet?' she shouted anxiously, her heart thumping.

'Look' she gasped, pointing a shaking finger towards the part of the pool where the body was floating.

'Ooer' whispered Ada 'oo the 'ell is it? You know - that blonde 'air don't 'arf look like Dave Fisher's.'

'Can't say from 'ere Ade, and I ain't gonna go no nearer to find out.'

'Better get the law' said Betty, seriously 'and I'm ready for that cuppa – me knees is like bleedin' jelly.'

It normally took quite a lot to shake these two hardened campaigners. They had stayed in London throughout the war and survived all that Hitler's bombers could throw at them. During that time they had seen many dead bodies.

But this wasn't wartime and if that body was Dave Fisher's then it was a bit too near home.

With shaking fingers Betty dialled 999 from the office. They both collapsed into chairs and waited for the police to arrive.

It wasn't long before the local Area Car arrived, with two officers, followed closely by an Inspector who was the Duty Officer from the local station and who immediately assumed control. There wasn't much doubt that the man was dead, a quick examination confirmed this, but following strict procedure the Inspector put out a call for the Divisional Surgeon to be contacted and at the same time for the senior Detective Superintendent to be notified, as the overall responsibility for the investigation would be his.

Having set the wheels in motion, the Inspector posted his men to ensure that nothing at the scene would be touched or interfered with and gratefully accepted the cup of tea on offer.

******

Detective Chief Inspector Robert McKay groaned and turned over reluctantly as the phone rang at his bedside. With difficulty he eventually located the bedside lamp and switched it on. Propping himself up on one elbow, he squinted at his watch. Christ! It was 7.15 am and it was Saturday morning and, what was more important, it was his weekend off. So who the bloody hell was ringing him? He knew before he picked up the phone that it could only be trouble. He was right. After exchanging a few brief words, he replaced the phone, sank back on the pillows and groaned again.

'That was the Chief Super, love' he said apologetically to his wife, who had drawn the covers back over her head when the phone had rung 'I'm afraid we'll have to have that trip out another time.'

His wife, Margaret, had never been able to come to terms with continually having their private lives spoiled by what was known in police jargon as the 'exigencies of the service'. She appreciated the fact that it was all part of the job but invariably she was the one who had to explain to Ian, her disappointed son, that their father would be missing again. This was to have been his first weekend off for ages and the intention was for them all to go out as a family – to the Jubilee Celebrations - now, as usual, it would all be left to her.

She considered expressing her feelings, decided that no good could come of it and instead got up, put on her dressing gown and slippers and said 'I'll get you some breakfast before you go.'

'Thanks, love' replied McKay, gratefully 'Just toast

and coffee will be fine.' Sitting now on the edge of the bed, he picked up the phone again and dialled.

The news was received at the other end of the line in much the same disappointed way by his partner, Detective Sergeant Charles Bennett, whom he arranged to pick up as soon as possible

McKay yawned, stretched himself and then suddenly jumped up and headed for the bathroom.

He was awake.

McKay, as the name implies, was a Scot and fiercely proud of it. He was thirty-two years old, just under six feet tall and in exceptionally good shape for a CID officer with thirteen years service. He wasn't a fitness fanatic, the long unsociable hours he had to work being hardly conducive to 'the healthy mind in the healthy body' maxim. However, he did work out whenever possible and tried, not always successfully, to keep the drink down to the minimum.

Looking in the mirror, as he moved his electric shaver round the dark stubble on his chin, his face showed disappointment at having his weekend spoiled, but the dark eyes glistened with anticipation. This latest assignment sounded interesting. He quickly brushed his black wiry hair, which was beginning to recede a bit, and couldn't fail to notice the tell-tale streaks of grey alongside the temples. At the same time he thought 'I'm getting older.' His nose had suffered during his rugby days, when he had clashed with a huge front row forward, not to mention several adjustments to his eyebrows where stitches had been inserted. His face was beginning to have that lived-in look.

Back in the bedroom, he dressed with just a little more care than usual, knowing that the first day of any case was likely to attract considerable attention from the press and photographers. It was this kind of attention to detail which he found paid off - looking ahead and trying to some extent to anticipate future events. He made his way downstairs.

Passing his elder son Jamie's bedroom, he had an idea. Opening the door, he could see him fast asleep, half hidden under the crumpled duvet. The ringing of the telephone next door had not affected him in any way.

'Jamie ... Jamie ' he shook his shoulder gently at first – and then harder.

His son's brow frowned with displeasure, one eye opened, he blinked and said 'What is it, Dad?'

'Jamie, I want you to do me a big favour. I've been called to a murder at the Leisure Centre so I won't be able to take your mother and Ian to the Jubilee Celebrations – will you take my place?'

'Oh, Dad' he replied, sitting up in the bed and rubbing his eyes 'I was going out with my mates to see the new James Bond film.'

'Yes, I know, but your Mum and Ian were looking forward so much to us going out together. I'll make it up to you' he added quickly 'I promise I'll get you some tickets for the Calcutta Cup Match at Twickenham, so that you can take your mates.'

'OK, well that sounds alright' Jamie replied, grudgingly 'but you realise I'll have to support England!'

'I can't do anything about that' said McKay, with a grin 'Thanks, son, I must be off. Have a good time. See you later.'

McKay left the room feeling guilty that he had had to bribe his son in this way but, on the other hand, he was used to his wife being fed up with having family arrangements spoiled. He made his way downstairs and was greeted by the smell of toast and fresh coffee and his wife bustling around the kitchen. He kissed her quickly, saying 'Sorry I'm going to be missing, love, but Jamie has volunteered to take my place today, so maybe it won't be so bad after all.'

Margaret looked surprised 'Volunteered? How did you manage that, Robert McKay?'

'Well, maybe he had to be persuaded a little. It looks like a fine day' he added 'any marmalade, love?'

After a hurried breakfast and, after a few more inadequate words of sympathy to his dejected wife, he was off.

Margaret waved as he backed the car out and drove away. McKay or Mac, as he was known to his friends, headed for Charlie Bennett's house. Inevitably his thoughts turned to the case ahead. Would it be straightforward and over quickly, or much more difficult and drag on for months or even years, with little to show at the end of it?

As he pondered, the adrenalin started to flow. Whatever lay ahead it would be a challenge - and there was nothing McKay enjoyed more than a challenge. As far as he was concerned, that was what police work was all about and the reason why it was his chosen career.

Detective Sergeant Charles Bennett, known to villains and colleagues alike as Charlie, made his way down the garden path as the car pulled up. Forty-five years old and grey haired, he was older and shorter than McKay and was in his 25th year in the Force - always a milestone in a policeman's career, because it was possible to retire at this stage on a limited pension. Charlie, however, had no such intention, as he enjoyed life and his work just the way it was at the moment.

Like McKay, and despite his much longer service, he looked forward eagerly to the job ahead. Charlie was a

South-East Londoner, as anyone would easily have discerned as he piped up cheerfully 'Mornin', Guvnor, know what the job is?'

'How the hell can he be so cheerful at this time of day?' thought McKay, as he smiled and answered 'Morning, Charlie - only that it's a suspicious death in that new leisure pool at the Sports Centre.'

Charlie's bushy eyebrows shot up as he exclaimed 'Blimey, Guv. I know most of the blokes down there, we've played against their darts team many times. I wonder who it is?' They were soon to find out.

CHAPTER TWO

The Leisure Centre had been built seven years earlier in 1970 and, situated adjacent to a local park, had rapidly become a very popular amenity in the borough. It was the main social centre for many of the local community and seemed to succeed in its aim, which was to improve the quality of life of children and adults of all ages.

The whole complex was divided into two main areas. On one side was the huge main hall, the sheer size of which led one to think in terms of an aircraft hangar. It was built in attractive red brick with dark grey pointing, as were the small gymnasium, squash courts and projectile hall, where the shooting, archery and gymnastic vault took place.

On the other side, leading off a spacious reception area,

were the sauna and solarium suites and the huge leisure pool. Its roof of metal and tinted glass was enormous and resembled the shape of the Astrodome in Texas; it contained many innovations, not the least being a tall palm tree surrounded by numerous exotic plants.

The Council was justly proud of the leisure pool; one of the first swimming pools in the London area to be built in free form, basically a circular shape, and containing a wave-making machine, much enjoyed by children and adults alike.

Pulling into the Sports Centre car park, McKay noticed the Area Car and another which belonged to the Duty Inspector, who met them and took them to where the body lay.

Suddenly a strange, unaccountable feeling came over Charlie. Most of his service had been spent in the CID and he had dealt with death on many occasions, but somehow at this moment he felt strangely uneasy. As soon as he saw the body and the long blonde hair floating out from the head he knew why.

'Christ, Guvnor' he whispered 'It looks like Dave Fisher, the Deputy Manager. He runs their darts team.'

'Well, if it is him, he won't be running any more darts teams, that's for sure' commented McKay, his Scottish brogue rolling the r's in the words 'more' and 'darts'.

The Inspector spoke next as they gazed down

hypnotically at the body, which was still gently rocking up and down with the movement of the water. 'Apparently they had something called a 'Caribbean Evening' here last night. Oh, and one of the cleaners seems to think that the body looks very like the Deputy Manager - a David Fisher.'

'Right, thanks' said McKay briskly 'Who have you informed?'

'The Detective Chief Super, as you know, and the Divisional Surgeon - he said he would be along quite soon.'

'Fine. Just make sure your boys keep everyone out of the Centre till we can go over it' replied McKay.

Turning to Charlie, he said 'Give SOCO a ring, will you? Tell them it's urgent, we can't do much till they arrive. Oh, and ring CID and get them to organise a Murder Room.'

'OK Guvnor, will do' replied Charlie and departed with the Duty Inspector.

McKay looked around him. He, too, had dealt with death on many occasions but seldom in such pleasant surroundings; he was amazed at the colour and beauty of the leisure pool. His eyes stopped searching when he noticed that the tables and chairs, which had obviously been used the night before, were still in position at one side of the pool. He moved towards them. All of the table tops had been cleared except for one, and as McKay approached he noticed a pint glass lying on its side. Beer from it had stained the table top and the floor beneath. Next to it was a whisky glass with some yellow liquid still at the bottom. McKay bent down and sniffed - it was whisky alright - being a Scot, he was not averse to a 'wee hauf' himself. A chair behind the table was lying on its side and a crumpled blazer with the Sports Centre badge on the pocket was hanging, half off the back.

He eased carefully away from the scene. Various thoughts raced through his mind as he tried to imagine what might have happened at this spot the night before. This was only natural, but he knew that it was fatal to have preconceived ideas before the body had been thoroughly examined and an autopsy performed. So much could be revealed in the pathologist's report, that he had to keep an open mind.

One thing, however, was abundantly clear - Fisher had not received those injuries at the pool side. The lack of blood confirmed this. The injury to the ear alone would have sent blood spurting all over the place.

Charlie appeared in the company of a tall, distinguished-looking man aged about thirty-five, with sleek black hair and a clipped moustache. He was wearing grey flannels and a blazer with the Sports Centre badge on the pocket - similar to the one McKay had seen on the back of the chair at the pool side.

The man was visibly shaken. As he reached McKay, Charlie introduced him, saying 'This is Mr. Veale, Sir. He's the Centre Duty Manager for the weekend.'

McKay nodded a greeting, saying curtly 'I'm afraid it looks as if there is some very bad news for you, Mr. Veale. Would you mind making a positive identification for us?'

'Certainly. Anything at all to help' replied Veale, his voice shaking 'But I can't believe what I've heard. What on earth happened?'

'We have no idea at the moment' replied McKay, as they made their way back to where the body lay.

Ted Veale stared down at the body for a long time, unable to accept what he was actually seeing.

Eventually, he replied quietly 'It's Dave Fisher alright, even without seeing his face properly I can tell it's him. I just can't believe it' he repeated, shaking his head slowly.

'When did you see him last?' asked McKay.

'I've been off for a couple of days prior to working this weekend - so it must have been on Wednesday afternoon.' As he looked at the body, his mind went back to the Wednesday just past. The time was almost 3.15 pm and he pictured himself sitting beside Dave Fisher in the Manager's office. He had been alive enough then, relaxed and sitting with one leg crossed over the other. He had a cigarette in his stained fingers as usual - balancing a clipboard on his knee.

It had been nearly time for the ritual weekly Management Meeting.

Mike Weston, the Manager, had been sifting through a pile of papers on his desk when the phone rang - he answered it. Suddenly his rugged features changed. His eyes narrowed perceptibly, his lips pressed together tightly and the knuckles of his left hand turned white as he made it into a fist. After several protestations he slammed it down.

'Sod it' he exploded, smashing the fist down on his desk top, causing a wooden pipe rack to leap into the air and rattle as the pipes settled down 'Those buggers from the Treasury Department have done it again.'

'Done what, Mike?' queried Fisher.

'They've got computer problems at the Town Hall' Weston replied 'and they only want us to produce the last three month's figures of the bar and cafeteria takings for the Borough Sports Council meeting tomorrow night.'

He ranted on 'They're sorry they couldn't give me more notice - sorry be buggered - they're always dropping bombshells like this.'

He gritted his teeth, sucked air noisily through them, sank back in his chair and looked up at the ceiling, as if searching for inspiration.

'Those sods will all go home from their ivory towers at five o'clock tonight. They haven't got a bloody clue about the sort of hours that we have to work or what's involved in running a Centre of this size.'

Dave Fisher, who had remained silent throughout his Manager's outburst, smiled sympathetically. He had heard it all before. He was quite used to the running battle which Mike kept up with the Town Hall officials.

Mike thumped the desk again with anger and frustration.

'I'm Duty Manager tonight, Mike' piped up Dave Fisher 'I'll give you a hand if you like.'

'Thanks very much Dave, I'd appreciate that.'

Weston reached for his pipe, filled it with tobacco from a small leather pouch, snapped on his lighter and puffed hard. Finally he sat back in his chair and relaxed saying 'I'll have to see if Barbara can stay on for a while - she will be pleased! I only hope she hasn't got a date or anything fixed up for tonight.'

Barbara Johnson was his secretary and was the next one to appear. She was thirty years old, tall, slim, very attractive and well-groomed, but after a failed marriage and an acrimonious divorce she was beginning to look more than her age. She was also a very competent secretary and had worked at the Centre since its opening. She handed minutes to those who needed them and a copy of the agenda to everyone. Then she sat down and, by carefully crossing her slim legs, she achieved maximum effect. Smoothing her skirt, she remained, pencil poised, waiting for her Manager to begin.

Mike puffed gently on his pipe; he had calmed down now and was ready to start the meeting.

He welcomed everyone as usual and then went quickly through the minutes of the previous week's meeting and invited comments. He checked that one or two items had been dealt with and went straight on to 'Today's Agenda.'

On reaching Item 8, 'The Caribbean Evening' to be held on Friday 16th, he said to Dave 'You're Duty Manager on Friday. Any problems?'

'Everything's under control. It's the crowd from the Bank so there shouldn't be any trouble, and the catering has been arranged.'

'Fine' replied Mike 'I've been invited and I'll be there.'

He returned to the agenda and, after dealing with 'Any Other Business', closed the meeting.

******

As Veale stared down at the body of Dave Fisher, he particularly remembered him saying how lucky he was to be on duty on the night of the Caribbean Evening. It looked as if his luck had run out. Suddenly his thoughts were interrupted - someone was talking to him.

It was McKay, who repeated 'I shall want you to formally identify the body later, if you wouldn't mind, Mr. Veale. Meanwhile, the Centre will obviously have to remain closed. Will you organise a notice to the public to that effect?'

'Cer-certainly' replied Veale, coming back to reality 'I'll get one of the attendants to see to it right away. Oh, by the way, has the Manager been informed' he added.

'No, not yet' replied McKay.

'I don't know how he's going to take all this. Look, he doesn't live very far away, would you like me to ring him - or call round' enquired Veale.

'Thank you, but that won't be necessary. I shall be seeing him myself.'

'Just as you wish' said Veale and, after taking one more look at the body of his colleague, he walked slowly away shaking his head and murmuring 'I still can't believe it.'

******

Veale now recollected that, after the Management Meeting the previous Wednesday, he had left the room at the end of the meeting with Fisher, who had said 'Christ, Ted, my mouth's dry, I could murder a pint'.

'Well the bar isn't open yet, but come upstairs and I'll

buy you a coffee' Veale had replied.

Fisher had accepted the offer. It was a poor substitute as far as he was concerned but it would have to do. Fisher loved his drink. He had no respect for his kidneys at all - in fact he was at the stage of having a serious drink problem and wasn't worried one bit. The slightest excuse to have a good drink, as he put it, was seized upon and very often ended up with him legless.

The drink had already begun to take its toll, as he looked more like forty than thirty. He had also become unpredictable - a real Jekyll and Hyde character. Pleasant and helpful when sober - awkward and nasty when in his cups.

It wasn't that he was unintelligent - he had a good brain. His present position in the management structure proved this. His area of special responsibility, the leisure pool, was well run and he had a sound knowledge of the recreation scene. He had spent a year of his life attending college acquiring a Diploma in Management Studies, which had helped him with his promotion.

However, what let Dave Fisher down was his theory that business could only be transacted in the relaxed atmosphere of a bar. This was all right up to a point, but he always carried it too far. He could never decide where work finished and socialising began and by the time he had put away a few pints he was past caring anyway. His

27

excessive drinking had already led to his being officially warned by the Manager.

******

The Scenes of Crime Officer arrived - he was well known to McKay. He was a short, fat, middle-aged man with grey hair, which curled at the nape of the neck and he was wearing jeans, sneakers, a shirt and a casual jumper. He was accompanied by a tall, more formally dressed, young man, laden with photographic gear.

With Charlie's help, they began, in a very efficient manner, to photograph the body, the surroundings and finally the area of the poolside where the tables and overturned chair were situated. They meticulously dusted every item which might offer up a fingerprint of some sort, no matter how remote.

The Divisional Surgeon arrived, none too pleased either at having his Saturday morning disturbed. After a quick examination of the body which had been moved up on to the shore part of the pool, he pronounced life extinct and departed.

Next to appear was the Coroner's Officer, in the huge shape of Brian Jolly. His initial and name, coupled with his present occupation, was one of those strange legacies created by unthinking parents. Still, as he was quick to point out when ribbed by his colleagues 'If my name had been De'ath I wouldn't have got the job at all.' His name certainly fitted his character because he stood 6 feet 2 inches tall, weighed 15 stones, and always seemed to be happy. Perhaps it was the constant dealing with death, in all its horrific complexities, that forced him to adopt this attitude in order to remain sane.

He was, in all respects, a gentle giant. His pleasant manner in dealing with the relatives of the 'sudden deaths', which he came across in the course of his duties, had led to numerous letters addressed to his Superintendent, expressing gratitude for the sympathy and understanding shown by the big man.

He was well known to the CID and Uniform Branch alike, as their paths crossed so many times in the course of everyday police work. He also enjoyed the power which the position gave him. Late in his service he had discovered the niche which suited him. Never a promotion seeker, he found the work rewarding. It also gave him a certain amount of freedom and bound him more to the rules and procedures relating to dead bodies than the Police Act or Discipline Code. In a way his allegiance was more to the Coroner than to his own Superintendent. The latter often sought his advice and direction - a unique situation in the police service.

A typical example of this was McKay's request 'What

do you think, Brian - is there much point in getting the pathologist down to examine the body in situ?'

'Not really, Sir' replied Brian, cheerfully 'He's obviously been well washed by now. But what about your Chief Super, is he coming down?'

'I'm just going to ring him, as a matter of fact.'

'We could get on much quicker if we didn't have to wait for him to see the body here, you know.'

'Yes, I realise that Brian. I'll arrange for him to see it down at the mortuary.'

'Good' agreed Brian 'Then we can get the body bagged up and moved down there as soon as the boys have finished with him.'

McKay called the Station and the team, assisted now by Brian Jolly, continued their various tasks. Then he approached the body once more.

Once turned over on its back, there had been no doubt it was Fisher. The longish blonde hair had fallen away from his face on either side and hid the marks on his neck. However, it did not hide the right ear which clung perilously to the side of the head, while the lifeless steel-blue eyes stared heavenwards in disbelief.

The SOCO and Charlie were busy making various tests in the pool. The most important being the recording of the ambient temperature of the water at various depths, together with the surrounding air temperature. Both facts would be invaluable to the pathologist in his assessment of the probable time of death - a factor eagerly awaited by McKay.

The bagging-up had begun, in order to protect the body and all its clues until a more thorough examination could be made. It started with each hand being carefully enclosed in a polythene bag and sealed at the wrist in order to protect the fingers - particularly the scrapings from under the fingernails. These would be microscopically studied later in the police laboratories. The procedure ended with the whole body being wrapped in a huge plastic sheet and secured, ready for transportation to the mortuary.

McKay took one last look at the spot where Dave Fisher had come to rest. Normally, with the injuries it had received, the body would have been covered with blood, but the warm waters had cleansed the wounds and saved the mortician a job. He also made a mental note to speak to the Manager about the filtration system which had removed all signs of blood from the pool. Unless Fisher had been killed elsewhere and dumped in the pool, then someone, somehow, had delivered vicious blows to his head whilst he was in the water. The dislocated thumb and finger seemed to indicate that he had probably tried unsuccessfully to protect himself.

Detective Sergeant George Turner, one of Charlie's

colleagues, appeared with an assortment of boxes and polythene bags. He was to be the 'exhibits officer', a vital link between the investigating officers and the forensic side of things. Turner took possession of every item of Fisher's property, which he meticulously recorded, labelled and placed carefully in polythene bags. Then, under McKay's direction, he followed the same procedure with every other item found at the scene which could have the slightest connection with the murder.

Finally, they all filed out, carrying their gruesome load and accessories, to board different vehicles and make their way in procession to the mortuary.

McKay considered the next steps to be taken. Obviously the leisure pool would have to be searched and this would mean calling upon the services of the Police Underwater Search Unit. He could just imagine their delight at the prospect of working in such pleasant surroundings with the luxury of being able to actually see what they were looking for. A unique situation, because almost without exception their work was carried out by feel alone. Usually in pitch darkness, in the cloying mud and slime at the bottom of rivers, canals or gravel pits amid such hazards as vicious clinging weed and roots. Closer to home there was the additional problem of negotiating old bedsteads, prams, barbed wire and other items which Londoners disposed of in a hurry.

Yes, it would be a pleasant change for them and McKay looked forward to giving them a decent job for once.

Next, as soon as sufficient troops could be mustered, every inch of the poolside and surrounding area would have to be searched. McKay looked disconsolately at the hundreds of exotic plants, all growing profusely in the warm atmosphere, any one of which could easily be hiding the murder weapon. It was going to be a monumental task, and one which he could easily leave to whoever was in charge of the Murder Room, soon to be established. He had other fish to fry.

The pool seemed strangely silent once more. All that could be heard was the pleasant lapping and bubbling of the clean, filtered water as it recycled the old, which disappeared into grilles to repeat the process again. It must have been quiet and peaceful like this as Dave Fisher sat enjoying his last drink before he was disturbed.

But by whom?

McKay's thoughts were interrupted by Charlie's return. Together they searched Fisher's office for a suicide note or any indication that he intended to take his own life. This was, of course, one possibility that had to be checked.

McKay had itchy feet 'Charlie, I'm going to break the news to the Centre Manager myself - I want to see his immediate reaction. He doesn't live very far away and we need him here anyway. I shouldn't be long.'

'OK, Guvnor. Where do you want me to start?'

'Cop a statement from Veale, as the first person to identify the body. Oh, and you might as well get one from the cleaning ladies as well.'

McKay was already on his way to the door.

CHAPTER THREE

McKay arrived at the Manager's flat within minutes - the first joint of his index finger showed white as he kept up the pressure on the bellpush.

Inside, Mike Weston in his subconscious state was trying desperately to decide whether the ringing he could hear was in his head or if it was the doorbell.

He raised his head from the pillow, opened his eyes, and listened. It was the doorbell. He had enjoyed himself immensely the night before at the Caribbean Evening, but part of the enjoyment was the knowledge that he could lie-in the following morning.

Like McKay earlier, he too wondered who the hell was disturbing him at this early hour. Actually it was about nine o'clock by this time, but it seemed much earlier to

Weston. Whoever was ringing the bell was certainly persistent. The continuous ring gave the impression that they were unlikely to go away till the door was answered.

He sat up in bed grudgingly, yawned, rubbed his eyes and dragged himself out of bed. He looked at his partner, Jenny Marlowe, who was sleeping soundly, completely oblivious of the noise. He smiled to himself; in sleep she looked even more gorgeous, with her dark tousled hair contrasting with the pink silken pillows.

Pulling on a dressing gown, he headed for the door.

'Alright, alright! I'm coming, you impatient bastard' he grumbled, as the shrill note of the bell became louder in his ears 'You'll wear the bloody thing out.'

He opened the door and immediately screwed up his eyes as the bright sunlight attacked them. He blinked and raised a hand as a shield, at the same time trying desperately to clear his head.

The face he saw in front of him was vaguely familiar.

'Mr. Weston?' demanded the person.

'Yes, what is it?' replied Mike, grumpily.

'Detective Chief Inspector McKay' the person announced, thrusting a police warrant card in his direction 'I'm afraid I've got some rather bad news for you. Mind if I come in?'

'Yes - er, do - please' stammered Mike, who stood back with one arm outstretched to admit his visitor.

Closing the door behind him, his thoughts raced. What on earth could be wrong this time to warrant the visit of a Detective Chief Inspector? He was only too well aware that his large staff at the Centre was truly a mixed bag. It wouldn't be the first time that one of them had got into serious trouble.

'Come in here, please' he said, leading the way into a comfortably furnished lounge.

'Take a seat.'

McKay chose one of two armchairs which were close to each other.

Weston stopped beside the mantlepiece and selected a pipe from a polished wooden rack. The familiar feel of his favourite Meerschaum gave him comfort as he braced himself.

'OK. Tell me the worst' he said, easing down into the other armchair.

McKay turned his chair to face Weston and asked casually 'Dave Fisher, your deputy. When did you see him last?'

'As a matter of fact, it was late last night' replied Mike, calmly 'Why?'

McKay ignored the question and continued 'Where was that?'

'At the Centre, he was duty manager last night at the Caribbean Evening - why what's happened?' he demanded, in a louder puzzled voice.

'I'm afraid he was found dead in the leisure pool just after seven o'clock this morning' said McKay in a slow deliberate voice, watching the Manager's face intently.

Weston's mouth opened, the pipe dropped into his lap. His face was one of total disbelief as he gasped 'Dave dead. I don't believe it.' Then, realizing that a senior detective was unlikely to get such things wrong, he hastily enquired 'How on earth did it happen?'

'There hasn't been time to establish that yet' replied McKay. 'I was rather hoping that you might be able to assist me on that score.'

'Certainly – anything, anything' gabbled Weston, hastily.

'What was he like when you saw him last?'

The question remained unanswered. Mike Weston suddenly felt very cold. He stood up, crossed to a drinks cabinet in the corner of the room and poured himself a large scotch.

'Can I offer you anything?'

McKay shook his head and said quickly 'But you carry on, by all means.'

Weston raised the glass to his lips, threw his head back and swallowed hard. The yellow liquid burnt all the way down. His body shook and then the feeling of inner warmth comforted him. In his mind he could visualise

Dave Fisher standing at the bar the previous night, downing a scotch, just the way he had done.

McKay waited patiently for an answer to his question and eventually he suggested 'Perhaps it would help if you take me carefully though your movements last night?'

Weston nodded. Unhurried, he helped himself to another scotch, relit his pipe and settled down again in the armchair. He started at the point where he and Jenny were approaching the leisure pool to attend the Caribbean Evening. Proceedings had been well under way. The coloured lights shone upwards through the domed roof giving a pleasing inviting effect and the sounds of a lively West Indian steel band could be heard coming from within.

Mike remembered drawing Jenny closer to him in anticipation of the pleasure to come and the way she had looked up at him, her face radiant. Considerably younger than him, she was slim and very attractive with dark hair and brown eyes. They had met at a time when Mike's marriage was on the rocks and stayed together. He had never been able to believe his luck that, just when he was at his lowest after the breakdown of his marriage, she had come along.

They had been together for two years now and were both very happy. They had made their way jauntily along the corridor, through the large swing doors and on to the poolside.

The atmosphere felt electric. The reflection of the coloured lights, which had been hung all around, sparkled on the surface of the water. Even the plants had taken on a different aura, some looked mysterious as their outlines cast shadows around the pool. The whole scene was dominated by the huge palm tree whose vast leaves partially blocked out the night sky. The air was filled with lively music and movement from the steel band. The musicians in their red silk shirts with black-frilled cuffs added further to the colour. Their gyrating bodies seemed to be completely consumed by the music. The darkness of their faces broken only by the flashing of white teeth as they smiled and laughed.

'Have you noticed that they almost seem to be in another world?' remarked Mike.

Jenny laughed easily - the atmosphere had been so friendly and the gaiety infectious.

He remembered looking towards the side of the pool where the scene was completed by the dancers themselves. Some women wore bikinis, others brightly-coloured blouses and skirts, while the men wore mostly light summer attire.

'As colourful as possible' had been the dress of the day order and, because it was expected that the temperature would be pretty high because of the plants and the warm water, 'As scantily dressed as possible' for comfort.

Mike and Jenny had edged their way through the tables to where their friends from the bank were sitting. Jonathan Maynard, the Bank Manager, had risen to greet them. They knew most of the bank people, as they had attended numerous social functions in the past. The formalities over, Mike automatically looked around the possible trouble spots. Everything seemed to be going smoothly. The bars were busy but the two bar girls and Bob Forrester, who was really the Centre Plant Engineer, seemed to be coping adequately.

'The usual, Jenny?' said Mike, after enquiring round the table.

'Yes' she replied 'but with a slimline tonic.'

Mike smiled to himself as he eased his way to the bar - he was the one who needed to cut down on the intake - as the tell-tale bulges around his midriff told the story of too much desk work. 'But not tonight' he thought, as he collected the drinks.

Tony Lopez, the Catering Manager, had appeared; he was short and dark with large bags under his eyes, testament to too many late nights dealing with functions.

'Has Dave Fisher been in yet?' enquired Mike.

'He was in earlier, but went back over the other side.' This meant the sports side of the Centre.

Mike had returned to the table and they sipped their

drinks and chatted to their friends till Jenny could stand it no longer; the beat of the music was so infectious that she jumped up saying 'Come on, Mike, let's dance.'

Joining the other dancers, they were quickly into the swing of things. The music was terrific to dance to. They had both enjoyed the dancing very much, as did the rest of the crowd present who were obviously out for a good time.

Mike then noticed Dave Fisher had come in, gone straight up to the bar and downed what appeared to be a large scotch.

'That's funny' he had thought 'He usually sticks to lager' but he was then immediately caught up in the dance again.

The evening had continued until the band took a break and it was refreshment time. Tony Lopez and his staff handled an excellent buffet, while sales at the bar seemed to be doing well.

Mike always had difficulty in divorcing himself from the proceedings on occasions such as these. He was off duty, but still felt that the ultimate responsibility was his. Jenny was usually the one who reminded him that his staff could manage perfectly well without him and, reluctantly, he had to agree.

Dave Fisher was back at the bar again, being served by Bob Forrester, and Mike made mental note to have a word with him about his drinking. Mike was more than happy to employ Forrester in the bar situation because it meant that, should anything technical go wrong, Bob was at hand to deal with it. He was one these really practical men who could turn his hand to anything and was a very useful member of the leisure centre team.

The evening wore on and everyone seemed to be enjoying themselves.

'Another drink, Jenny?' asked Mike.

'No, I'd rather not' she replied and looked at Mike in such a way that made him ask 'Do you want to go then?'

She nodded. They had made their excuses, said goodnight to their friends and headed for the door.

'Everything alright?' said Mike to Dave Fisher, as they passed the bar.

'No problems, Mike. Everything's going fine' he replied 'Hope you enjoyed yourself, Jenny. Goodnight.'

Weston brought himself back to the present and looked straight at McKay, saying slowly 'Those were the last words Fisher spoke to me.' Feeling his eyes start to water, he blinked several times. Then, raising his glass, he threw the rest of the contents to the back of his throat, turned his head and stared out of the window.

McKay remained silent until Weston was more composed.

'You said that Fisher had downed a scotch earlier. Did

he seem upset or worried about anything?'

'No, he seemed quite normal.'

'Thank you for being so helpful, Mr. Weston - what happened next, after that?'

'Why, we returned here, of course, and went to bed, that is until you disturbed us just now.'

'You didn't return to the Centre for any reason?'

'No, of course not' replied Mike angrily, not liking the line of questioning.

'Don't get upset, Mr. Weston' said McKay, quickly 'These questions have to be asked. I suppose your girl friend can verify what you have just said?'

'Naturally' snapped Weston 'She's in the bedroom asleep. Have a look if you want to.'

McKay accepted the offer and put his head round the bedroom door. Sure enough she was fast asleep, oblivious to everything that was going on.

'Do you want me to wake her' asked Weston, coldly.

'No, that won't be necessary - I'll speak to her later' replied McKay, closing the door quietly. He headed for the front door, where he stopped and faced Weston again, saying 'We obviously need you down at the Centre for a variety of reasons, not the least being a full statement of what you have just told me.'

'Yes, of course' replied Weston, in a much calmer tone of voice 'Just give me time to change and I'll be right down.'

'Thanks again for your co-operation, Mr. Weston. I'll see you shortly.'

Weston closed the door behind McKay, turned and went back to the lounge and flopped into the armchair feeling shattered.

CHAPTER FOUR

Back at the Sports Centre once more, McKay was relieved to see a much-respected colleague in the shape of Detective Inspector Thomas Rogers, who was in charge of the Murder Room. They had worked together on many occasions and were good friends. This kind of work was Tommy Rogers' speciality and he was well known throughout the District as methodical and calculating. What was more to the point was the fact that his brain seemed to operate differently from his colleagues; he could see a connection between two scraps of information where no one else could. One of his prime duties was to supervise each reporting to the Murder Room, referred to in police terms as an 'action.' Each action being carefully logged and then allocated to a member of the Murder

Squad and the result of that action reported back personally to Tommy Rogers.

This careful logging and cross-checking of tiny scraps of information and statements could make all the difference between a speedy result and one which dragged on for months or years involving hundreds of hours of valuable police manpower.

Rogers had also managed to round up the beginnings of a squad of Detective Constables who would work under his direction and conduct the house-to-house enquiries. They would also take statements from everyone, no matter however unconnected to the crime they seemed to be, and generally do all the foot slogging. Judging by their faces, a few more weekends had been spoiled.

McKay was also pleased to see Tommy Rogers for another reason because, along with Charlie, he could now move out and get on with the investigation. But first he wanted a word with Ted Veale.

'Sergeant Bennett, here, tells me that Fisher wasn't married. But did he live alone?'

Veale thought for a moment and replied 'Difficult to say really. He always had a girl friend in tow, but I don't think any of them stayed at his flat permanently.'

'I see. Can you let me have his address?'

'Certainly. It's 45, Blackshore Road - only about fifteen minutes from here.'

'Thank you again, Mr. Veale. I shall no doubt want to see you again later.'

'Well, that's not a problem, I'm here for the weekend.'

As McKay and Bennett left the Centre they were greeted with flashlights, clicking cameras and a flood of questions, since the Press had got wind that something was up.

Particularly persistent was the young blonde-haired reporter from the local rag. Being local, he naturally expected a better deal than the others.

'Give me a break, Mr. McKay' he pleaded 'We saw the body come out - is it a man or a woman?'

McKay had always made a point of maintaining a good relationship with the Press and had found them useful many times in his career. However, on this occasion, he confined his reply to 'You've seen a body come out but you know that I can't give you anything till the next of kin have been informed.' Getting into Charlie's car he said 'There'll be a press conference later.'

Charlie put his foot down, leaving the rest of the questions unanswered. They were heading for the mortuary, where McKay wanted to get hold of the key to Fisher's flat. He had noticed a fairly worn Yale key on a bunch of keys found in the blazer pocket of the jacket which was lying at the poolside. A quick word with the Laboratory Liaison Officer and McKay obtained the bunch of keys, which had already been dusted for prints.

Within minutes Charlie was turning the car into Blackshore Road. They stopped outside number 45. It was a large detached house, built about the turn of the twentieth century - no doubt in earlier times it had been a large family house with servants and possibly stables at the rear. Now, like so many others, it had been taken over by a property developer and converted into flats and bedsits.

Working their way through the names beside the bell pushes, they found that Fisher's flat was on the third floor. Climbing the stairs, they paused for breath outside the door of the flat, which McKay was anxious to inspect before anyone else had the opportunity to blunder in and disturb things.

He pushed the key into the lock, turned it and the door opened. He sighed thankfully and they entered.

The first impression was not favourable. McKay wrinkled his nose at the smell of stale beer and cigarette smoke. The main room of the flat was poorly furnished, run down and mostly untidy.

Charlie broke the silence 'Doesn't strike you as being the domesticated type, Guv.'

'You can say that again' replied McKay, noticing the dirty dishes piled high in a sink in the curtained-off area which served as a kitchen.

Suddenly they heard a noise coming from behind a closed door, which had to be the bedroom. They instinctively spread themselves either side of the doorway. McKay cursed to himself that neither of them was armed, not even with a short truncheon. If it was bother, then it was going to be every man for himself. He glanced quickly round the room for something to protect himself with.

Another noise came from the room. Both men stared hypnotically at the door, waiting for it to open. Then a frightened girl's voice came plaintively from the room 'Is that you, Dave?'

McKay and Bennett both heaved a sigh of relief and smiled at each other.

'It's the police' said McKay 'Come out, will you.' Charlie was on the opening side of the door and they both watched as the handle turned slowly, followed by the opening of the door.

Out of the room came a poor specimen of womanhood, blinking her eyes as she tried to get used to the light. She was small and slightly built and her thin hand moved automatically to her head as she tried to tidy her scruffy, mousey hair. She was young and wore only a pink slip and pants. Her tiny nipples pushed out the slip where there should have been breasts. She looked anxiously from one to the other and, gaining confidence, demanded 'What the bloody hell do you lot want?'

The anger in her voice surprised McKay, who ignored the question and asked 'Are you alone?' at the same time looking past her into the bedroom.

'Yes, of course I am' she replied, angrily 'Look, what the hell is going on?'

This time McKay answered 'Would you mind telling me who you are and what you are doing in Mr. Fisher's flat.'

'I don't see what it's got to do with you, but I happen to be his sister' came the reply 'and I often stay here.' McKay could just discern a slight north-country accent.

'Where's Dave? He was supposed to come back last night. I must have fallen asleep waiting for him.' She looked from one to the other and repeated 'Where is he - nothing has happened to him, has it?'

'Put some clothes on' said McKay 'and we'll have a chat.'

As she turned, Charlie said 'Shall I make some tea?'

'Yes, please, over there' she replied, pointed to the curtained-off area, and disappeared into the bedroom. Charlie crossed to the cooker area, filled an electric kettle and plugged it in. Eventually he found some tea and, after hunting unsuccessfully for a clean cup, washed one of the dirty ones lying near the sink.

McKay had a quick look around the lounge to see if

51

there were any envelopes or notes which might have been left by Fisher, but without success.

Fisher's sister re-appeared wearing faded jeans and a sloppy thick knit jumper with a huge rollover collar; she had also tried and failed miserably to do something with her hair. It was a mess. She flopped down into an armchair and gratefully accepted the tea offered by Charlie. Placing her hands around the mug as if to warm them, she took a few sips of tea, looked up at McKay and said anxiously 'Something has happened to Dave, hasn't it? That's why you're here.'

'I'm afraid so, Miss Fisher' replied McKay 'When did you see him last?'

'One evening during the week. I think it was Tuesday, Yes, it was Tuesday.'

'Thank you. When did you arrive here?'

'Last night after work. I knew Dave was working 'lates' so I let myself in with my key.' Her voice changed, as she demanded 'Look, has he had an accident?'

'Yes' said McKay, quietly 'He has - a fatal one I'm afraid.'

She repeated McKay's words slowly '...a...fatal...one? Do you mean he's dead?' Her face showed real concern for the first time.

McKay nodded.

'No! I don't believe it' she said, shaking her head, her

eyes darting from side to side 'Dave...I don't believe it.' Her voice rose, hysterically 'What's happened – how did he die?'

McKay ignored the question, reached forward and relieved her of the cup.

She placed both hands over her face and started to cry. Soon her frail body shook with sobbing, the tears running through her fingers as she gradually accepted the fact that her brother was really dead.

McKay and Bennett offered what words of sympathy they could, always sounding inadequate. It was one of the necessary aspects of police work hated by all policemen alike and they were no exceptions.

She stopped crying almost as suddenly as she had started. Wiping her eyes and face with a crumpled piece of tissue, which she had produced from her jeans, she looked up at the two men and said 'I'm alright now - what happens next?'

'We understand that your mother lives up north. She will have to be told.'

'That's right, but I'd like to tell her myself, it will be better coming from me.'

'We would also like a full statement from you, if you feel up to it. I'll send a policewoman and a car to take you down to the station. Oh, and in the meantime I must ask you not to touch anything in the flat. It will have to be tested for fingerprints, and we'll have to take yours, I'm afraid, for purposes of elimination.'

'Yes, certainly - anything you say' she replied, having regained her composure 'Can I ring my mother from the station then?'

'Yes, that would be better' agreed McKay.

Charlie contacted the station for a policewoman to attend, made arrangements for the flat to be dusted for fingerprints and, at the same time, requested the attendance of the Exhibits Officer.

Before long, a smart young WPC arrived in a Panda Car. After a few brief words with her, Charlie and McKay made their way downstairs. Neither spoke till they were in the car once more.

'She still doesn't know what happened, Guvnor' remarked Charlie.

'I thought it could wait' replied McKay 'She was a poor scrap of a thing, wasn't she? Looked as if she hadn't had a decent meal for a month.'

As they drove along, they outlined the known facts of the case so far.

These two came from completely different backgrounds, but together they made a highly successful team. McKay, with his astute mind, did most of the talking, and Charlie contributed his 'nose' and years of experience of thief-catching.

Back at the mortuary, the Detective Chief Superintendent of the Division had just finished formally identifying the body to the pathologist. McKay was surprised to see the pathologist; they were fortunate indeed to have obtained his services so quickly.

Further photographs of the body had been taken, with special close-ups of the injuries. McKay was particularly interested in those injuries. He felt that, if he could establish how and when they had been inflicted, he would be well on the way to discovering who had inflicted them.

The pathologist had already begun his gruesome task. His report would be anxiously awaited by McKay, as would those of the Toxicology and Forensic Departments. The latter should reveal evidence of blood and alcohol levels. The link man would be the Laboratory Liaison Officer.

Returning to the Sports Centre, McKay and Charlie realised that they hadn't eaten since breakfast. It was Charlie who remarked 'When're we gonna eat, Guvnor - me stomach thinks me throat's been cut.'

They found the cafeteria and sampled the fare, which wasn't at all bad.

Feeling more human, Charlie headed for the Murder Room to check with Tommy Rogers that the house-to-house enquiries were under way. This was a hard slog, as every house or business in the vicinity would have to be visited by the teams of detectives. They would systematically interview all householders to ascertain if anyone had seen or heard anything unusual during the night. A small open park, adjacent to the Centre, was a favourite place for late night couples and dog walkers, so the possibility of people coming from further afield had to be considered.

McKay meantime sought out Mike Weston, who had been waiting for him. He had recovered from his rude awakening and was ready to talk. The formalities over, McKay got down to business right away.

'What I would like first is a list of names and addresses of every member of staff, including part-timers, starting with those who were working at the Caribbean Evening.'

'I'll get Ted Veale on it straight away. My secretary is, of course, off for the weekend, but we can get the information from records and I can tell you who was working last night.'

'Thank you, we need that information as quickly as possible.'

Picking up the phone, Weston gave Veale the necessary instructions.

'Before we talk about Dave Fisher, there is one point which you can clear up concerning the leisure pool where he was found.'

'Certainly - anything at all to help' replied Weston.

'There was hardly a trace of blood in the pool, yet with the injuries that Fisher had received one would have expected a considerable amount.'

Weston replied without hesitation 'Oh, that's easy to answer. I'm not an expert on pools but I do know that the water circulation system is the very latest and is highly sophisticated. The water at the deepest part changes every two hours and, in the shallow part where you found Fisher, every hour.'

'As quickly as that?' interjected McKay, in astonishment.

'Hang on, that's not all' boasted Weston, warming to his task 'It is then treated with a dosing of sodium hydrochlorate before being re-circulated, so I'm not surprised you couldn't find any blood. The sanitation aspect has to be of a very high standard these days, you know. And nowhere higher than the Parkdale' he added, proudly.

McKay smiled at the plug for the Centre and said 'Thank you, Mr. Weston, that's clarified the situation, but I don't think that it's going to help us very much. Never mind' he continued 'let's get round to your Deputy Manager. What can you tell me about Dave Fisher?'

Mike Weston reached for his favourite pipe; he seemed to have them all over the place. Lighting up, he puffed clouds of smoke ceilingwards, settled himself comfortably in his large office chair, cleared his throat and began 'He came to us from another sports centre about two years ago when the post of Deputy Manager was advertised and, apart from deputising for me, his area of special responsibility was the leisure pool.'

'Have you been satisfied with his work?'

'Basically, yes. He's worked hard, the pool is well promoted, has a high usage and is very successful.'

'At the time, did anyone from here apply for the post?'

'Yes, as a matter of fact. Ted Veale, the assistant manager you've already met, also applied.'

'How did he take it? Not getting the job, I mean.'

Weston puffed on his pipe before answering 'Naturally he was disappointed. He saw it as his clear line of promotion, as he has been here since the beginning. But he didn't interview well on the day and Dave Fisher was brilliant. He really impressed the Councillors on the interview panel.'

'I see' McKay paused and then asked 'Did they get on with each other.'

'I never had any reason to think that they didn't.'

'Did you have any problems at all with Fisher?'

'Only one' he replied, in a resigned voice 'He was good at his job, but he drank too much. In fact, I had to warn him officially about overdoing his socialising whilst he was on duty - it's on his record.'

McKay made a mental note to check out Fisher's employee record and continued 'He was really quite young - do you know if there was a reason for him drinking so much?'

Weston shook his head 'I really don't know. If he had a reason he kept it to himself.'

'He was single, wasn't he?'

'Yes, but he had an assortment of girlfriends who he used to bring to our functions. And he always seemed to enjoy himself.'

'He had a sister living in London, do you know much about her?'

'Not really. I've only seen her a couple of times, but I think they were quite close. Although she never struck me as being a very sociable person.'

'Finally, Mr. Weston, do you know if Fisher had any enemies?'

Mike Weston thought for a moment, again sucking his pipe 'I suppose you'd have to say that he was a bit of a Jekyll and Hyde character. Nice as pie when sober but could turn nasty when he'd had a few drinks. He has upset one or two people but, as far as I know, never enough to make enemies.'

He shook his head again and added slowly 'No, I would have to say that generally he was well liked.'

McKay rose, saying 'Thank you, Mr. Weston,

obviously we are going to see quite a lot of each other during the investigation. I can only assure you that we are just as anxious to complete our job, get out of the Centre and leave you in peace, as you no doubt would like to see the back of us.'

Weston, heading for the door, stopped, turned and, in a voice full of feeling, replied 'My only wish at this moment is for you to find out how he received those terrible injuries and to catch the bastard who did it. If there's anything the staff can do to help don't hesitate to ask.'

McKay closed the door behind the worried manager and sat down at the desk which had been put at his disposal. It was ironic that it was the one usually occupied by Dave Fisher. He looked around the room, the walls of which were covered with charts and lists of duties to be performed by the staff in the pool.

'Well' he thought 'at least I know a bit more about the man floating in the shallow end of the pool, the man lifted from the warm waters and wrapped ignominiously in the sheet of plastic, the man who had no further need of the chair I'm occupying at the moment.'

He suddenly felt whacked - it had been quite a day.

He contacted Charlie in the Murder Room and together they headed for home, stopping only for a quick one at the local near Charlie's home. After arranging the time of their meeting the following day, McKay dropped Charlie off outside his home.

Alone in his car, McKay's thoughts automatically turned to the events of the day. What he dreaded most was that the case would drag on for months without success or, even worse, be placed on file, to be re-opened over the years at regular intervals. He was tired and mentally drained - he shook himself out of this mood - it was negative thinking and McKay always took the positive line of approach. It had paid off in the past and was one of the reasons for his undisputed success. His track record in the detection of crime spoke for itself. Six Commissioner's Commendations with his length of service were a clear indication of someone special.

Robert James McKay had been born and raised in Dunfermline in the Kingdom of Fife, a small town that is the burial place of the famous King Robert the Bruce. So McKay more than qualified as a 'Fly Fifer', an expression frequently used to describe a Scot coming from the county just north of the river Forth.

He had been educated at the local High School and, after a year of sheer boredom in a surveyor's office, joined the Edinburgh City Police for some excitement. By dint of hard work and study, he had passed the examinations for Sergeant and Inspector. There was only one snag - after five years service, his chances of making Sergeant, let alone Inspector, were nil. It was a case of filling dead men's shoes.

McKay, fiercely ambitious and confident that he was capable of better things, now had the added responsibility of a wife and child to support. He had no choice but to do what many of his predecessors had done, which was to leave his beloved Scotland and transfer down to the 'smoke'. Down South to London to join the Metropolitan Police. Here, the promotion system was entirely different and, for someone as capable as McKay and as willing to study, almost guaranteed.

First though, he was required to attend the Metropolitan Police Training School at Hendon, where he had to learn the major differences between Scottish and English law and procedure. Not to mention the famous Metropolitan Police Act, applicable only in the London area. Wisely, he treated his time at Hendon as promotion study time and considered himself fortunate to be able to study in the firm's time. The following year saw his name heading the Sergeant's examination results. He was on his way. His position on the promotion list almost guaranteed him a place on the Special Course and a year at Bramshill Police College followed. After a short spell as a Sergeant, both in uniform and CID, he was promoted to Inspector.

His natural aptitude for CID work had led to his present position of Detective Chief Inspector with the authority to investigate murder. Everything he had worked so hard for in Scotland and his diligence and study after coming South had paid off handsomely.

His wife Margaret, also a Scot, had, in the beginning, been very unhappy with the move to London, mainly due to strong family ties. Now, with many friends, and her two children happy and attending good schools, she had come to accept and enjoy life in the 'soft' South.

McKay entered his house at the end of the first day of the murder enquiry, which coincided with the Jubilee Celebrations. Margaret, despite her full day with the two sons, had managed to prepare a welcoming meal for her husband. He kissed his wife lightly and enquired 'How did the day go, love?'

'We had a wonderful time and Jamie was a very dutiful escort. The crowds outside the Palace were all so good-natured – every nationality under the sun – and the boys did enjoy it.'

'So it doesn't sound as if I was missed at all' said McKay, thankfully.

'No, not really' quipped Jamie, with a smile 'I also got a chance to talk to one or two of the Cadets on duty and I can't wait to get out there.'

'That's good, all you have to do is get through your interview, which shouldn't be a problem. Thank you, Jamie, you obviously did a very good job taking my place' he said, proudly 'I shall have to look to my laurels.'

'What about your day, Dad?' Jamie asked, keenly.

'It was a murder – the victim was the Deputy Manager who was found in that beautiful swimming pool at the Leisure Centre – I really can't tell you much more than that.'

Jamie and his brother Ian were disappointed as they had hoped for more gory detail.

Margaret could see that her husband was tired and she said 'All right boys, it's been a long day, give your father a break and let him have a bite to eat in peace.'

'Good night, boys' said McKay 'See you in the morning' and added 'and thanks again, Jamie.'

Margaret poured a glass of Famous Grouse as her husband settled himself into his favourite armchair and relaxed.

It had been quite a day and McKay knew that, when they went to bed, sleep would come easily for her but for him. Tired though he was, it would be different. The pattern was always the same on the first night of a new case. He would lie there in the darkness, wide awake, re-living the events of the day in chronological order, considering every detail carefully until he was satisfied that nothing had been missed.

CHAPTER FIVE

When McKay and Charlie met the next morning, McKay said 'Look Charlie, there are a few things still to be done around here, but as soon as possible I want you to go up to Manchester and check up on Fisher's early days, see his mother and so on. You'd better take someone with you and stay overnight'.

'OK, Guv. I've got a good mate up there who used to be at the Station and transferred to the Manchester lot because his wife couldn't settle here'.

'Charlie, you've got mates everywhere. Now I think we should go and see Ted Veale.'

When they got to the Sports Centre, Ted Veale, the Duty Manager, sat opposite McKay and Bennett in the office allocated to the CID at the Sports Centre.

Prior to the meeting, he had been busy making sure that all the schools who normally attended for swimming lessons had been informed of the circumstances; also the coaches of various sports.

McKay opened the questioning 'Exactly how long had you known Dave Fisher?'

'About two years altogether. He came here from another sports centre on promotion to Deputy Manager.'

'Was he easy to get on with?'

'Most of the time, yes.'

'You say most of the time. When wasn't he easy to get on with?'

Veale squirmed in his seat and replied reluctantly 'Well…I imagine that you have heard by now that he used to drink quite a lot. When he did, he could be very awkward.'

'Did you fall out with him at any time?'

'Yes, once or twice, but it never amounted to anything serious.'

'Did you like the man?'

Veale replied without hesitation 'When he was sober - yes. He had a good brain and there wasn't much about the recreation scene that he didn't know.'

'Can you think of any reason why anyone would want to kill him?'

Veale thought for a moment, shook his head, and

replied 'As I said before, he used to upset people sometimes when he had been drinking, but I honestly can't think of anyone who would want to see him dead.'

'What about staff relationships?'

'He was very good with the staff. In fact, I would say that he had a very sympathetic nature. They would often go to him with their problems.'

'Do you think that maybe he was too friendly?'

Veale pursed his lips and the corners of his mouth turned down. He moved his head from side to side, before answering 'Possibly...he certainly was more sociable with staff than with the rest of the management team.'

He shrugged his shoulders and, staring into space, said 'But that's the way he was.'

'Thank you very much, Mr. Veale' said McKay, adding 'Oh, by the way - who do you think will be in the running to take Fisher's place as Deputy?' He watched Veale's face, knowing full well what the answer would be.

Veale frowned, but answered calmly 'That's a loaded question if ever there was one. It's no secret that we both applied for the job as Deputy and that I was runner-up.'

'Were you very upset about that?'

'Naturally, I was very disappointed at the time. It meant that my main avenue of promotion was blocked for several years to come. It also meant that I would probably have to look outside the Borough for any further promotion.'

'In the same way that Fisher had to move here for his promotion?' interrupted McKay.

'Yes…I suppose so. It's just that I've got a good record here - and everyone thought I was favourite for the job.'

'I see. Thank you, Mr. Veale, you've been a great help' said McKay.

Charlie saw him out of the room and, after closing the door, said 'What do you think, Guvnor?'

McKay pondered for a moment 'He's the obvious one, Charlie - too obvious. The one with everything to gain by Fisher's death, but I can't see him committing murder to achieve it. Unless there's more to Mr. Edward Veale than we've seen so far.'

'He certainly seems a straightforward bloke' said Bennett 'He always looks after our darts team well when we play at the Centre.'

'Oh well, that's got to be a good recommendation, Charlie' replied McKay, sarcastically, with a smile on his face.

They were interrupted by a knock on the door and in came Tommy Rogers from the Murder Room looking mighty pleased with himself 'I thought you would like to see this straight away, Mac' he said, handing McKay several sheets of computer printouts 'It looks a bit useful.' They clustered around as McKay spread the sheets out on the desk top. It was the result of the Criminal Records check on every person employed at the Centre, including part-timers.

McKay had not been too hopeful when he asked the manager for the list the previous day, because the references of most council employees are checked out thoroughly before engagement, or else they come well recommended. But, judging by Tommy Rogers' comments and the look on his face, he was about to be pleasantly surprised.

Most of the names on the list were clean, as McKay had predicted. One, however, almost jumped off the sheet.

RICHARD WILLIAMS, age 39 yrs

CONVICTIONS - six

MALICIOUS WOUNDING - one

ASSAULT- four

This looked like one that had slipped through the net - Williams must have worked a fiddle somehow.

'Cor...Guvnor. He looks a bit tasty' commented Charlie, enthusiastically.

'Certainly does' replied McKay, nodding in agreement.

'Well done Tommy, can you get a hold of his file? I'd like a complete rundown on Mr. Williams and any known associates, as soon as possible.'

'Sure, I'll get someone on it straight away' replied Rogers, making his way out of the office with a satisfied look on his face.

McKay, his heart beating just that little bit faster, produced a copy of the list compiled the previous day by the Manager.

'Now…what job does this character do at the Centre' he asked eagerly.

He ran his finger down the list, stopped and announced 'Richard Williams, Assistant Plant Manager. Obviously spends most of his time dealing with maintenance and the running of the leisure pool. Quite a strong connection there, Charlie.'

'Do you want me to find out when he's next on duty?'

'Yes, will you' answered McKay, adding 'Veale should know.'

Charlie scuttled off while McKay checked through the list once more. Apart from Richard Williams, there were only a few minor offences listed against the staff. Nothing to worry about.

Charlie was back in no time 'Guess what, Guv?' he said excitedly and, without waiting for an answer, continued 'Chummy's wife rang through earlier this morning and reported him sick – said he'd been involved in an accident.'

'What kind of accident?'

'You'll never guess, Guv. She said that he had fallen down some stairs.' He almost laughed as he said it.

'I've heard that one a few times' said McKay, smiling,

as much at Charlie as anything else.

'I think we should pay Mr. Richard Williams a little visit. After all, now we've got two Sports Centre employees out of action at the same time. One obviously murdered and the other fallen down some stairs.'

'Bit of a coincidence, isn't it?' commented Charlie.

'I believe in coincidence' replied McKay 'but not to that extent. No, there's got to be some credible explanation. Come on Charlie, there's only one way to find out.'

******

Richard Williams' flat was on the third floor of a small block called Brookdown Mansions. It was surrounded by neat lawns and shrubs in a quiet road. McKay and Bennett made their way up the clean stairs towards Number 18. Turning on to the third floor balcony, they could see a man working in the doorway of one of the flats. As they approached Number 18 they realised that he was working on the door jamb of the address they had come to visit.

He looked up and eyed the two men suspiciously – he had them sussed out as coppers straightaway.

McKay spoke first 'Richard Williams live here?'

'Who wants him?' replied the man, abruptly.

'Detective Chief Inspector McKay' came the answer, as

he produced his warrant card. Pushing it towards the man he asked 'Who are you?'

'Frank Williams. I'm his brother...but he's not seeing anyone at the moment. He's had an accident and he's not feeling too good'. The words came tumbling out as the man's brain tried desperately to work out how the law had put in such a quick appearance – and a Detective Chief Inspector at that.

'Who is it, Frank?' a woman's voice enquired anxiously from inside the flat.

McKay answered for him 'It's the police. Can we come in?'

A small woman of about thirty-five appeared immediately. She was quite attractive in a blowsy sort of way, ostensibly blonde but the roots indicated otherwise. She was wearing a tight fitting, well-filled sweater, a neat grey skirt and introduced herself as Gloria.

McKay took this in at a glance but his eyes focused on her face. One side was red and swollen and the eye on that side was puffy and discoloured. He had seen that type of injury many times before. It was, without doubt, the result of a backhander.

She looked at the two men defiantly, as if she felt obliged to offer some kind of resistance - instead she heaved a loud sigh, shrugged her shoulders and said 'Oh alright, I suppose you'd better come in.'

She turned and led the way into the lounge, followed by McKay, Charlie and, eventually, the brother. McKay looked quickly round the room, which was spotless and comfortably furnished, as was the kitchen beyond.

The woman crossed her arms tightly, hugging her body as if for comfort, then turned and faced the two men.

'We've come to see Richard Williams' announced McKay 'Where is he?'

'Well er...he is here' said the woman, nervously 'but he's had an accident and he's asleep in bed. Why do you want him?' - the words came tumbling out.

'Are you his wife?" asked McKay, ignoring the question. She hesitated before answering 'No, we live together, but what's that got to do with anything?'

'Look, there's been some trouble at the Sports Centre and I want to speak to Mr. Williams about it - that's all.'

'When was this?' she demanded.

McKay remained silent.

'He hasn't been near the Centre - it's his weekend off anyway' she continued, slowly gaining confidence.

McKay still remained silent.

'Look. What is all this about?' she blurted out, angrily. She lodged her hands on her hips and glared at McKay defiantly.

'It's very important that I see Mr. Williams' insisted McKay, firmly 'I won't disturb him if he's asleep' he added.

'Oh, alright then' grumbled the woman, starkly 'If it's as important as all that.'

She led the way into the hallway and quietly opened a bedroom door 'He's in here' she whispered, standing aside.

McKay and Bennett entered the room cautiously. It looked like a disaster area. Hurried attempts had been made to tidy up, but without much success. Piled up in one corner were the smashed remains of a chair, only one good leg remaining, the back hanging off. A bedside lamp lay on its side, most of the pottery base missing and the shade damaged beyond repair. The centre mirror of the dressing table had been shattered and the pieces crunched into the carpet. A picture hung at a crazy angle, its glass also broken, and the frame almost touching the bedhead. Beside it on the wall were splatterings of what appeared to be blood, giving the area a red, stippled effect.

There was an overpowering smell of surgical spirit in the room and the reason for this became suddenly apparent as a pile of bedclothes moved and a voice said, painfully 'What the bloody 'ell's going on?'

McKay and Bennett gaped with amazement as a figure covered with bandages slowly emerged from under the bedclothes. It tried to sit up, only to fall back again with a loud curse which turned into an agonising scream of pain.

'Blimey, Guv' whispered Bennett 'The poor sod really has been in an accident.'

The figure before them resembled one of those cartoons of someone in a hospital bed swathed in bandages. Both eyes were blackened and stitches closed several wounds around the cheek bones.

'Cor...Guvnor. He looks a bit tasty' commented Charlie, enthusiastically.

'Certainly does' replied McKay, nodding in agreement.

His swollen top lip and nose looked as if he had unsuccessfully fought ten rounds with a boxer several stones heavier than himself.

After a few minutes, he struggled to sit up again and McKay noticed that the whole of his rib cage was strapped. Despite the terrible injuries, McKay had the distinct impression that he had recognised his visitors as being the law. Not surprising, really, because with all those previous convictions Richard Williams must have had considerable dealings with them in the past.

He suddenly yelled with pain and collapsed back into the bed again screaming 'Fuck off and leave me alone, you bastards.'

McKay turned to the woman 'He should be in hospital.'

'He's been there most of the night, but he discharged himself' she said, bursting into tears 'He just wouldn't stay.'

McKay looked at Charlie and, with a nod, indicated that they should leave the poor sod in peace. It was obvious that no one was going to get anything sensible out of Williams for some time to come.

Back in the lounge, the woman continued to sob uncontrollably and they were quickly joined by the brother Frank, who put his arm around her, to comfort her. Looking at McKay, he spat aggressively 'Can't you leave us alone? There's been enough aggravation for one night.'

McKay answered quietly 'Look pal, I can see you've had aggravation here, but I'm conducting a murder enquiry and one of you two is going to answer some questions - and I don't care which one.'

'What are you talking about?' blazed Frank Williams 'My brother was the one that was nearly murdered. Christ, you saw that for yourself.'

'Exactly when was he nearly murdered?'

'Yesterday evening, of course - we've spent most of the bloody night at the hospital.'

'Where was your brother on Friday night, then?' asked McKay.

Gloria, who had recovered somewhat by now, was making a cup of tea in the kitchen. She had been listening and came back into the lounge to answer the question.

'It was his weekend off and we stayed in and watched a video. And on Saturday night we all went to the pictures.'

She looked towards Frank.

'Yes, that's right' confirmed the brother 'Me and my wife, brother Dick and Gloria all went to the pictures together Saturday night - to the Astoria.'

'And afterwards?'

'We had a drink till closing time and all came back here for a game of cards. Must have been about three in the morning when we finished. I lost money as usual' the brother added.

'What did you do then?'

'Me and my wife walked home, it's only round the corner.'

McKay looked at Gloria, who replied 'And me and Dick went to bed when they went home' she added defiantly, hands on hips again.

McKay and Bennett looked at one another, both realising that the state of the man lying swathed in bandages in the other room had nothing whatsoever to do with the Sports Centre murder. Then McKay remembered that the brother had been repairing the door jamb when they arrived. That, coupled with the fact that he had already decided that Dick Williams' injuries were more consistent with a 'good kicking' than falling downstairs, made him demand 'Look, who was it who broke in here last night and gave your brother such a hiding?'

'Don't say anything, Frank' pleaded Gloria, grabbing his arm 'Dick will never forgive you.'

'I don't care' said Frank, his eyes blazing with hate 'He's a bloody animal - he could easily have killed Dick, and look at your face.'

Her hand went automatically to her damaged face 'It's nothing' she said 'I've had far worse than that.'

'That's why I'm saying the bastard should be put away' he persisted, hysterically, and his face reddened as his anger mounted.

McKay already had the answer.

'Have you ever been married?' he asked Gloria.

For the second time during their visit she suddenly dissolved into tears. The pain and anguish she had experienced during the past few hours caught up with her again.

Her hands came quickly to her face as she sobbed 'Yes, yes...to a right bastard.'

'And he was the one who broke in here last night and did that to Dick?' McKay asked, quietly.

Unable to control himself any longer, the brother burst out 'Him and a couple of his bloody mates - all tooled up with pickaxe handles they were. My brother could have managed him on his own, but they came mob-handed. It was only that Dick's so strong that he's still alive - least that's what they said at the hospital.'

'But why?' asked McKay, guessing the answer.

Gloria answered 'He always was a jealous bastard. He could never believe that I'd leave him and go and live with someone else.'

She looked a sorry sight, with her swollen face, hair untidy and neglected and eyes red-rimmed with black mascara streaks running from them.

McKay rose to go. The local CID could handle this job. The last thing he wanted, at this stage of the proceedings, was to involve himself in an eternal triangle, even though things did seem pretty desperate at the flat.

'I'll send someone round to get a statement from both of you, and him when he's better' said McKay, nodding towards the bedroom 'And with any luck you'll get your wish' he continued, addressing the brother 'The bastard will be put away alright.'

As the car pulled away, Charlie spoke first 'Well, Guvnor, bang goes our chance of tying the job up quickly.'

'Yes, I thought it was too good to be true - never mind, it was interesting though.'

'I wouldn't want to be that poor sod under those bandages, though' said Charlie, with feeling.

McKay thought for a moment and then answered grimly 'Judging by all those previous convictions for causing GBH, he was in the habit of dishing it out. Now he knows what it's really like to be on the receiving end - actually, as far as I'm concerned it couldn't have happened to a nicer feller.'

Charlie grinned 'I just had a thought, Guv, that's two of the staff out of action. If the guy we're after is also from the Sports Centre they could end up with a real staffing problem before we've finished.'

'Maybe' replied McKay, seriously 'but we've still got to find the bastard, and we're no nearer now than we were at the beginning.'

******

They related the story to Tommy Rogers back in the Murder Room. His disappointment was apparent.

'Sorry, Mac, I thought we were on to something there.'

'Yes, well that's the way it goes, Tommy. It should be another one or two for the crime figures, at least.'

'Any joy with the house-to-house enquiries, Sir?' asked Charlie.

'Nothing yet, I'm afraid' replied Rogers 'But it's early days yet. We've started to check further afield, quite a lot of people walk their dogs in the open parkland at the side of the centre and some even come by car. So we've got plenty to be going on with.'

'Keep me posted, Tommy' said McKay.

Charlie was receiving messages again from his stomach. 'I'm starving, Guv – you realise we've missed our Sunday dinner.'

'I'm hoping to get mine this evening' replied McKay 'But if the Centre bar is still open we might be able to get a glass of lunch.'

In the Centre bar, they found Mike Weston and his girlfriend Jenny Marlowe. Over a sandwich and a pint, McKay took the opportunity to check out, with Jenny, Weston's version of the events of the Caribbean Evening. She was not at all surprised that McKay had looked in on her as she had slept the previous day, as she was such a heavy sleeper.

She was unable, therefore, to say with any certainty, whether Weston had left the house that night after their return.

'So' thought McKay 'the Manager cannot be ruled out.'

******

McKay and Bennett took the opportunity over the next few hours to consider and discuss all the information gathered so far, and to plan their course of action for the forthcoming week, before agreeing to call it a day. The Sports Centre had closed when the murder investigations began, so they took advantage of the situation and shut up shop themselves.

This time, Charlie dropped McKay off and turned the car towards his own house. He was feeling tired but stimulated. He considered himself fortunate indeed to be working with such a good Guvnor as McKay. An expression frequently used in the police is 'you can't do enough for a good Guvnor'. Usually it is said tongue in cheek, but as far as Charlie Bennett was concerned it was true.

Detective Sergeant First Class Charles Bennett had been in the Force for nearly twenty-five years and had spent most of that time in the CID. A south-east Londoner, born not quite within the sound of Bow Bells, he considered himself a true Cockney and proud of it.

As a youngster, brought up in a rough area, he had had to be quick witted and tough to survive. Both of these qualities, although he did not realise it at the time, were to be invaluable in his work as a CID officer in the metropolis. Early in his police service he had shown an aptitude for catching villains, which was not surprising really because he had met quite a few whilst growing up and he knew what made them tick.

He had long since given up the idea of ever making Detective Inspector and had settled for the life he loved, which was detective work at the grass roots. Just to be part of the team suited him - not that he hadn't had his moments.

When he was younger he had worked out of Scotland Yard in the Flying Squad and Cl 1.

Now he was happy to settle for the camaraderie which exists in most police forces, and particularly the working relationship he enjoyed with McKay.

It was strange how these two, a Scot and a Cockney, brought up at least four hundred and fifty miles apart, had formed such a successful partnership. Bennett had only just managed to enter the Force at the minimum height limitation and educationally it had been a struggle.

In the early days as a young police constable he had painstakingly studied the 'black book' and eventually passed the various examinations for Sergeant - but it hadn't been easy.

Charlie's forte was the practical side of police work, he wasn't cut out for studying or the finer points of law or, as he would put it so succinctly 'We can't all be Chiefs, there has to be some Indians.' Charlie had the usual aggravation at home to contend with. Normal police hours of duty are bad enough; but a CID officer can never spend enough time at home, especially if he's attached to a busy nick.

His wife Rose had accepted all this when she was younger and their marriage had been a happy one. His family of two children had grown up over the years, but his wife, who did not have the best of health, had always found the hours worked by Charlie in his various postings very trying. The son had already left home, had joined the Army and was serving in Germany. His daughter worked in a local bank and was about to be married. This would leave a big gap in her mother's life, as they had got on so well together, almost like sisters.

As Charlie drove home, his thoughts turned to the job ahead the next day, which was to co-ordinate, with Tommy Rogers, the taking of statements from every person who had been present at the Caribbean Evening. McKay would tackle the Sports Centre staff. A monumental task for all those involved. This side of detective work could be boring and repetitive, but it had to be done thoroughly to ensure that nothing was missed. Every piece of the puzzle had to fit.

But that was tomorrow.

CHAPTER SIX

Charlie Bennett arranged with DI Rogers at the Murder Room to release Detective Constable Stephen Wade from the house-to-house enquiries, so that he could go with him to Manchester. They had worked successfully together on several occasions, despite the difference in their ages.

Steve was young in service, aged 25, good-looking and very popular with the opposite sex. He was inclined to be a bit cocky at times, but in Charlie's book this was no bad thing. There was no doubt that he had a soft spot for Steve, perhaps because he reminded him of a much younger Charlie Bennett.

They had got on well together right from the start and Charlie had more or less looked after Steve when he was posted to the Station as a Detective Constable. Steve was keen, fit and a very useful member of the Metropolitan Police Judo Club. A very handy lad to have around if there was any bother. However, bother was the last thing on Charlie's mind as they drove north to Manchester.

After an uneventful journey, they booked into an hotel near where Fisher's mother lived. Next, Charlie contacted his old colleague Geoff Thomson, explained the reason for his visit north, and asked him if would find out if anything was known about Fisher's early days in the area. He also arranged for them to meet the following evening to exchange notes and have a meal together before their return to London.

The next morning saw them in a pleasant street of terraced houses, knocking on the door of Fisher's mother's house. It was answered by a small woman, soberly dressed and whose grey hair was tied back neatly in a bun, and who greeted them solemnly.

Charlie produced his warrant card and introduced both of them, explaining that they were from the Metropolitan Police in London.

'Mrs. Fisher?' queried Charlie.

'Yes… have you come all this way to talk to me about my David?'

'It's nothing to worry about, Mrs. Fisher. We would just like to talk to you about David's early days and to offer our condolences. Can we come in?'

'Certainly' said Mrs. Fisher, standing aside 'Just go straight into the lounge.'

Charlie and Steve walked down the passageway into a large, cluttered room in which many framed photographs were displayed. They settled themselves down in armchairs and waited.

Having taken a seat on the sofa, Mrs. Fisher collected her thoughts and then said 'Well, David was a bright boy and went to the local grammar school but he didn't study. He was more interested in sport, especially cricket and football, and he really enjoyed himself in the gym. His father died of cancer when David was about ten years old and it was very hard bringing up two youngsters. Mother helped me out as much as she could, but with no money coming in I had to go out to work and couldn't keep an eye on him, as I should have done, maybe. Anyway, he got through his exams alright but fell in with a bad crowd, who were up to all sorts of things. It was mainly high spirits I think. He was smoking and drinking when he could earn money doing odd jobs for people; I certainly didn't give him any, but at least he kept away from the drugs. Funnily enough it was the sport which saved him in the end.'

'How was that, Mrs. Fisher?' interrupted Charlie.

'He saw an advert in the local rag. They were looking for attendants to work in the Trafford Sports Centre which had just been built in the area. He applied, and was accepted. I was very relieved, I can tell you. After that, he settled down and was no more trouble.'

'He didn't find the unsocial hours a problem?' asked Charlie.

'No, he enjoyed working in the sporting atmosphere and I was proud of him. Eventually he got down to studying again and got a Diploma in Management Studies. Unfortunately for me, this led to him getting his first management job down South.'

'So apart from being with the bad lot after school, he was never in trouble of any kind.'

'No' she replied, hotly 'he was a good boy.'

Charlie had heard that many times during his career. A mother claiming that her son couldn't possibly have done what he was accused of, when the evidence clearly indicated otherwise.

'Thank you, Mrs. Fisher. Now, would you please give me the address of the Sports Centre where he worked when he left school and then we will leave you in peace.'

Steve noted this down and they took their leave.

Back in the car and heading for the Sports Centre, Steve said 'What do you think Charlie?'

'I feel sorry for her, it couldn't have been easy bringing up those youngsters without a dad, and then for one of them to have been murdered after all the sacrifices she must have made.'

'I agree, but it hasn't given us anything new to go on. As far as she was concerned, it was a case of 'local boy makes good.'

'Maybe we'll find out more at this Sports Centre' said Steve, consulting his map 'It's not far away.'

Before long, despite considerable traffic, they pulled into the car park of the Centre, a smaller, and older, building than the one that they had left in London.

They contacted the Manager without any difficulty and, as luck would have it, he had been at the Centre since its opening. They explained the reason for their visit and he seemed more than willing to help them. He immediately organised some coffee and biscuits for them, which was gratefully received.

'I heard the terrible news, it was in all the papers up here, him being a local lad and all that. David was no different from any lad from school, full of energy, a bit cocky but no trouble. He had been with a bad crowd, but what impressed me most about him was that he was so keen. He really settled in well and was hardworking - you could give him any job to do and know that it would be done well. It must have been difficult growing up without a father and I think he felt that he was part of a team here. I gave him a good reference when he applied for the Assistant Manager's job at Waltham Cross in Essex.'

'Did you see or hear from him again?' asked Charlie.

'Yes, as a matter of fact, he used to call in and see us whenever he visited his mother and he seemed quite happy. When he got his promotion to Deputy Manager at the Parkdale Centre, he came in again and we had a drink on it. I was very proud of him. That kind of thing doesn't happen every day, and I was devastated when I heard the news of his death.'

'Look, we needn't take up any more of your time' said Charlie, rising 'You've told us all we need to know. Thanks for your help.'

'It's a pity we had to meet under such unhappy circumstances' replied the Manager.

They took their leave and then killed time until their meeting with Charlie's mate, Geoff Thomson, planned for that evening. They met in a local restaurant and, quite quickly, it appeared that Geoff had come up with much the same information that Charlie and Steve had found out – that Fisher was the best of the bunch that he had knocked around with, and that there were no convictions of any kind against him.

Having got this out of the way, they settled down to enjoying themselves. As the two old friends reminisced, after a good meal and a few drinks, Steve learned a few things about Charlie that he didn't know before.

First thing the next morning, Charlie phoned McKay and told him that Fisher had moved from the Manchester

Trafford Centre to the Waltham Centre in Essex and suggested that he and Steve called in there on their way back to see what they could find out. McKay agreed, saying 'Complete the job you started when you went up to Manchester, but don't take all day about it.' And the two were soon on their way heading for Essex.

At the Waltham Leisure Centre, which also was not as modern as Parkdale, they had no difficulty in finding the Manager. In his office, Charlie explained the reason for their visit and asked him if he had any knowledge of Fisher's drinking and, if so, whether he could account for it.

'He used to drink, but never to excess, and it was no problem while he was here. He worked well and, as he wanted to better himself, I gave him time off to study and, in fact, I gave him a very good recommendation when he applied for the job at Parkdale.'

'Did he have any particular friends in the Centre who we could speak to?'

'Yes, as a matter of fact he was very close to one of our young Assistant Managers called Tom Richardson - they seemed to have a lot in common. He just happens to be Duty Manager this morning, so you're in luck. I'll page him.' He duly put out a call for Richardson to come to the office.

'Thank you' said Charlie 'It would be better if we could see him on his own, if you don't mind - he might find it easier.'

'Certainly, you could see him in his office.'

When Richardson appeared, he was young and fresh-faced and dressed smartly in a blazer and grey slacks. After the introductions, they made their way to his office. When they had settled down, Charlie opened the questioning 'I understand that you and Dave Fisher were quite close.'

'That's right, we got on well together, we actually shared a flat when he first came South. I couldn't believe it when I heard the sad news. Are you any nearer to catching his killer?'

'We are making progress' replied Charlie 'But we hope that you can help us with what Fisher was like when he was here.'

'Sure, I'd be only too pleased to help - fire away.'

'What can you tell me about his other friends, if he had any, outside the Centre?'

'His only real friend seemed to be his sister, but she was a weird one.'

'What do you mean?' pressed Charlie 'Anything you can tell us would help.'

'Well, I was invited, along with Dave, to a party at his sister's flat, which she shared with several other girls. It turned out to be quite a rave-up. I'm pretty sure half of them were on drugs and I had a great time, but Dave was worried about his sister. He was very protective of her. Apparently he felt responsible for her following him down South and he had promised his mother that he would look after her.'

Charlie's mind went back to the morning when he and McKay had gone round to Fisher's flat and the sister had appeared from the bedroom. If she was on drugs that would explain the pathetic creature she had become, and would certainly be news for McKay.

'Dave seemed to worry about her and started drinking more than he usually did. Several times I turned down offers to go drinking with him because, although I like a drink in moderation, I also try to keep myself fit. Then Dave got his promotion and I didn't see much of him after that. He told me he had bought a flat near the Parkdale Centre and was getting on well.' He paused before asking 'What happened to his sister by the way, she must have taken all this badly?'

'Well, she followed him to London and when we saw her recently, she was shocked, but otherwise seemed OK.' Charlie saw no need to elaborate any further and, thanking Richardson for his help, he brought the interview to an end and they took their leave.

Back in the car once more, Steve said 'It seems that Mrs. Fisher's fears about her daughter have been realised. You saw her, Charlie, what did she look like to you?'

'When McKay and I saw her on the day after her brother died, we both thought that she was a pathetic thing, but neither of us suspected that she was into drugs. At least now we've got something to report back about.'

In London again and reporting to McKay, Charlie had to admit that they had got plenty of background on Fisher's early days, but nothing that was going to help them with the investigation.

McKay said 'You seem to have enjoyed yourselves by the look of you – guess what?'

'I know, we've got to go and speak to the sister.'

'That's right, but not today. I've got work for you here.'

CHAPTER SEVEN

As McKay entered the Murder Room at the Sports Centre the next morning, Detective Inspector Rogers handed him two large buff-coloured official-looking envelopes.

It was just what he had been waiting for. One contained a report from the Forensic Science Laboratory and the other was the Pathologist's report, complete with photographs.

Sitting down at his desk, McKay eagerly opened the latter. He quickly thumbed through the photographs of the dead man. The close-ups of Fisher's injuries looked interesting but mostly served only to remind him of the first morning of the case, which already seemed like ages ago.

Next, he turned to the report and, after he read through the preliminaries, there it was in black and white, what McKay had to know before he could proceed with any certainty, namely the amount of water in the lungs that had led the Pathologist to conclude that the cause of death was drowning. At least he now knew where he stood. It was now reasonable to assume that Fisher had been drowned in the pool and not killed elsewhere and dumped there.

He read on. The time of death had been established as between one and two o'clock in the morning, which suggested that Fisher had been murdered whilst finishing his drink after everyone, or nearly everyone, had left the Centre.

After studying the rest of the report, McKay returned to the photographs. He had been pretty sure that the marks on the neck were inconsistent with manual strangulation and the report confirmed this. In fact all the injuries to the head and throat appeared to have been caused by blows with a thin metal object and the dislocation of the thumb and finger was consistent with the hand being held upraised to protect the head.

McKay felt happier - no further forward, but happier. Two other items of real interest were contained in the report. One was that the alcohol level in Fisher's blood, although high, was insufficient for him to have been very drunk on the night. The second was that his kidneys already showed signs of disease, which came as no surprise. All indications that he had received from the staff interviewed, so far, pointed clearly to Dave Fisher's drink problem.

It looked as if death had caught up with him sooner, rather than later.

McKay was disappointed that there was nothing in the laboratory report of any assistance concerning Fisher's clothes or personal effects.

After studying the reports for some time, he made his way along the corridor to the Sports Centre side which was in full morning session. Fortunately, the police had spent the previous day searching the whole pool area and the rest of the Centre and had cleared it in time for the local schools to attend for their recreational periods. Happy laughter and excited chatter seemed incongruous to McKay in the middle of a murder enquiry. On the other hand, being a family man, he was pleased to see the youngsters enjoying their outing so much.

He stopped outside a door marked 'Catering Manager', knocked and entered. He was in luck. Tony Lopez was alone in his office, almost hidden behind mountains of invoices and receipts. He looked up and greeted McKay in a friendly manner 'Take a seat, Chief Inspector. I expected a visit sometime today and you've picked a good moment - anything to have a break from this endless paperwork.'

They chatted about the murder in general terms for a few minutes and then McKay asked him specifically about the occasions he had seen Fisher during the Caribbean Evening.

Lopez replied 'I saw him several times during the evening, because he was the Duty Manager for the whole Centre, and then I saw him twice, I think, standing at our bar.'

'This was normal, was it?'

'Oh yes. He would have to visit all areas of the Sports Centre, including the pool, to make sure that everything was running smoothly.'

'Would he have visited the Sports Centre bar?'

'Definitely. Apart from the usual supervision, part of his job on the late shift is public relations - getting to know the users of the Centre by socialising. It all helps to bring the customers in and create a friendly atmosphere.'

'I understand' replied McKay 'And when was the last time you saw him that night.'

Lopez thought for a moment before answering 'Well we were pretty busy most of the evening and there is always a lot of hard work to do at the end of a function, cleaning the counters, washing and drying all the glasses, cashing up the tills, and so we all get stuck in. The sooner we get tidied up the sooner we get home to bed, so I didn't really notice him again till I was leaving.'

'And where was he then?'

'He had obviously got himself a couple of drinks just before the bar closed and was sitting at one of the tables at the poolside, waiting for everyone to go home so that he could lock up.'

'Was he the only one in the building when you left?'

'As far as I know he was - there was no one else about.'

'What about your staff?'

'Oh, Bill Forrester took the two sisters who work in the bar. They left just before I did. They were the only other ones to stay right to the end - the band had long gone.'

'Did you speak to Fisher?'

'Only to say goodnight and to let him know that I was leaving.'

'What did you do next?'

'I went out, got into my car and went home.'

'Were there any other cars left in the car park?'

'No. Mine was the last to leave.'

'What about Fisher?' he queried 'How was he going to get home?'

'He usually walked, or got a minicab depending on how he felt.'

'I see' pondered McKay 'When you were leaving did you notice anyone hanging about - anyone who might have been at the Caribbean Evening?'

'Not a soul. You see, the bank crowd had organised themselves a couple of big coaches to bring them and take them home. It's a good idea really - they can drink as much as they like without having to worry about your boys stopping them on the way home.' He grinned and continued 'It works out very well for both sides.'

McKay nodded in agreement 'One last question, Mr. Lopez. Did you get on well with Fisher?'

'Most of the time I did, but occasionally he would try to interfere on the catering side and I wouldn't have that at any price. He fancied himself as a bit of a chef, just because he was interested in cooking and could prepare a variety of bachelor meals. Also, as his favourite pastime was drinking, he liked to think that he was an authority on the running of bars. Sometimes we clashed, after all I think I'm the expert, but the rows never amounted to anything serious, I can assure you.' He spread his hands out expansively and sat back in his chair.

McKay nodded 'I see' and continued 'Finally, I have to interview every member of your staff who was working that night.'

'That shouldn't be a problem, except that the two sisters who were working in the bar went to Italy on holiday the next morning. So I'm afraid they will be away for ten days, but Bill Forrester should be available and then there are two others from the cafeteria that you could see anytime.'

'Thank you very much for your help, Mr. Lopez' said McKay, bringing the interview to an end.

Leaving the office, he made his way back to the Murder Room for a conference with Charlie, Tommy Rogers and the rest of the team who were doing all the leg work. It was a get-together to consider exactly what they had achieved in terms of facts and to decide which line of action to take next.

The large blackboards, hurriedly assembled, were still mostly bare, and in the end McKay had to admit that they had achieved very little. But it was early days yet.

Charlie had just returned from an interview with Jonathan Maynard, the bank manager. The purpose of his visit was to make arrangements for all of the bank's staff who had attended the Caribbean Evening to be interviewed and he had taken the opportunity to check on the state of Fisher's bank balance, which proved to be very much in the red.

When questioned by Charlie, Maynard went to great lengths to explain that his employees used the Sports Centre regularly for badminton, five-a-side football and the leisure pool, not to mention social evenings with the Sports Centre staff. He had encouraged this and they had such a good relationship with Mike Weston and his staff, that the fact that Fisher's bank balance was continually in the red was seen as really a minor detail. Naturally, Fisher had to be reminded from time to time when he was excessively overdrawn but Maynard knew that, being a council employee, Fisher's account would automatically be credited with a month's salary, regularly and without fail.

******

Mike Weston, working his way through a pile of papers on his desk, stopped for the third time, unable to concentrate. The events of the past few days kept flooding back to him. Just when he had reason to anticipate a period of stability with the staff at the Centre, everything had been turned upside down.

He was already one Assistant Manager short, which had meant that Weston himself had had to take his turn as Duty Manager, including working at weekends. He hadn't minded the shift work whilst on the way up, but having reached the position of manager he felt that he had earned the right to a spell of regular hours. One of the drawbacks with the leisure industry was that it invariably meant working when everyone else was relaxing and enjoying themselves.

The unsocial hours had already played havoc with his marriage, which had ended in divorce and, although Jenny was younger and more adaptable, she too hated it when he was missing on her return from work.

Looking on the bright side, a new Assistant Manager had been appointed and was due to start soon. Taking some consolation from this fact, he picked up his pipe and started scraping black shards from the inside into an ashtray. He stuffed shreds of tobacco into the bowl and, satisfied that all was well, applied the flame of a lighter and relaxed back in his chair.

Glancing round the room, his mood changed. His eyes rested on the framed certificates on the wall, his Diploma in Management Studies (Recreation) which had taken a year out of his life to achieve, but which had set him on the road to his present position. Alongside this was his Membership of the Institute of Leisure and Amenity Management and, finally, a framed photograph of a much younger Mike Weston dressed in an Army Physical Training Corps working uniform. How smart he had looked in it! The white vest with red piping and the famous crossed swords contrasting with the black, narrow, cloth trousers.

'Those were the days' he thought to himself, being fiercely proud of his twenty-one years in the Regular Army, most of it spent in the Corps. His service included several tours abroad and had ended at the Army Physical Training Corps Depot at Aldershot where, for five years, he had been an Instructor. He remembered with pleasure the roads and woods around the Depot, all of which he knew like the back of his hand. He closed his eyes and recalled the sound of pounding boots on a clear frosty morning as he took his latest squad of budding Assistant Instructors for an early morning run, their panting breath rising like steam in the cold air.

He was still in pretty good physical shape, but in those days he had been super fit. He had taken part with pride in many occasions such as Royal Tournaments and displays at the Albert Hall on Remembrance Sundays. Always a good gymnast from school days, he had been recommended for the Corps during National Service and had literally jumped at the opportunity. The life had suited him so much that he had signed on and made a career of it. At the end of his service, with his vast experience of sport and recreation in a practical sense, he decided to use this knowledge in a management situation. His full-time course in Recreation Management was followed by a spell as an Assistant Manager at a Sports Centre in the south of England. His knowledge and experience in gymnastics had led to the post he now held at a Centre which specialised in gymnastics.

He drew hard on the pipe, realised that it had gone out, considered re-lighting it but instead placed it carefully in the holder on his desk and returned to his paperwork.

******

McKay and Bennett, anxious to acquaint themselves with all aspects of the Sports Centre, made their way towards the Plant Room hoping to find Bill Forrester, the

Plant Engineer, there.

A large Sports Centre, such as the Parkdale which included one of the latest leisure pools, had to have a huge filtration and heating system. It followed, therefore, that the room which housed the enormous gas boilers, which fed these systems, was also on the grand scale. McKay had anticipated this but, even so, he was amazed by what he saw on entering this plant room. A vast, brilliantly lit cavern which contained a labyrinth of silver-coloured pipes of all sizes which criss-crossed the ceiling before branching off to feed different machines at floor level. Each machine was brightly coloured and spotlessly clean with various dials showing temperature or pressure. Other pipes led to huge boilers covered with silver lagging and these provided the hot water for the whole complex. Alongside, were the giant storage tanks used for the pool water and sanitation system.

Charlie was the first one to speak, a look of amazement on his face 'Blimey, Guvnor, it beats the old school boiler house where we used to go for a crafty fag. That was a filthy old place - the boiler was black and everywhere was covered in dust and cobwebs. Mind you, I suppose it was fired by coal.'

'I know just what you mean, Charlie. This looks like the inside of a spaceship' replied McKay, equally impressed.

In a small office leading directly off this room, they found Bill Forrester meticulously recording figures on various charts, which covered one wall and meant nothing to the uninitiated. He was a short, stocky middle-aged man, going bald with dark wiry hair which curled at the back and sides. Somehow he fitted in well with the surroundings. This was the man that Mike Weston had referred to as a very valuable member of his staff who could turn his hand to anything and McKay wondered if anything might possibly include murder.

Forrester looked up from under thick bushy eyebrows, surprised that two strangers should enter his office uninvited.

'Detective Chief Inspector McKay and Detective Sergeant Bennett' announced McKay 'I believe you are William Forrester?'

'That's right, although most people call me Bill' he answered, his face breaking into a smile, not at all impressed by the status of his visitors. Here in this domain, he was top dog - nobody knew as much about the workings of those machines outside as he did.

'Can you spare us a few minutes?' said McKay, returning the smile.

'Certainly - take a seat' said Forrester, who hurried to pull up another chair for Charlie.

'Just a few questions about the Dave Fisher business'

said McKay, once they had settled.

Forrester, sitting back comfortably behind his desk, replied sympathetically 'Poor Dave - a terrible business - and it had to happen in my pool of all places.'

'A typical reaction from a plant engineer' thought McKay. In the way that farmers have great regard for their beasts, this type of person seemed to have almost an affection for the mechanical monsters they had just seen. It must have something to do with working daily with the machines and making certain demands on them, followed by the feeling of pleasure, reward even, when they responded successfully.

'How long have you worked at the Sports Centre, Mr. Forrester?'

'Ever since the place opened five years ago.'

'And where did you work before that?'

'I was Plant Engineer at one of the swimming pools on the other side of the Borough.'

'Was this a promotion for you, then?'

'Oh, yes. There isn't another set-up like this in the whole of the Borough. In fact, this leisure pool with its wave-making machine was one of the first in the London area' replied Forrester, with obvious pride.

'So it's a full time job for you and your assistant' said McKay, pointing to the second desk.

'Yes, my assistant, Dick Williams, and I are kept pretty busy. Actually I've just heard that he's been involved in an accident but I haven't had time to go round and see him yet. No doubt you will want to see him as well. I'm afraid I don't know how bad he is or how long he will be off work.'

'It's pretty bad' commented McKay 'He won't be back at work for some time.'

Forrester's bushy eyebrows shot up 'You mean you've already seen him?' he gasped, sitting bolt upright in his seat.

'Yes, as a matter of fact we saw him yesterday.'

Forrester thought hard for a moment and then queried 'What made you go and see him first?' adding 'If I may ask?'

'We just thought it rather strange that Dave Fisher should be killed and your Richard Williams involved in an accident about the same time.'

'You mean you suspected him of being involved?' gasped Forrester.

'In a murder enquiry we have to consider everyone' replied McKay, pointedly 'But, as it happened, the murder occurred in the early hours of Saturday morning and your colleague had his accident in the early hours of Sunday morning.'

'So there was no connection then?'

'No. None at all.'

'Thank God for that' said Forrester, relaxing back in his seat once more 'But what happened to him. What kind of accident did he have?'

McKay had no intention of relating the tale of how Williams came to be beaten up, so he replied in a casual manner 'Oh, he'll tell you all about it when you see him. But let's get back to business and the Caribbean Evening. I believe you work part-time, when required, behind the bar?'

'Yes, that's right, just to earn a little pin money - and it is little, believe you me' he paused before saying 'Actually I quite enjoy working behind the bar. One of my dreams is to run a little pub in the country, if I could ever save enough.' He smiled self- consciously.

'And you were working behind the bar on the night of the Caribbean Evening?'

'Yes. That's right.'

'Did you see Fisher that night?'

'I saw him several times during the evening - once or twice at the bar.'

'Did he seem upset, or any different from normal?'

'No. Not really.'

'What did he drink?'

'His usual lager.'

'Anything else?'

Forrester paused 'I believe he may have had a scotch.'

'Did you have much to say to him?'

'Very little. We were very busy that night – that lot from the bank can certainly drink!'

'Can you remember any of the conversation you had with him. It could be very important' stressed McKay.

Forrester thought hard for a moment, his bushy eyebrows coming together in the middle of his forehead 'As far as I can remember it was only shop, about how the evening was going - nothing out of the ordinary.'

'I see' said McKay 'And when did you see him last?'

Again Forrester paused and replied slowly 'It must have been after we had washed up all the glasses. Yes, I was getting ready to leave and I noticed him at one of the tables with a drink.'

'When you left, were you alone?'

'No, the two girls were with me. I dropped them off on the way home.'

'The girls? That would be the sisters who were working with you that night?'

'That's right, a couple of real nice girls who work part time in our bars. I usually give them a lift home. They'd have to pay for a taxi otherwise and it's not much out of my way. I expect you know that they've gone on holiday, the lucky devils.'

'Lastly Mr. Forrester, you must have had quite a lot to do with Dave Fisher in the job situation, with him being responsible for the swimming pool side of the Centre. Did you get on well together?'

'Yes, quite well really' answered Forrester, immediately 'He came here from a Sports Centre which didn't have a swimming pool so he picked my brains a lot to begin with. I didn't mind that. I mean we've all got to learn, and he learned fast. He was quite bright, you know, and once he'd settled down he made a very good job of running the pool.'

McKay thanked Forrester and rose to go.

Charlie replaced the chair he had been sitting on to its original position behind the empty desk. Seeing him do this McKay pictured its usual occupant, lying in bed covered in bandages and blood spattered above him all over the wall. 'Yes' he thought to himself 'you're in for a big shock the next time you see your mate Dick Williams.'

'What do you think, Charlie, he seems to be well on top of the job?'

'I'm not sure, he seemed a bit too full of himself for me.'

CHAPTER EIGHT

Every sizeable sports or leisure centre employs a number of Sports Assistants, usually referred to as 'the boys', despite the fact that there are girls as well. They are invariably young, fit, and interested in sport; so the idea of working in a sporting environment appeals to them. Without them the Centre could not function efficiently, as they are responsible, amongst other things, for the 'change-overs'; this means ensuring that the change from one sport to another takes place as quickly and efficiently as possible. At times the equipment which has to be handled is heavy and complicated and calls for considerable effort.

During the course of their work they have a good deal of contact with the general public using the Centre, therefore each one tends to be a public relations officer in his own right.

One of the Parkdale 'boys' was, at this very moment, taking part in a public relations exercise or, at the very least, trying very hard to improve staff relationships. His name was Mark Tyndall and he was in bed with the Centre secretary Barbara Johnson.

He had been unable to believe his luck. What had started as just a casual invitation for a drink in the Sports Centre bar had led to this. Along with the rest of his mates he had fancied Barbara alright - who wouldn't? But this was completely unexpected - he didn't think he stood a chance. Besides, she was always seemed to prefer older types - not that he was complaining - he just couldn't believe his luck.

Unknown to Mark, Barbara had been very attracted to him. Normally she wouldn't have had anything to do with the attendants but he was a cut above the others. His qualifications as a PE teacher proved this. She just hadn't got around to doing anything about it but, after their drink in the bar, she had invited him back to her flat for a nightcap, and what a nightcap it was turning out to be.

'God, she's terrific' thought Mark, not stopping to consider how she had acquired this expertise. Like most young bloods he was making the most of the occasion by giving it his undivided attention.

Barbara Johnson, away from the office, looked even more beautifully put together. Her eyes were dark and, at the moment, wild looking. Her long black hair had been loosened from the neat, complicated style she used during the day, when she was the efficient secretary. She was strikingly attractive, and she knew it. For someone on the wrong side of thirty-five years, she was in remarkable shape.

Mark Tyndall's young muscular body, tanned and firm, contrasted with her soft white skin. He had decided to move into the leisure field when the kids at his large comprehensive school had begun to get him down. He knew that it was going to be a retrograde step to begin with, but planned that once he had gained experience in the Centre, he could then move eventually on to the management side.

It occurred to him that at the moment he wasn't doing too badly, certainly gaining experience in the recreational field, whether it led to a management situation or not. Barbara's long slender fingers moved sensuously over the muscles of his back, tracing their outline. Suddenly her fingernails dug in viciously almost piercing the skin. Her long legs clamped around his body and he could hold back no longer. In the excitement of making it with Barbara, it was all over before he had really even started.

She was visibly disappointed and so was Mark, but he wasn't going to show it.

'Never mind, Mark' she moaned 'It was a good start. You're not in a hurry to get away are you?'

'Christ' thought Mark 'she'll be giving me marks out of ten next.'

Barbara Johnson had been satisfied, up to a point, but she wasn't about to let him escape without making a better job of it than that. He was young, good-looking and fit. He was also more intelligent than most of those she had been with lately, including Dave Fisher who had usually been available after the Sports Centre functions. She shook the thought from her mind and turned all her attention to the situation in the room.

'Would you like a drink?' she asked, as they parted.

Mark lay back in the bed feeling at peace with the world. The silken pillows and sheets felt so luxurious compared to those back at his miserable shared flat.

'Yes please' he replied 'Er...scotch and water if you have it.'

She slipped out of bed and Mark's eyes followed every movement as she pulled on a deep-red, silk dressing gown and tied the belt tightly around her waist, accentuating her figure. Then, crossing the room to a drinks trolley in the corner, she busied herself with the glasses. Mark watched in amazement - he had never been with a woman who was so well organised.

He looked around the room. It certainly was a wonderful pad. Especially the bedroom, which had an oriental look. Several Japanese wall hangings and the twin bedside lamps with wicker, coolie hat shades helped to create this effect. The curtains and pelmet were richly coloured and made of a silky material. A light beige carpet with a soft deep pile covered the floor and completed the picture.

'Yes, it's all rather nice' thought Mark.

In no time, Barbara was back with the drinks. Handing him both, she eased herself down beside him. She crossed her long legs, causing the gown to part either side revealing her shapely legs and ankles. She reached across to take her drink and the top of her gown slipped open giving Mark a glimpse of her fully-rounded breasts. Normally just the thought of this alone would have had Mark pushing out his trousers - but it was too soon. She lit two cigarettes, the way they did in the old movies, and handed one to him. They chatted for a while and inevitably the Sports Centre came into the conversation.

Then Mark, with the tactlessness of youth, said 'Barbara, you've been at the Centre a long time. What was Dave Fisher really like?' adding 'I heard that you had a thing going with him at one time.'

Barbara was completely taken aback for the moment,

but she managed to disguise it well. The last thing she wanted to do right now was to talk about Dave Fisher. However, she wasn't about to spoil the way things were going either. So, as politely as possible, she answered 'When he first came to the Centre we used to get on well together' then she paused and drew hard on her cigarette, as if carefully considering what she was going to say next.

Impatiently, Mark pressed 'So what happened to change things?'

She answered, calmly 'Well, he didn't drink so much at the beginning and he was quite good fun to be with. After a while he seemed to need more and more drink.'

'I understand that - but he could handle it, couldn't he?'

Barbara had had enough of this conversation. She looked straight at him and the eyes seemed to bore right in 'Let's put it this way, Mark. The more he drank the less use he was to me.'

'Christ...at least she's honest and to the point' thought Mark, readily accepting her answer.

Barbara, in her calculating way, could sense that the situation was in danger of becoming morose. She was much more concerned with the living than the dead, and the living was right beside her, within reach. Without saying another word she placed her drink on the bedside table and crushed out her cigarette in the ashtray. She untied the belt of her gown and with a quick movement caused it to slip off her shoulders. Tilting her head slightly to one side, she looked at him with her eyebrows raised questioningly.

Mark swallowed hard and considered finishing his drink, but decided against it. Before he had finished stubbing out his cigarette, he felt her body tight beside him. Her soft skin sent wild feelings throughout his body. He swallowed hard again and reached for her, but she was first. Her hand automatically moved across his chest, the fingers caressing gently. Then down over his stomach muscles and they bunched in anticipation of what must surely follow. She kissed his eyes, face and neck, her soft lips moist and probing. Reaching his ear, she bit hard with a groan of pleasure. She was breathing hard by now and her lips covered Mark's roughly. He kissed back as hard as he could; she was overpowering, her perfume filled his nostrils and made him feel lightheaded.

Her hand finally reached its destination and she moaned with delight on finding him as ready as he was ever likely to be. There was no question of him getting off so lightly this time.

Suddenly, much to her surprise, Mark felt the need to dominate; he had held back long enough. Turning her over roughly, he forced her to follow his lead. She cried out with excitement, loving every minute of it.

This time Mark felt that he was never going to stop as they moved in unison. Barbara screamed with delight, her head thrashing from side to side as Mark tried desperately to continue for as long as possible. Eventually they reached a painful, but excruciatingly wonderful, climax for Mark and the last of many for Barbara. She was in another world - it was just what she had wanted - needed. They both sank back exhausted. Mark wanted only to relax and keep still but Barbara still moved slowly and rhythmically, as if to savour each last second of pleasure.

Barbara spoke first 'That was wonderful, Mark - aren't you glad you came in for that nightcap?'

Mark was still in that euphoric state when all his limbs and muscles tingled from sheer exhilaration. He mumbled a few words in reply which he felt must have been totally inadequate. 'God, she was marvellous. Unlike anyone before' he thought to himself. It couldn't possibly be any better than that. He gazed at her with such admiration in his eyes, which were only just beginning to focus properly again, that Barbara knew without doubt that she had made a conquest.

Mark Tyndall would be back for more.

******

It was a Wednesday afternoon again and Mike Weston had just finished holding a very solemn management meeting. It seemed incredible that only one week before they had all sat in this very room and discussed the Caribbean Evening which had ended so disastrously.

The weekly ritual had been observed. With Dave Fisher's untimely death and the accident to Richard Williams, who was likely to be off work for some time, there were adjustments to be made in staff duties. Weston had called for greater co-operation and extra effort from everyone, in order to carry on the efficient running of the Centre. Morale was naturally low and he struggled bravely to raise them from their gloom.

At the end of the meeting, as the others were leaving, he asked Ted Veale to remain behind. When the door was closed he said 'Ted, one piece of good news that I can give you is that the new Assistant Manager arrives in two weeks time.'

'Thank goodness for that' replied Ted, with relief 'Although it still leaves us one short.'

'That's true, but when the new chap arrives I intend putting him in charge of the Sports Hall side of things - and you know what that means?'

Ted Veale nodded his head and answered slowly 'Yes Mike, it means that you want me to take over Dave Fisher's old job in charge of the pool.'

'That's right, I can't give the new chap that job, he's not experienced enough and anyway you've got the qualifications.'

'Alright, Mike' he replied 'if that's what you want.'

'It's the only answer' he paused, spreading his hands 'I take it that you will apply for the Deputy's job when it's advertised?'

'I suppose so.'

'You were very close to getting it last time, and you know that you will have my backing' Mike added.

'Thanks very much. I might be a bit luckier this time, but it's a pity it's got to be under these circumstances.'

'I agree, but we just have to get on with it' replied Weston, reaching for his pipe. He pressed the butane lighter which sent out a huge flame as he lit the pipe and he said, in between puffs 'I was just thinking - only the other day - how well things were going' a huge cloud of smoke wafted towards the ceiling 'and how well we all got on together - now everything has been turned upside down.'

'Do the Police have any idea who killed Dave?'

'Apparently not' replied Mike, looking concerned 'What bothers me most of all is that, if it wasn't an outsider who killed him, it must be someone who is still working in the Centre.'

'Yes, I know' again Veale nodded in agreement 'I've racked my brains trying to think who could possibly have done it and why.'

Mike Weston's gut feeling was that, however much he hoped that it was an outside job, it was much more likely to be someone that Fisher had upset at some time or other. He had been an awkward man to deal with, sometimes brilliant and at other times edgy, impatient and over-officious. Customers and staff alike had complained of this at times.

Mike Weston could appreciate their feelings more than most, coming from a Service background. He had found great difficulty, himself, in adjusting to the civilian outlook. The mere fact of having to persuade people to comply, rather than order them, was one of the problems. This was even more important in the leisure industry, where success depended so much on having the right attitude towards customers who are out to enjoy themselves. Mike considered that he had coped well with the problem and was surprised to find this flaw in Fisher's character – after all, he had never even had to do National Service. Maybe it was ambitious drive, or perhaps, just the drink talking - one thing was sure, there would be no way of finding out now.

He looked up at Ted Veale, who was waiting patiently 'Sorry, Ted' he said hastily 'I've sorted out most things over at the pool, so it should be fairly straightforward. Any queries, you know where my door is. And thanks again' he added, with a smile, as Veale left the room.

******

McKay and Bennett settled themselves comfortably in a quiet corner of the Sports Centre bar with a drink and some sandwiches in front of them. It was Charlie who spoke first, despondently 'We don't seem to be getting very far at the moment, Guvnor. We'll be running out of people to interview soon.'

McKay sampled his lager with relish and then replied slowly 'Come off it, Charlie, it's early days yet and if we do run out of people to interview, we'll just have to start at the beginning again. Somebody in this place knows more than they are saying - we'll just have to dig deeper, that's all.' He took another pull at the lager and continued 'I don't believe that a stranger came in off the street and killed him, it's got to be someone in this place with a reason for wanting him dead'.

'Alright, Guvnor, but everyone who was on duty the night of the Caribbean Evening has been checked out and their movements verified. The rest of the staff are all in the clear. We've ploughed our way through all the crowd from the Bank without success.' Charlie was beginning to sound desperate.

'What about the house-to-house enquiries?' McKay queried.

'A blank there as well, I'm afraid. Nobody seems to have seen or heard anything.'

'Well, they'll just have to keep at it and widen the area. Even though I have this feeling that it was an insider, somebody could have come to the Centre by car or to walk a dog in the park. Perhaps a courting couple might have been there late and seen something. As I said before, it's early days yet.'

'Alright, Guv, let's go through what we've got already.'

McKay collected his thoughts and in a quiet and precise manner said 'Fisher, a single man with a good brain and a responsible position in the Centre as Deputy Manager, is found dead in the leisure pool after a Caribbean Evening. He had consumed a considerable amount of alcohol during the evening, but wasn't drunk. The pathologist's report shows that death was due to drowning, and this despite the fact that Fisher was a reasonable swimmer and had basic life-saving qualifications.'

He paused to drink again and continued 'He had severe bruising and lacerations to his head and throat, the latter inconsistent with manual strangulation. How did Fisher receive these injuries and what caused them? The dislocated thumb and finger, and the ear almost severed from the head, suggests that he was holding his hand up in order to protect himself.'

He paused again 'Alright so far, Charlie?'

'Yes, Guv, but there was more in the report wasn't there?'

'Right - his liver showed signs of damage through drink. From our own enquiries we know he was a hard drinker who could turn nasty when he'd had too much.'

Charlie interrupted 'I wonder where else he drank. I don't suppose he spent all his spare time in the Leisure Centre bar. He must have had a local. I'll make a few enquiries at the pubs in the area of his flat.'

'Good idea. He might have made some enemies there - oh, and check out any clubs at the same time' McKay continued 'He doesn't appear to have had any real enemies at the Centre, although we know he could be an awkward bugger at times. There appears to be no real reason for his heavy drinking, at least nothing we have come across so far. Maybe he started when he was young and it just became a habit. There is no suggestion that he was gay; he seems to have had various girlfriends but no one regular.'

McKay paused and, almost thinking aloud, suggested 'We could make a few more enquiries along those lines, Charlie. There could even be some female we haven't heard about with a grudge against him.'

Emptying his glass slowly, McKay said 'You know there's still something bugging me about that sister of his, but I can't put my finger on it. What do you think about her?'

'She certainly did seem a poor scrap of a thing. One of the world's losers I'd say.'

'It might be worth you paying her a visit to see if you can find out more about her.'

'Okay. I'll go as soon as I can' replied Charlie, picking up the empty lager glass which had been placed carefully in front of him. He smiled and made his way to the bar.

They usually discussed their cases in this fashion, one hoping to feed off the other. It really amounted to mutual respect and played a major part in the success of their partnership. However, if either had been pressed at this moment, they would have had to admit that they were no nearer discovering who killed Fisher than they were at the beginning. They were still waiting for a breakthrough. Suddenly McKay, who had been deep in thought while Charlie was at the bar, said to himself 'Somebody in this bloody place knows more about Dave Fisher than they've disclosed so far and I've got an idea how I might get one of them to open up.'

At that moment Charlie returned with the drinks. Placing one in front of McKay, he said cheekily 'You know what they say about people who talk to themselves, Guvnor?'

'Okay. All very well, but I've been thinking that I might get something out of Ted Veale. I've heard that he's a keen golfer and I think I'll try and get something out of him on the golf course.'

'Good idea. It might work and you might even enjoy it.'

McKay smiled, raised his eyebrows and said 'Never mind that, big spender, where are the crisps?'

CHAPTER NINE

'Hello, Charlie. I'm told that her ladyship, the boss, wants to see me this morning. It can only be bad news.'

'It's early days yet, so why should she be getting her knickers in a twist?'

'When you are as promotion-minded as she is, nothing ever moves fast enough - and don't forget that there's a Board next month. The appointment is at 10.30 am so I'll have to leave you to look after the shop.'

'OK, Guv - and rather you than me' he grinned.

McKay made his way to headquarters, parked his car in the yard and climbed up to the second floor. On reaching the door which had the plate 'Detective Chief Superintendent Janet B. Marshall' on it, he checked his watch. It showed 10. 28 am.

He knocked and, on hearing the invitation to enter, opened the door and stepped into the room. She was standing behind her desk and McKay was greeted by a cheery 'Good morning Mac, and how are you?' her hand outstretched. McKay clasped the hand, which returned a surprisingly strong grip for such a slight figure.

Janet Marshall must have been just on the borderline of the height restriction for joining the Force but she had an aura about her, which left no one in doubt that she was in charge.

She had short, cropped fair hair, was wearing a smart well-tailored grey suit and oozed confidence. McKay couldn't help thinking that she must be good, very good, to have reached this rank by the age of 38.

With a wave of her hand she indicated a seat for him to take and McKay, with a bit of old-world charm, waited till she was seated before sitting down himself. He noticed that her white skin with very little makeup contrasted with her black, piercing eyes.

'I'm very well, Ma'am, and I hope you are too.'

A few pleasantries followed 'How are your family? I hear that your son is going to join the Cadet Corps - following in his father's footsteps, eh? – maybe we have a future Commissioner here?' she quipped.

'They are all very well, thank you.'

McKay looked around the room, which was furnished in much the same way as any other Senior Officer's, but Marshall had added a few feminine touches by means of colourful plants. 'Maybe she's not so hard after all' he thought.

He waited patiently for the reason for his summons and then it came 'This Leisure Centre murder, Mac – are you making any progress? Only I've had the Commander on my back wanting to know how things are going.'

'Yes, but I'll bet you're the one who really wants to know' thought McKay.

'It's early days yet, Ma'am. All the staff have been interviewed and their alibis checked. The Path Report showed that the murdered man had a bit of a drink problem and we've gone into his background to try and find the reason – and this is ongoing.'

'I hear that another member of the Leisure Centre staff has been beaten up. What's that all about?'

'We thought at first that it may have been connected, but no such luck. It turned out to be the eternal triangle - husband takes revenge on wife's lover with the aid of a few of his mates. They've all been arrested and appeared in Court, but it will be some time before the husband is fit to give any evidence.'

'Well at least the crime figures will show 'clear-ups', so that's good.'

'Yes' thought McKay 'that's all you're interested in - figures.'

'You've got Bennett with you, I believe - how's he working out?'

'Fine, he's very experienced, nothing much gets past him.'

Marshall tidied up some papers on her desk, drew herself up as tall as she could and McKay thought 'Here it comes.'

'We have to put this to bed as soon as we can, Mac. I can't stress how good a result would look on your CV, especially with a Board coming up soon.'

'Yes' thought McKay 'and it would do wonders for yours as well.'

She smiled, extended her hand again and said 'Best of luck'.

'Thank you, Ma'am' said McKay, as he rose and pressed the hand a little firmer this time. Relieved that the interview was over at last, he turned and left the room.

Making his way back to the car, he considered what had just taken place. He had long ago accepted the fact that policewomen were no longer assigned to dealing with children and young persons and now competed with colleagues of all ranks, but, being a Scot, he found it difficult to have one as a boss. However, like it or not, she must have been exceptional to have reached that rank in such a short time.

Back in the car heading for the Leisure Centre, he thought to himself 'Yes, a result soon would be more than welcome, if only to get Janet Marshall off my back.'

******

It was Thursday evening and the Sports Centre was buzzing with excitement. People of all ages made their way cheerfully through the turnstiles and into the main sports hall.

The reason for their attendance in such large numbers was the finals of the Five-a-Side Soccer League. Throughout the winter, every Thursday evening, twenty-eight teams had taken part in league matches and tonight would see the culmination of all their hard work.

All the Centre Staff were on duty. The reason for such devotion to duty was the fact that the Sports Centre Assistants' team was second in the league and had high hopes of carrying off the trophy and taking part in the celebrations afterwards.

The team, captained by Mark Tyndall, could truly be described as a League of Nations and included Dai Williams, a short, stocky Welshman with long black curly hair who, at 27, was the oldest and Bob Easton, the goalkeeper who, tall and thin in physique, was the youngest at 18. He was blonde-haired with pimples and was trying desperately to grow a moustache to make him look older. Also in the team was Winston Macdonald, aged 26, a second generation West Indian, born in Willesden. He was a nippy player with very good ball control, but inclined to overdo things. His nickname 'Flash' was partly due to his speed and style of play and partly due to his liking for natty clothes, which swallowed up a good deal of his wages each week. The fifth member of the team was Big Jock. As the name implied, he was the biggest and heaviest of the players, aged 25, from Glasgow, with flaming red hair and a temper to match. A little short on skill, he was more at home on the large pitch where his ability as a stopper could be put to full use.

The team, resplendent in the Centre colours, were all keyed up and ready to go. They were drawn early for the first of their games, which was against the fourth team in the League, a team from the Architect's Department at the Town Hall.

McKay and Bennett arrived just as the teams were warming up. The chance to observe so many of the Sports Centre staff together socially at the same time was too good a chance to miss. They sat down next to Mike Weston and Jenny, having passed Ted Veale, who was Duty Manager for the evening, on the way in.

McKay glanced around the noisy crowd arranged down one complete side of the Hall. Just behind them sat most of the catering staff and the girls from the office together with two of the receptionists and the remainder of the sports assistants. They were very voluble already - obviously the time between finishing work and attending the football had been spent in the bar.

The referee called the captains together and the game got underway to enthusiastic encouragement from both sets of supporters - those from the Sports Centre easily drowning the others. It was obvious from the start that the strength of the Architect's team lay in their skilful, intelligent passing moves and young Bob Easton was called upon several times to make good saves. The Centre team relied heavily on the quick breakaway, using the speed of their coloured striker, Winston, who came close three times during the first half.

They turned around with no score, with Mark Tyndall encouraging his team to greater efforts and the Centre supporters adding theirs. Within seconds the ball was in the net - one of the Architects had turned Big Jock easily and the young goalkeeper had no chance with the shot. The second half continued with both goalkeepers busy and time was running out when Big Jock, well aware of the fact that they had scored through a mistake on his part, put in a fine tackle. The ball rebounded luckily to Mark Tyndall, who immediately passed it almost the length of the hall into space. Winston Macdonald showed his speed and, just beating the opposition to the ball, cracked in a beauty.

The Centre supporters went wild, as did the team, and before the game could be restarted the final whistle went. The Centre players heaved a sigh of relief, as a draw meant they were still in with a chance.

During the interval McKay, Charlie and Mike Weston, accompanied by Jenny, made their way to the bar where a very colourful scene met their eyes. The local brewery were using the occasion to advertise their latest brand of lager and the whole of the cafeteria and bar was covered with posters, beer mats and ashtrays extolling the virtues of the lager, which by that time was flowing freely. The brewery representative, Steve Jameson, came forward to greet them and, after the introductions, a round of drinks quickly appeared.

Before long, McKay's mind turned to business and the reason for their presence in the Centre. He noticed Bob Forrester providing an extra pair of hands in the busy bar, as he had done on the night of the murder. Looking around he saw Mike Weston's secretary, wearing a silk blouse and silver lurex jeans, which looked as if they had been poured on. With shiny high-heeled shoes, her shapely legs appeared longer than ever and she attracted considerable attention.

Meanwhile, Charlie had wandered over to speak to the two remaining supervisors. Not being in the team and not being on duty, they were drinking the new lager as if it was going out of fashion. They were keen to get a head start on the others before the games ended.

McKay excused himself and sought the company of Tony Lopez, whom he had noticed bringing in some fresh sandwiches to the bar. 'Hello, Mr. Lopez' he said 'It looks like a very busy evening for you and your staff.'

'It certainly is' he replied 'but all the preparations have been made and it's really just a case of keeping the bar going.'

'What about later?'

'We'll be inundated at the end of the competition when all of the crowd from downstairs come up for a drink, not to mention the teams – they'll be dying of thirst.'

'I see you've got Bob Forrester behind the bar. I suppose you're missing the two sisters who are on holiday?'

'Actually, it's not too difficult to get extra bar staff, but those girls are good. We trained them ourselves so they know the ropes - and they're honest' he added, with a knowing look 'Which is invaluable these days.'

'When are they due back?' queried McKay.

'They should be back this weekend. They promised to be available for a function early next week.'

'So I should be able to see them on Monday?'

'Yes, provided they can tear themselves away from those Italians. They're a couple of good-looking girls you know.' A smile broke over his usually serious face.

'Right, thanks' said McKay 'I'll see you later this evening, no doubt.'

He made his way into the bar area, collected Charlie and together they made their way back to the Main Hall where the Final was about to take place. The Sports Centre team was already in the hall warming up for what was likely to be a very tough game. They had been drawn against the second team in the League, a local pub team who had lost their earlier game. To win the League, the Centre team had to get two points from this game - a draw would be no good this time as the other team had a better goal difference.

Mark Tyndall called his team together for a final reminder of the tactics they had discussed earlier, saying 'Remember, this team is not as skilful as the Architects, but they're hard and play more the way we do, so keep it tight and don't give anything away. We can do it' he clenched his fist and said, forcefully 'Now put it together.'

They lined up determinedly against the other team. The supporters yelled their encouragement; probably more of them in favour of the Centre team as they were well known and popular with the Centre users.

The first attack from the pub team led to a warning for Big Jock as he up-ended one of their players, who rolled over several times in the accepted dying swan act. The player recovered miraculously with the aid of the magic sponge and was soon on his feet, though limping badly. No doubt when the ball next came to him he would be able to sprint after it as if nothing had happened. The referee made it plain to Big Jock, who towered over him, that he would stand for no more of that, and that he had better watch it. Big Jock stood listening with a surprised look on his face, all innocence, his hands spread out as if it had been a pure accident, However, a word from Mark Tyndall reminded him also to watch it because, if he was sent off, that would be the end.

The game restarted with boos from the pub team's supporters every time Big Jock played the ball. It was the kind of situation that he revelled in, as it suited his image to be cast in the role of villain.

The Welshman, Dai Williams, came more into the game, combining well with his team-mate, Winston, and was close to scoring several times. The opposition goalkeeper, however, was in great form and pulled off some fine saves, which were much appreciated by the crowd who were really enjoying the game.

As forecast, the teams were very even and, when half-time arrived with no score, it looked as if it would be the odd goal that would settle the match. Mark Tyndall called his team together, the sweat pouring down his face, his shirt drenched, but determined to win this game 'Look lads, there's nothing in it - keep going hard' he urged 'Let's try the fast break as we did in the first game, only this time we'll vary the end of it. Feed Winston fast down the hall. Taff, you and I will follow up equally fast. They'll expect you to shoot, Winston, so dummy and back-heel to the centre. Either Taff or myself will pick up the backpass. Right? Now, come on, we've got to win this' he urged, as forcefully as he could.

The second half was hard, the pub team being equally determined to win. Both teams, urged on by their supporters, were trying desperately to produce that little bit extra from tired limbs and aching lungs.

From the fitness point of view, the Centre team had the edge. They had the facilities at hand and the odd half-hour could always be found during their shift to train in the Centre's fine fitness and conditioning room. Mike Weston allowed them to do this, provided the privilege wasn't abused; it was, after all, good publicity for the Centre and helped to keep the boys happy. Time was running out - a draw was no good – and Mark Tyndall urged his men to a last effort; they were obviously fitter at this stage and the pub team was looking tired. The young Centre goalkeeper dived full length and just parried a fierce shot - Mark pounced on the ball immediately and cracked it down the hall in desperation. Whether by luck or good judgement,

Winston, situated well, took off as if his life depended on it, won the ball and dummied as if to shoot past the advancing goalkeeper. Instead, hoping for the best, he back-heeled the ball into space. Mark Tyndall, following up fast with an opponent closing, lunged for the ball but he was too late and cursed his lack of speed. However Dai Williams, following up as planned, met the ball beautifully with his right foot and crashed it into the net before the goalkeeper could get back.

The team was elated and Taffy disappeared under first three bodies, and then four, as the goalkeeper arrived to add his congratulations.

The Centre supporters went mad; they shouted, whistled and jumped up, arms raised aloft - this was what they had been waiting for. It was the final blow for the pub team whose heads were down, arguing amongst themselves. Their captain tried to raise their spirits, a near impossible task. All the Centre team had to do now was to keep them out for about sixty seconds more and the trophy was theirs.

After the longest minute they had known, accompanied by loud whistles from the Centre supporters, the referee finally blew his whistle for full-time. The Centre team threw their arms in the air - all of them shattered with the effort, but all smiles as they shook hands with the opposition and the officials. The crowd cheered and whistled, both sets of supporters agreeing for once, that it had been a good clean game and that the best team had won.

Mike Weston made a short speech, thanking the crowd for attending and making the evening a success, and invited the crowd upstairs to sample the lager for themselves after the presentation.

Led by Mark Tyndall, the Centre team stepped forward to receive the handsome trophy, which he held aloft in true Wembley fashion, to the delight of the staff and supporters.

Mike Weston was naturally pleased with his team's success. It meant more good publicity for the Centre, which was always welcome. He excused himself and made his way quickly to the bar to organise a bottle of champagne for the boys.

'Charlie' said McKay 'I think I'll push off now - but do you think you could stay and get something out of the staff?'

'Yes, I'll stay, Guv. You never know what might be said when their tongues are loosened after a few lagers – not to mention champagne.'

'Okay. I've organised that game of golf with Ted Veale for tomorrow morning, so I'll be in late. Somebody in this place must know more about the murder than they are saying and I intend to find out. Oh, and I'll have my portable phone with me. Anything urgent, just give me a buzz.'

After a while the team came into the bar red-faced and shiny, hair plastered down and still wet from the shower, but looking very pleased with themselves. Mark Tyndall was carrying the cup which he raised again above his head, to cheers from the supporters.

Mike Weston called them over to one corner of the bar where he had poured a glass of champagne for each of them to celebrate their victory. He made a short speech, again congratulating them on winning the trophy, and they all raised their glasses triumphantly. Big Jock felt embarrassed holding the slender glass in his huge hand and commented to Taffy, in a thick brogue 'This is a real poofters drink, my mouth's as dry as the bottom of a parrot's cage. I canna wait tae get ma fist roond a pint jug.'

Finishing the champagne quickly, they pulled several low tables together and settled down to enjoy themselves. Part of the time was spent re-living some of the better moments in the matches which they had just played and there was the inevitable leg-pulling over any mistakes or funny incidents which had occurred and, for some time, they were in that euphoric state which follows once a team has fought hard and ended up the victors.

Charlie was included in these celebrations. He already had a good relationship with most of the staff, having played darts against the Centre team on many occasions. His presence was accepted by them automatically. On such an occasion all thoughts of the murder, which had taken place not many days ago, were forgotten.

The lager promotion was going well and Steve Jameson was much in evidence presenting such items as table cigarette lighters, T-shirts and caps, all suitably endorsed with advertisements, to the winners of a draw in which every ticket holder had been included. The first of the team to win a prize was Winston, much to everyone's delight. The cap with the large peak made him look like an American baseball player.

The party progressed with a swing - all enjoying themselves as the alcohol gradually took effect. Soon, one of the cafeteria girls called Sandra was on her feet, her hips gyrating to the music, and trying to encourage others to join her. She pulled the young goalkeeper Bob Easton on to his feet and proceeded to cover him with her ample body. In fact Sandra protruded excessively in all the right places and the poor lad looked most embarrassed, although inwardly he had to admit to a certain amount of pleasure as they danced to cheers and shouts of encouragement. Sandra was a very friendly girl who was out to enjoy herself and after a few gin and tonics there was no holding her.

The cash registers were ringing continuously and Tony Lopez was busy behind the bar, with his jacket off, helping to deal with the impatient, thirsty customers. Mike Weston was pleased with the profit being made and Steve Jameson more than happy with the way the lager promotion was going. In fact, the evening was turning out to be an unqualified success. Charlie was finding it difficult to keep up with the boys as far as the lager was concerned, despite years of practice. He wanted to stay reasonably sharp.

Some people had already left and those remaining tended to be the hardcore of the staff from the Centre. Mark Tyndall had left some time ago accompanied by Barbara Johnson and it was obvious that even more demands would be made on his stamina before the night was over.

'Last orders' was called and, finally 'Time'. Ted Veale approached the remaining members of the team and said, in a friendly manner 'Come on, boys. We've had a good time tonight, let's start to make a move, eh?'

'Aye…rightho, Boss' slurred Big Jock, his eyes trying desperately to focus under heavy lids. Turning to Taffy, with a far from delicate dig in the ribs, he continued 'At least we hav'na got that bastart Fisher trying to push us aboot this time.'

'You're right there, Jock, that poor sod won't be spoiling our fun again, that's for sure' replied Taffy slowly, in lilting tones.

Charlie's senses froze on hearing this. So, there had been trouble last year at this competition. Just when he was thinking that all his socialising had been in vain, out of the blue came something which just might have made it all worthwhile. He would certainly have to tackle Big Jock and Taffy tomorrow, when they were sober.

Jock and Taffy, with their arms around one another for support and singing happily, together with two other Recreation Assistants equally unsteady on their feet, made their way down the stairs. As usual, Tony Lopez and his bar staff were the last to leave. The hectic football finals evening was over for another year.

Charlie called a minicab and Ted Veale headed for home.

CHAPTER TEN

Early the next morning, McKay left Charlie Bennett in charge of the shop while he carried out his plan to encourage someone in the Sports Centre to 'open up'. As arranged, he had challenged Ted Veale to an early game of golf at his own local club. An unorthodox approach perhaps, but McKay was ever willing to bend the rules if he thought some good would come of it.

He suspected that Veale, who he had been told was a keen golfer, would find it impossible to resist his challenge. McKay was no mean player himself. Encouraged by his father, a low handicap club player, he had started young and achieved considerable success at his local club in Fife. The Edinburgh Police Team had always been more than pleased to have his services and, after his transfer South, he had

146

continued to play, winning several competitions whilst a member of the Metropolitan Police Golf Society. Unfortunately, the long demanding hours of CID work, not to mention cancelled weekends, had reduced his play to purely social golf these days.

He pulled into the car park and looked forward with pleasure to the game in prospect, especially as the weather was dry and the forecast good. He met Ted Veale in the clubhouse and, after changing their shoes, they were soon on their way to the first tee.

Both men were immaculate, with McKay sporting his favourite tartan 'Tammy' and wearing a dark blue jersey with matching slacks. Veale wore white shoes, grey slacks and a red pullover displaying his club crest.

After a few warm-up swings, they were off with two good drives. There wasn't much difference in their handicaps but Veale was the player in form as he played regularly for his club.

After the first few holes, the game was fairly even, with Veale winning the longer holes. The sun had come out, it was a fine bright morning and McKay was enjoying himself. As far as he was concerned there was nothing like the open air and the beautiful contrasting greenery of a golf course to take his mind off work, especially if he was in the middle of a particularly difficult case. He had used this method before to clear his mind and found he was able to go back refreshed and much better able to concentrate.

Between holes the two men chatted amicably, mainly about golf. Veale had played many of the courses in McKay's part of the world so they were able to swap stories of famous holes at St. Andrews and Gleneagles. The atmosphere between the two was so convivial that McKay began to wonder how on earth he was going to introduce the real reason for the outing without spoiling the enjoyment.

He had, however, underestimated Ted Veale and was therefore taken a little out of his stride when the problem was solved for him. 'Look Mac' said Veale seriously 'I'm enjoying the game immensely but the suspense is killing me. I know that a Detective Chief Inspector in the middle of a murder enquiry doesn't take the morning off to play golf without a very good reason. If it will make things easier - just what is it that you want to know?'

'OK thanks, Ted' said McKay, as they were on their way to the next green 'You've been at the Centre a long time, what I really need is more background information on the staff, if you don't mind.'

'Sure, fire away' replied Veale 'I'm just as anxious as you are to get this terrible business cleared up, especially now that I find myself doing Dave Fisher's job in the Leisure Pool.'

They played out the rest of the game and for the next three or four holes McKay probed, Veale answered and McKay's game suffered – so much so that by the fifteenth Veale had won the game 4 and 3. McKay shook Veale's hand warmly and said 'Thanks for the game, Ted, I enjoyed it very much, even though we had to mix business with pleasure. Perhaps when the investigation is over we could have a rematch and concentrate solely on the golf.'

'Yes, I'd really like that, but don't put in too much practice in the meantime' replied Veale, laughing.

However, as they made their way back to the clubhouse, McKay continued to probe 'What about Barbara Johnson, Ted? What can you tell me about her?'

'Well, Barbara is one of the originals, like myself - been at the Centre from the beginning and knows the admin side backwards — she's also a very efficient secretary.'

'It wasn't so much her secretarial skills that I was interested in. I understand that she was very thick with Dave Fisher at one time. Is that true?'

'Yes, that's true, for quite some time in fact.'

'Do you know why it finished?'

Veale's eyebrows wrinkled as he replied slowly 'Strange you should ask - I've never really known.'

'Isn't that rather unusual? I get the impression that it's a very close-knit community at the Centre.'

'Yes, it is.' He thought for a moment before answering 'The only unusual thing that happened about the time they packed up was that Barbara was off sick for about ten days.'

'What was so unusual about that?'

'Well, Barbara was never off sick. It was a matter of pride with her - almost an obsession.'

'Do you know what was wrong with her?'

'She was supposed to have been involved in an accident of some kind, but didn't want to talk about it.'

'Didn't you think that was strange?'

'Not really - it fitted in with her hatred of being sick, she just never talked about being ill.'

'Did they go out together after that?'

'Not as far as I can remember. I certainly never saw them together again - apart from at work, of course' he added.

'I see' pondered McKay 'Thanks again, Ted, you have been most helpful.'

By the time they had showered and changed, the bar was open. 'Just in time' said Veale 'All that talking has given me a terrible thirst - I only hope it was worth it.'

'I hope so, too. Here, let me buy you a drink.'

******

'How did it go, Guvnor?' asked Charlie, as McKay arrived back at the Centre, soberly dressed and with the golf clubs well hidden in the boot of his car.

'We had a good game and I lost, but I think I may have won some useful information.'

'Good, good, as long as all that exercise was worth while' said Charlie, tongue in cheek.

'What about you last night, Charlie. Any luck?'

'Well, I saw it through to the bitter end, Guvnor, and I felt I was on to something almost at the last minute.'

'Go on' said McKay.

'Apparently there was some trouble last year at the same competition between Big Jock, one of the Sports Assistants, and Dave Fisher.'

'What happened?' asked McKay, anxiously.

'I tackled Big Jock this morning and it appears that Dave Fisher was Duty Manager last year at the Final and he had celebrated enthusiastically with the others. When the time came to clear the bar he foolishly picked up Big Jock's half-drunk pint glass.' McKay winced. Being a Scot he could well imagine what happened next.

'Yes Guvnor, you've guessed - to put it in Jock's own words 'We didna hae a fight - I just panned him - he should hae kent better than to touch a man's drink.' Charlie tried hard to imitate Big Jock's Scottish accent without much success. McKay smiled at the terrible effort.

151

'So you thought that Big Jock might have had cause to hate Dave Fisher.'

'I thought so at first, but after questioning him and Taffy Williams, his team-mate who was also present at the time, I came to the conclusion that it was all down to the drink. Blows were struck, but the incident was certainly nothing out of the ordinary as far as Big Jock was concerned - and nothing ever came of it.'

'So no luck, then?' said McKay.

'But hang on, there's more. They said at one stage that Fisher would not be giving Winston any more grief. I tried to get them to open up some more about this but they both clammed up.'

'So what did you do?'

'I managed to get hold of Winston when he was coming on duty and directed him to our room. He bounced in looking very confident, all dressed up in the latest gear, before he'd had a chance to change into his T-shirt and track suit.'

'He asked straightaway 'Why have you picked me out?'

I got him to sit down and said 'A little bird told me that you had a bit of aggravation with Fisher – you didn't say anything about that in your statement.'

Winston looked surprised, but replied confidently 'It was nothing really and anyway it was just between the two of us.'

'You'd better let me decide whether it was nothing or not' I said.

Then he said 'Obviously, someone has told you that I play a lot of snooker and pool, sometimes before I come on duty and quite often after – I can earn a bit of extra money that way.''

'OK, but where does Fisher come in?'

'Well, on the odd occasion the game over-ran my duty starting time and I was late –it's difficult to leave in the middle of a game, especially if there's money on it.'

'So Fisher caught you coming in or you were missing when the change-overs had started?'

'That's right, but it wasn't by much and the others always covered for me – so it was no big deal.'

'I imagine that it was more than just the odd occasion that you were late, if Fisher got upset about it. After all, anyone can be late, what with London Transport the way it is. Are we talking about the snooker hall in the High Street?'

'Yes, so I was never very late.'

'I can imagine that Fisher was just doing his job when he was taking you to task for being late. So I suggest that there was much more to it than that?'

'Well maybe, but he went over the top.'

'How do you mean?'

'Well, one day he came down to the hall and caught me playing when I should have been on duty. He didn't kick up a fuss or anything at the time but he had a good look at the people there and later asked me if I could get him some grass and then he wouldn't put in a report on me.'

'So what did you do?'

'Well like I say, it was no big deal, so I got him some. He said it was for that wacky sister of his. Did you ever meet her?'

'So I said 'What went wrong to change this cosy little arrangement?''

'With an exasperated sigh, he replied 'Well, grass was one thing, but after a while he wasn't satisfied with that, he wanted something stronger.''

'And he obviously thought you could get it for him.'

'Maybe, but I'm not stupid and no way was I going to get in any deeper - that's a completely different ball game. I've seen what happens to people who go down that road. That sister of his must have been putting the pressure on him.'

'So what happened after that?'

'Things turned a bit nasty, we had a flaming row and he threatened to put me on a report for being late on several occasions. That was a shitty thing to do, especially after I had done what he wanted.'

'So how was it resolved in the end?'

'Well, I reckoned that he had much more to lose than me, so I threatened to go to the Manager and tell him the whole story. He didn't like that, but it shut him up and I never knew whether he got any coke or not. But he seemed determined to get hold of some, somehow. Anyway it got him off my back and look what happened to him. I don't know if he got mixed up with any drug dealers or not in the end. And all for his sister!'

'He seemed to be relieved to get it all off his chest and then he said 'It was a shame really, because apart from this incident, he treated all of us very well, and that's all I can say.''

'I realised that this was a good time to finish the interview and said 'You may not have heard the end of this, Winston. You've been skating on very thin ice dealing in drugs and we'll see what my Guvnor has to say about it. You can go now.''

'And without another word he left.'

McKay said 'Well, I'm glad to see that you have been busy while I have been enjoying myself - now it's my turn.' His tone of voice had changed 'Find out if Barbara Johnson is free, will you Charlie? I want a word with her.'

******

Barbara Johnson had been interviewed earlier, along

155

with the rest of the Sports Centre staff, mainly to establish alibis for the night in question, and she had been cleared.

Charlie Bennett showed her into the office. McKay rose to his feet to greet her, smiled, and indicated a chair saying 'Take a seat, Miss Johnson, it's good of you to see me at such short notice.'

Barbara Johnson returned the smile uneasily, her beautifully even white teeth only just showing between full red lips. This was an unusual role for her, she was much more used to being in the driving seat and in full control of the situation when it came to dealing with men. She was exceptionally well turned out, as usual, in a pastel shade cashmere sweater which accentuated the shape of her breasts and waistline. The skirt, with a slit at the front, parted and showed her knees and some thigh as she crossed her long slim legs. An expensive perfume reached McKay as he took all this in at a glance, his eyes moving quickly down her legs.

She placed her hands neatly together in front of her, gaining confidence as she realised the impression that she was creating.

McKay noticed her long fingers adorned with several rings and a heavy gold bracelet encircled one wrist. His immediate thought was that this little lot must have cost a fortune and quickly decided that it was all well out of his price range. On the other hand, being comparatively young and red-blooded, he decided that, if he had the money, she would certainly be worth it. She certainly was a cracker, there was no doubt about that.

Charlie looked as if he was about to enjoy this interview more than most. The situation was rather like that of a doctor about to examine a beautiful patient - so many of his routine examinations are carried out on the female form full of imperfections, so that when one like Barbara Johnson comes along, the moment has to be savoured.

She enjoyed the admiring glances and replied 'You're very lucky you caught me just at the right moment. The weekly panic to get the pay sheets completed and off to the Town Hall is over, so I've got time to relax.' Then, looking straight at McKay with querulous eyes, she asked pointedly 'So what can I do for you then?'

Ignoring the obvious inference and trying not to look at Charlie, whose eyebrows had shot up a good two inches, McKay replied 'I'll come straight to the point, Miss Johnson. In an enquiry of this nature we have to consider every possibility, every link no matter how small.' He paused before adding 'It's your past association with Dave Fisher that we are really interested in.'

Barbara Johnson's face remained impassive and she replied calmly 'I guessed that you would get around to it sooner or later and I couldn't think of any other reason why you would want to see me again.' Looking straight at Mc Kay, she asked 'What is it exactly that you want to know?'

McKay seized the opportunity 'I realise that it may be painful for you, opening old wounds, but we really need to know as much as possible about Dave Fisher's character if we are to find the person who killed him. So, perhaps, would you mind taking it from the beginning?'

She sighed audibly, but settled herself more comfortably in her chair, drew a deep breath and began 'Our friendship started shortly after he came to the Centre on promotion. As the Deputy Manager he assumed responsibility whenever the Manager was on holiday or absent for any reason, so we worked closely together at times. Having been at the Centre since it opened, I was able to familiarise him with some of our procedures, which were different from those at his last Centre. We hit it off very well together and at the end of the day we often had a drink in the bar upstairs before going home.' She paused, her hands trembling slightly 'Do you mind if I smoke?' she asked, reaching quickly into a small handbag which she had placed beside one of the chair legs.

'By all means do' replied McKay 'Make yourself comfortable.'

She fitted a cork-tipped cigarette into a black holder and, taking a gold-coloured lighter in her carefully manicured fingers, applied the flame to the cigarette and puffed hard. With a quick movement of her head she blew the smoke ceilingwards and continued 'One evening, after we had worked later than usual, he asked me out for a meal. I accepted, and that's how it all started.' She paused for a moment, then shrugged her shoulders and, looking straight at McKay, added 'It was all pretty straightforward, there was nothing unusual or dramatic about it.'

McKay nodded and said 'Thank you, Miss Johnson, and how often did you go out together and for how long?'

'I suppose about two or three times a week over a period of about a year.'

'A year?' exclaimed McKay 'You must have got to know one another very well during that time?'

'Naturally - we had some good times together.'

McKay looked at Charlie and then asked the sixty-four thousand dollar question 'So what went wrong?'

Barbara drew nervously on her cigarette, looked down at the floor and answered reluctantly 'At the beginning he was good fun to be with and we had a lot of laughs, but after a while he seemed to change.'

'In what way?' pressed McKay.

'He started drinking more than usual.'

'Do you know why?'

'No. I asked him several times if anything was wrong but I never got a satisfactory answer. He always clammed up and became moody - so in the end I stopped asking.'

'What finally made you finish with him, then?' It was a loaded question and McKay had automatically assumed that she would be the one to terminate any affair.

He was right. She hesitated, coloured a little and answered uneasily 'Well, as I said before, he used to drink too much.' She paused, looked straight at McKay, and continued 'To be quite frank with you, Chief Inspector, a man who has had too much to drink is of no use to me.'

McKay looked at Charlie, whose face remained expressionless.

'Thank you for being so forthright - so what actually happened?'

'For God's sake, isn't that enough?' she answered fiercely, her dark eyes blazing with displeasure at being pressurised, her hands and fingers clasping and unclasping on her lap.

'Not really' replied McKay calmly, remembering what Ted Veale had told him on the golf course 'It would help us greatly if you could be more specific - even if it is painful for you.'

Barbara realised from McKay's determined look that he was unlikely to settle for anything less than the full story, so she gave in. Her body slumped in the chair and her hands dropped on either side of the seat. She spoke in a quiet resigned voice 'Oh well, if you must know everything, I suppose I'll have to tell you.'

Trembling even more, she lit another cigarette and continued 'One evening, we were out as usual and he had drunk too much. When we got back to my flat he tried to make love to me and couldn't. I suppose what happened next was partly my fault but I was all keyed up and felt suddenly let down. I said things to him that I probably shouldn't have. Anyway, he went berserk and started knocking me around. He slapped my face with the back of his hand, making my nose bleed and cutting my lip. I tried to protect myself but he was like a madman - he pulled my hair and punched me in the stomach.' Her eyes blazed and her face twisted with hate as she re-lived those terrible moments.

'Nobody, but nobody' her voice rose shrilly 'has ever done anything like that to me before. I was taken completely by surprise.'

'So what did you do?' asked McKay.

'I summoned up all my strength and did what my father told me to do, if ever I was attacked. I kicked him as hard as I could - right in the balls.' Her eyes narrowed as she spat the words out. 'Actually I nearly broke my toes doing it, but it didn't do his balls much good either. He yelled out, collapsed in a heap and was violently sick.' She paused, her eyes almost closed, and in a hushed voice continued 'I can still see him now, down on his knees on the bedroom carpet holding himself and moaning. I watched for a while spellbound - I couldn't believe what I had done. Then I realised that I had to get away from him and I ran out of the bedroom and locked myself in the bathroom. I prayed that he wouldn't come after me and, after what seemed like ages, I heard him moving about and then the front door slammed. I was shaking like a leaf and nearly passed out. I threw some water on my face and washed the blood off and looked in the mirror. My face was red and swollen, so was my nose. My top lip was split. I was sure that I would have black eyes in the morning.'

She nervously raised a trembling hand to her face as if she could still feel the pain 'I looked terrible.'

Suddenly, she lost the composure that she had fought so hard to maintain, dropped her head into her hands and started to sob, her dark hair falling over her hands. McKay offered a few words of comfort, waited till her sobbing lessened, and then said quietly 'So that's why you stayed off work and said that you had been involved in an accident.'

Her sobbing stopped. For a moment the room was silent. She dropped her hands from her face and made them into fists. She looked up at McKay, hate showing through eyes which were full of tears, black mascara marks on her face, and with venom spat out 'You bastard - you slimy bastard! You knew all the time - and you had to put me through all this. You're just as bloody bad as he was.'

She produced a handkerchief and wiped her eyes.

'No, you are wrong, Miss Johnson - I didn't know for sure' McKay assured her 'I just guessed that something had happened between you and him.' He wasn't about to disclose his source of information.

Barbara had regained her composure 'Well, now you do know for sure, I hope you are satisfied.'

McKay realised that he had gone as far as he could and, to break the mood, dispatched Charlie to get a cup of coffee for her.

She accepted the coffee silently and lit yet another cigarette. Gradually the situation was restored to normal.

McKay remained silent, while Charlie busied himself with notes. Suddenly Barbara, who had been deep in thought, blurted out 'What more do you want? I've told you everything. If you think I killed him, you must be bloody mad. It was the one and only time in my life that I've used violence to anyone - and that was in self-defence.' She was still very annoyed at having to re-live a painful incident, which she had tried desperately to forget.

McKay had one more question 'Do you know if he was friendly with other women during this time?'

'Look. I don't know what he did when he wasn't with me' she replied, impatiently 'You'd better ask that weird sister of his - she used to spend a lot of time at his flat - and there was only one bed.' She emphasised the last words.

McKay wondered whether she said them out of spite, but his mind flashed back to the first day of the case when they had entered Fisher's flat and found his sister there in bed waiting for her brother to return home.

'You're not suggesting...' started McKay.

'I'm not suggesting anything' Barbara interrupted sharply 'but she seemed to be around a hell of a lot. Oh, and by the way, I wasn't the only one here to have been close to Fisher – have a word with that receptionist, Mrs. Bryant.'

With that statement she closed her lips firmly together and McKay sensed that now would be a good time to close the interview.

He stood up and said politely 'Thank you, Miss Johnson for your co-operation, I hope it hasn't been too distressing for you.'

She stood up quickly, looked straight through McKay and without so much as a glance at Charlie, turned and hurried from the room.

McKay sat back in his chair - the adrenalin was flowing. He looked at Charlie who was still tidying up his notes. He smacked his fist into the other hand and said hopefully 'At last - at last, we're getting under the surface. She could easily have hated Fisher's guts enough for what he did to her, not only for the physical damage caused but mentally as well. Her self-confidence in her ability to deal with men must have taken a tremendous knock when he treated her that way.'

Charlie replied thoughtfully 'There's such a thing as being too trusting, Guv. You're bound to come unstuck sometime. I think that's what happened to our Barbara.'

'You're probably right, Charlie, but it still gives her a motive.' McKay fell silent, thinking of something that Barbara Johnson had said right at the end of the interview. He remembered what a lecturer had said on one of his courses at the Police College when dealing with the subject of Human Relations. He had said that, very often, the most important statement made by a person offering information or making a complaint was the 'throw-away line', the last thing the person said as they were going out of the door. In many instances the parting shot, made through pure spite, had more bearing on the subject than all of the conversation that had gone before.

She had made reference to Dave Fisher's sister and the receptionist at a moment when she was angry and under considerable stress. Perhaps it could have some significance. He would be the first to admit that he had looked upon Fisher's sister as just a pathetic figure, bewildered, shaken and in need of sympathy.

'Charlie' said McKay, thoughtfully.

'I know what you're going to say, Guvnor, - go and look up Dave Fisher's sister.'

McKay smiled, the double act was working well 'See what you can find out about her background from any flatmates, the landlady or anyone else in the house.'

'Leave it to me' insisted Charlie. Although usually content to assist McKay, he also looked forward to the prospect of carrying out his own investigations when the opportunity presented itself.

'While you're doing that, I'll tackle Mrs. Bryant.'

******

McKay caught up with Patricia Bryant as she was finishing her shift. She was in her early fifties, slim, dark-haired and attractive.

'Mrs. Bryant' he called 'I wonder if you could spare me a few minutes?'

'Certainly' she replied 'What's the problem? I've already made a statement.'

'Yes, I know, but this is something else' replied McKay, showing her into his office and indicating a seat to her. He sat down behind the desk and opened his briefcase, took out a single sheet of paper and placed it on the desk.

Mrs. Bryant placed her hands together, raised her eyebrows and gave McKay a quizzical look.

'You haven't been completely honest in your statement, have you?'

'What on earth do you mean – not completely honest?'

'You didn't divulge just how well you knew Fisher, did you?'

'Who says so?'

'Never mind, who says so, just answer the question.'

She sighed and replied 'No, I didn't, but it was nothing to do with your investigation.'

'Surely you can see that anything to do with Fisher's activities has to be thoroughly investigated?'

'I suppose so - but this was just between Dave and me.'

McKay sat back in his chair and said 'I suggest that you start at the beginning of the friendship and I'll decide whether it has any relevance - or not.'

She sighed and said 'Alright, if you insist. It all began almost the first day Dave arrived here on promotion. I was the duty receptionist and the manager asked me to take him through our procedures, duties and workloads - they can vary between Leisure Centres, you know. Anyway, I took a shine to him straight away, and it wasn't just a one-way thing – he seemed to like me. We got on very well in work situations, he could always be relied upon to deal with any awkward customers or trouble of any kind. He could also manage to calm down the situation and I admired him for the way he did it. I'd never been unfaithful in my marriage before but things hadn't been too good at home for some time, so that when he asked me out I was flattered - him

167

being so much younger than me. It's no excuse, I know. He also knew that I lived in the area and he asked me to help him find a flat near to the Centre. I agreed, and well, one thing led to another and we started an affair. Mind you, you didn't answer my question earlier regarding who told you that I had had an affair with Dave, but I've got a good idea who it was.'

'Have you?' said McKay.

'Earlier in the week, I saw you call Barbara Johnson in for interview and I've just put two and two together and I'll bet it was her. Come to think of it, she could have been the reason my husband found out.'

'What makes you think that?' queried McKay.

'Well, shortly after Dave and I finished, he started seeing her. I couldn't blame him really, she's much younger than me, but it made things awkward when we had to work together. I always sensed that she gloated a bit, but nothing was ever said...'

'Go on' encouraged McKay.

'I never knew why they split up, but they did - and the next thing I heard was that she was seeing young Mark Tyndall. I can't blame her for that either, he's the best of that bunch, an intelligent lad, good-looking too. She gives the impression that butter wouldn't melt in her mouth, with her good looks and great figure. OK, I'm jealous of that – I used to look like her once, but that woman is not whiter than white – I can tell you' she added, scornfully.

'Have you got any proof of anything against her?'

'No... but the more I think about it, the more I think that she was the one who let my husband know about my affair.'

'Maybe I'll find out when I interview him.'

'Do you have to see him?' pleaded Mrs. Bryant, 'Only things have been much better between us for some time now and this will only drag it all up again.'

'You're forgetting that this is a murder enquiry and I have to check all alibis for the night of the Caribbean Evening.'

'You surely don't think that he had anything to do with that, do you? I can see how your mind is working and, of course, when he found out we had a flaming row. He's a very quiet person really – too quiet, but he has a terrible temper and he was all for storming down to the Centre and confronting Dave and the manager, but I managed to talk him out of it.'

'How did you manage to do that?' queried McKay.

'Quite simple, really. I told him that I was bored with our marriage and that I would leave him if he went through with his threat. After a lot of soul searching, he agreed on the condition that I stopped the affair. I went along with that and that's when it ended. Some good did come from it though, he's much more attentive to me now and, anyway, Dave found somebody else.'

'Yes' thought McKay 'But he got more than he bargained for when he tangled with Barbara Johnson.'

'Thank you, Mrs. Bryant, you've tidied things up nicely. I shall have to see your husband but, don't worry, I shall be discreet. When would be a convenient time and place for me to meet him?'

She thought for a moment, before answering 'Not here in the Centre. Our house one evening would be the best.'

'Give me your home number and I'll ring and arrange it.'

******

One evening later that week, McKay knocked on the door of a neat semi in a tree-lined suburb and came face to face with Alan Bryant, a man of small stature with black curly hair. His horn-rimmed spectacles gave him a studious look.

McKay thought 'I can see why this individual wasn't measuring up to his bubbly, extrovert wife but in a marriage who can tell what really goes on between the two people.'

They went through the hall, into a lounge and sat down.

'Mr. Bryant' said McKay 'I really want to know what your movements were on the night of the Caribbean Evening'.

'When Pat said you wanted to see me, I anticipated that question. It doesn't take much to work that out. Actually, it's very easy, because Pat wanted to go but I'm not keen on dancing – I've got two left feet.'

'That doesn't surprise me' thought McKay, taking an instant dislike to the smugness of the man in front of him.

Bryant then said 'I'm a keen bridge player and on that night I was playing in a league match at my club - which we won' he said, proudly.

'What time did the match begin and how did you get there?'

'My usual partner picked me up and brought me home. The match started at seven and we got back about eleven o'clock.'

'And after that?'

'My friend came in for a drink – Pat fixed that and then went to bed. We chatted for a while, mostly about the hands we had played and how good an evening it had been, and then he left about midnight.'

'And your friend can verify this, I assume?'

'Yes, and about thirty to forty other people can verify that I was at the match.'

'I don't think that will be necessary' said McKay, caustically 'Just give me your friend's name and address. And you didn't leave the house again after your friend left?'

'No, of course not - why should I have?' Bryant replied, abruptly.

'You didn't go out and didn't go anywhere near the Leisure Centre?'

He stood up, eyes blazing, and said 'Look, when I heard about the affair Fisher wasn't my favourite man and, at the time, I was all for going down and sorting him out but this was the first time that anything like this had happened in our marriage and she threatened to leave me if I did. I was livid at the time but, thinking things over, I realised that maybe I was playing too much bridge. We sorted that out and things have been much better since.'

He smiled and said 'I play only twice a week now instead of three times.'

'Yes' thought McKay 'I can see how she was tempted when Fisher came along.'

CHAPTER ELEVEN

It was Sunday morning and at the Parkdale Sports Centre the usual quiet Sunday was disturbed by the South East England Schools Gymnastics Association, who were holding their 'Four Piece Individual Apparatus Championships' in the Main Sports Hall. The Centre was invaded by hundreds of enthusiastic school girls, all eager to lend their vocal support and encouragement to their particular favourite.

Another event was being held in the Rifle Range, with teams coming from as far away as 100 miles to compete in an 'Open Shoot'.

Starting at lunchtime, the sheer number of spectators and officials made extra demands on all of the staff, particularly those working in the cafeteria and the bar. Janet Simpson, the Catering Assistant, and her staff were coping well and both events were running smoothly.

This was one of the occasions that Mike Weston enjoyed most, but there was no doubt that it was hard work. The preparation had been considerable, but Mike was in his element with anything to do with gymnastics. He knew most of the judges and officials personally. It was like a reunion of old friends and, with his reputation in the gymnastics world at stake, he was determined to make sure that everything went smoothly. But, above all, he loved the atmosphere in the Sports Hall; it may have been only the English Schools Championships but, as far as the competitors were concerned, it could have been the Olympics. Gymnastics in the UK, and in many other parts of the world, had never been the same since the Munich Olympics in 1972 when Olga Korbut, the delightful young Russian, captured the hearts of everyone when she won her three gold medals in such style.

Today's young competitors, immaculate in their colourful, attractive, silken leotards, were full of grace beyond their years as they strutted to their particular exercise. With their heads high, and often with a pony tail streaming out behind, their young flexible bodies were the envy of many a spectator. They were encouraged by their coaches, who were delighted with a good performance, but angry and disappointed at the slightest mishap.

174

The strident notes of the inevitable piano used for the floor exercises echoed loudly around the hall before drifting upwards to be consumed by the maze of girders and cross-members which supported the roof.

The large knowledgeable crowd, silent during the exercise, voluble and appreciative afterwards, were enjoying the competition immensely. Weston, satisfied that all was going smoothly in the hall, made his way to the rifle range and into a completely different world. Instead of seeing young elf-like creatures, he immediately came face to face with men and women of all shapes and sizes, mostly wearing bulky ex-Army flakjackets, which reminded him of his army days. Round their necks hung black and orange ear protectors. These were the .22 Rifle people, a very popular club in the Centre, with some highly skilled members who were well placed in the British rankings. Weston immediately reached for a set of ear protectors and hung them round his neck.

The Range Officer, looking very military in his bearing and manner, was responsible for the safety and correct running of the Shoot. Suddenly he called for the next competitors to take up their positions on the raised shooting area. Satisfied that the targets down at the butts were correctly in position and that the entrance door to the range was securely locked, he gave the order to fire. Mike, along with those present in the range, automatically slipped the protectors over his ears. Almost immediately, the relative quiet of the range was shattered by the deafening crack of the rifles and the bullets as they struck the metal backing behind the targets.

Slowly the smell of cordite drifted back to the spectators, before the extractor fans could clear the air completely. That smell never failed to remind Mike of the Army - particularly the early days during basic training. Even then he had found the shooting interesting and now, after all these years, he still felt the same way about the sport.

Quickly checking with the officials that all was well, he made a hasty departure and, on his way out, was most surprised to bump into McKay.

'Hello, Mac' said Weston. They had become quite friendly during the investigation, despite the fact that he had to be considered a suspect along with the rest of his staff. 'What brings you here on a Sunday morning, when you could have been at home in bed?'

'No rest for the wicked' replied McKay, who was dressed less formally than usual, and who continued 'Actually I thought it would be a good idea to see the Centre at full stretch - apart from the fact that I'm quite interested in the Shoot anyway.'

'Of course, I'd forgotten. You have to be a marksman, don't you? But that's pistols, isn't it?'

'Mostly, yes, but we do fire other weapons as well.'

'Anyway, help yourself' said Weston 'But you will have to wait for the doors to be unlocked when this group of shooters has finished. If there's anything else you want to know you only have to ask.'

'As a matter of fact, there is something that I would like to have a look at and that's one of the charts on the wall above Dick Williams' desk in the office next to the plant room.'

'By all means' replied Weston, without hesitation 'Bill Forrester was on duty earlier, but I think you will find the office empty at the moment.'

'Thanks, anyway' replied McKay 'I'll just mooch around.'

At that moment, the door of the range was unlocked and McKay entered. He was very interested in the firearms scene and, although he shared the view of most coppers that it would be a sad day if all policemen were armed, he was also firmly of the opinion that in the modern war against crime, with firearms being used increasingly by villains, it was essential to have selected officers highly trained in the use of firearms. He enjoyed his regular trips to D8 Firearms Branch for training and re-classification as a marksman.

The training was highly professional and based on years of FBI experience in the training of agents. The present system had been in operation for fifteen years and had become more and more sophisticated in the light of the

British experience in the use of firearms. The Metropolitan Police Firearms Section had come a long way since that unfortunate day in the 1960s when three unsuspecting police officers, sitting in a patrol car in Shepherds Bush, were mercilessly shot. An outcry followed and, as a direct result, the present D8 Firearms Section had been formed.

On leaving McKay, Mike Weston made his way slowly back to the Main Hall wondering what on earth McKay could possibly want with the chart above Dick Williams' desk. In the end he gave up, shrugged his shoulders and was soon engrossed in the gymnastics once more.

McKay made his way down to the bar where he found Janet Simpson, the Catering Assistant. He bought a sandwich and a drink and approached the table where she was sitting.

'Do you mind if I join you?' he asked, with a smile.

'No, not at all. I'm glad of some company.'

'You seem to have your hands full today.'

'Yes, it's been hectic – we've really been at full stretch in the bar and the cafeteria. We're missing the two young girls who are on holiday and I've had to take on extra staff, which is always a problem.'

'Why is that such a problem? queried McKay.

'You have to keep a close eye on all casual staff – till you know that you can trust them. Sometimes they come well recommended, but you can never tell.'

'You've obviously had problems in the past – can you think of anything specific?'

'Well, strangely enough, I've been thinking about things since I made my last statement and there was one incident that came to mind in which Dave Fisher was involved, but I felt sure that Mr. Lopez would have mentioned it if it was important.'

'Refresh my memory, please.'

'He took on a barman, an ex-RAF chap called Geoff Young, who was a larger than life character. He was older, about 45, and I liked him. He was always jolly and a good person to work with – the trouble was he was too good.'

'What do you mean? – he was too good'

She thought for a moment before answering 'Look, I don't know all the ins and outs of the subject - all I can tell you was that he left under a cloud – and that Mr. Lopez didn't want to talk about it.'

'How long ago was this?'

'About six months ago, as far as I can remember. It was all hushed up and I can only think that Mr. Lopez was embarrassed because he took him on when we were pushed for staff and he prides himself on being a good judge of character.' She coloured slightly, saying 'I hope I haven't said anything out of turn.'

'No, no, it's nothing to worry about, perhaps it slipped his mind. Thank you, Miss Simpson, you've been most helpful.'

McKay rose and left the cafeteria thinking 'This sounds interesting. Lopez must have had a good reason for all this secrecy. I'll tackle him tomorrow.'

CHAPTER TWELVE

'Morning, Charlie – you ready for a bit of action?' said McKay cheerfully.

'He's got the bit between his teeth this morning' thought Charlie.

'Yesterday I found out from Janet Simpson that Lopez, her boss, had been involved in an incident involving Fisher and a barman who got sacked, which Lopez didn't mention in his statement.'

'Maybe he didn't consider it important' suggested Charlie.

'Anything, but anything, that involved Fisher and caused aggro around here recently might be important.'

'Let's pay Lopez a visit and see what he has to say.'

They found him in his office surrounded with paperwork as usual and he was, obviously, not too pleased to be disturbed first thing on a Monday morning.

'To what do I owe the pleasure of this visit' said Lopez, indicating seats for them to take.

'Mr. Lopez' said McKay, officiously 'during our investigations, it's come to our attention that there was some kind of incident involving yourself, Fisher and a barman called Young. You made no mention of this in your statement.'

Lopez was clearly taken aback by the tone of McKay's voice and he squirmed in his seat, embarrassed at being found out.

'Well…er…that's true, but who told you?'

'Never mind that' snapped McKay 'you should have told us instead of wasting our time - anything to do with Fisher has got to be important. I suggest you start at the beginning and tell us the full story.'

Lopez sighed, but composed himself and said' Look I'm sorry if I have caused you trouble, but the whole thing was down to me. We were short of a barman and Young's name came up. I interviewed him and he seemed OK, he had been in the RAF and was desperate for the job. I did my National Service in the RAF and maybe this swayed me a little. He was a bit larger than life, but I took him on. Casual staff for the bars and the cafeteria are one of my biggest headaches in this job and I pride myself that I'm a good judge of character - but with Geoff Young I came unstuck.'

'Just get to the point' said McKay, impatiently.

'He was nice enough, quick and got on well with the customers but after a while the takings didn't add up with the stock check and the suspicion fell on him. Fisher and I kept an eye on him but he always seemed to ring the correct amount on the till for the drinks and didn't take any more than he should have when the customer offered him a drink.

'So what was the fiddle?' said McKay, getting even more impatient.

'Young always tidied up thoroughly at the end of his shift and left the bar immaculate for the next bar-person. He emptied all the overflow of beer from under the pumps and then took the bottle-top container out to a sink in the little room adjacent to the bar to empty it and closed the door behind him. Fisher, who had cashed up with him and was still in the bar, thought it was a bit suspicious so he waited a few seconds and then suddenly opened the door – just in time to see Young separating the bottle tops from several one pound coins. It was obvious that as he opened a bottle of beer or coke and the top dropped into the holder, he would drop a one pound coin in at the same time, the sound of one covering up the other. It was ingenious - he could palm a one pound coin at any time during his shift

183

and ring up one pound less on the till when no-one was looking. At the end of the night, when cashing up with the duty manager, the money would tally with the till-roll.'

McKay, intrigued, now asked 'And what happened next?'

Lopez grinned triumphantly 'Well, Fisher told me that when Young was caught in the act he tried to bluster his way out of it by saying that it was the first time that he had done it and that it would never happen again. Fisher made certain of that – he sacked him on the spot. It certainly stopped his game.'

'So what was Young's reaction to being sacked?'

'Naturally he wasn't too pleased and turned nasty. He threatened to complain to the Council and take us to an Industrial Tribunal but we knew that he would never go through with it - he had been caught red-handed.'

By this time, Lopez, who had coloured up and was sweating profusely, pulled out a handkerchief and mopped his brow.

'You seem to be worried, Mr. Lopez. Is there something else you haven't told us?'

'There is, actually. I'm anticipating your next question. Did I tell the manager? Well, I didn't and there was a reason.'

'It had better be a good one' quipped McKay, scornfully.

'It is, from my point of view. You see I've applied for a higher catering position with the Council at the Town Hall and with my track record I stand a good chance of getting it.'

'So what's the problem?'

'I need to get a good recommendation from him and I didn't want him to hear about my mistake in hiring Young - it wouldn't look too good.'

'Strange' remarked McKay 'I would have thought that he would be pleased at the way that you and Fisher had dealt with the situation. Getting back to Fisher – did Young go quietly in the end?'

'Yes. Fisher escorted him off the premises and I never saw him again.'

'That may be so, but here's a man who had an altercation with Fisher, who is subsequently found dead in the Centre pool, and you don't think important to tell us about it?' blurted out McKay, his voice rising 'At the very least, it's withholding information that would have been useful to us in a murder investigation.'

'Yes, I'm sorry, but no-one could foresee how things were going to turn out' he pleaded 'and I suppose that I felt so embarrassed because I was the one who had hired him in the first place.'

'I don't buy that, Mr. Lopez' said McKay, getting even more officious.

'Well, I've already told you why I didn't tell the manager and it's much the same reason why I didn't tell you. I need this promotion and I wasn't prepared to take the chance of losing it.'

'Is there anything else that you haven't told us about?'

'No – honestly, you've seen the way things run here, it's a happy ship and everyone gets on well together. I take some credit for that' he added, proudly.

'Not everyone gets on, Mr. Lopez. You seem to be forgetting that the Deputy Manager was discovered dead in your swimming pool and that's the reason why we're having this little chat.'

'But surely you don't think that one of the staff did it, do you? It must have been someone that Fisher fell out with.'

'Someone like Young, who was sacked by him, perhaps?' pressed McKay.

Lopez, who realised that he had been boxed into a bit of a corner, replied 'No, I don't think that at all, you're twisting my words.'

'Well, you've brought this situation on yourself, by not being straightforward with us in the first place. Now is there anything else that we should know about' said McKay impatiently, looking straight at Lopez.

'There's nothing else – honestly' pleaded Lopez.

'OK' said McKay, rising 'but I can't guarantee that this will not get to the ears of Mr. Weston - that will depend on where our enquiries lead us. Now just give me Mr. Young's address and we'll leave you in peace.'

Lopez, glad that the interview was over at last, delved hurriedly into one of his desk drawers and produced a blue folder. He copied out the address quickly and sheepishly handed it to McKay.

'Thank you, but we may need to see you again' said McKay, as they left the room.

Outside the door, Charlie said 'You certainly put the wind up him, Guv. He doesn't come over whiter than white.'

'You're right, I want him to sweat for a while. He deserves it for messing us about. Now a quick cup of coffee and then we'll see if we can track down Geoff Young.'

******

Suitably refreshed, McKay and Charlie found themselves outside a run-down housing estate in the Harlesden area not far from the Leisure Centre. They parked some way away from the estate itself, to avoid the car being vandalised, and were soon making their way along a walkway till they arrived outside number sixty-seven.

Charlie hammered on the door, which was soon answered by a man who fitted the description of Young given by Lopez. He was wearing jeans and a T-shirt which could have done with a wash.

'Geoffrey Young?' queried McKay officiously, producing his warrant card 'I'm Detective Chief Inspector McKay and this is Detective Sergeant Bennett.'

'I am' replied Young, confidently 'but what on earth do you want with me?'

'We just want to have a little chat. Can we come in, it's private' said McKay, noticing several doors opening and heads peeping out.

'Sure' replied Young 'Follow me and close the door.'

He led them down a corridor into a poorly-furnished room and settled them down on an old battered settee.

'What's this all about then? I haven't done anything wrong.'

'I expect you've heard about the death of David Fisher at the Leisure Centre.'

'It was in all the papers - but what's that got to do with me?'

'In the course of our investigations, your name came up as being a barman in the Leisure Centre- is that true?'

'You know it's true, otherwise you wouldn't be here' Young replied, defensively 'but it was only for a short while' he added, quickly.

'Mr. Young, there are two sides to every story and we've heard one side, would you care to give us yours, up to the point where you were sacked.'

Young replied confidently 'It was no big deal. Lopez took me on, but Fisher had it in for me and I was sacked.'

'I think there was a bit more to it than that. Don't let's mess about. We know all about the scam you were working and you were caught red-handed.'

'Oh alright, the job was OK but the wages were so poor, I only tried to make a little bit extra, that's all, everyone does it.'

'But not everyone gets caught the way you did' quipped McKay.

'Look, I only did it because I've been having a bad time. I'm living with a young girl who has a boy of four, and my Air Force pension only goes so far. She's out at the moment and, as it happens, he's asleep in the other room.'

'It's not your domestic arrangements that we've come about. I want to hear from you what happened after you were caught and sacked. I hear you created quite a rumpus.'

'Well, obviously I wasn't too pleased – but Fisher was on my back and seemed to take great delight in catching me and giving me the push.'

'I believe he escorted you out of the building on that night. Tell me what you talked about.'

'Well, things got quite heated because he gloated rather, and said that he would make sure that I didn't get another job in the Borough.'

'What was your reaction to that?'

'I had a bit of a go at him, because it meant that I would have to pay fares to travel to any work – he was just being vindictive. There was no need for that, but we didn't come to blows or anything like that.'

'So you didn't pay him a visit on a certain night after a function at the Centre swimming pool?'

'Oh come off it! I'd heard that you weren't getting very far with the investigation. You must be desperate if you think you can pin that on me.'

'Can you tell me what you were doing on that Saturday night?'

'No I can't, but I was probably here. We usually watch a video and have a few drinks. I love those old movies, especially the Westerns with all the old stars. Louise goes out to work and I look after the boy, but she keeps a diary and should be able to tell you.'

'When is she likely to return?'

'Quite soon, actually. Look, if you think I had anything to do with the murder you must be mad.'

'Think about it – you had the motive, he sacked you and then turned the screw - you also know the set up at the

Leisure Centre and perhaps the way Fisher used to have a quiet drink after everyone had gone home.'

They were interrupted by the sound of the front door opening and woman's voice calling 'Is that you, Geoff?'

'Yes, come in. It's only the police' he rose to meet her.

'Why, what's happened - is Joe alright?'

Into the room came a young girl, wearing jeans and a white top. She slipped off her coat, shook her hair loose and looked round at the two policemen.

Young spoke up 'Don't worry, it's me they've come to speak to. They want to know what I was doing on the night of the Caribbean Evening at the Leisure Centre. I told them that you might be able to help with your diary.'

She felt around in her small handbag and produced a battered diary. Turning the pages her crimson nail stopped at an entry. 'That was the night we had a video out from Blockbusters. I always keep a check in case they say that we haven't returned it. I can't be sure, but it was probably one of your old Westerns – you can easily check at the shop.'

'OK' said McKay 'So what happened after the movie?'

'Quite often I go to bed. I'm usually tired and I leave Geoff to it.'

'Can you say whether Geoff left the flat that night after the video?'

191

'No, I can't say for sure, but I'm a very light sleeper and I'm sure I would have heard him.'

'Thank you' said McKay 'We'll leave you in peace.'

They headed down the corridor towards the door, followed by Young, whose parting words were 'Well, at least you know where I am if you want to find me. Oh, and by the way, that Lopez - you should have a look at him – he's not whiter than white.'

'What do you mean?'

'Well he's only a catering manager with the Council, so how can he afford to live in a bloody great mansion in Harrow?'

Young had McKay's full attention by now – was this just spite on the part of Young because he had been sacked or was this another example of the 'throw-away line' at the end of a conversation, which had some truth in it?

'Have you any evidence to back up what you are obviously alleging?

'No – all I'm saying is that, unless Lopez was left some serious money by a rich old aunt, the money to buy such a place must have come from somewhere – check it out.'

'Thank you, Mr. Young, for your assistance, we may do just that.'

Outside and on their way to the car, Charlie piped up, 'What do you think, Guv? Was he just trying to throw attention away from himself – he had reason to hate Fisher and Lopez.'

'Could be a bit of both, Charlie, but it's certainly worth having a look at. We've got time now, but remember I'll leave it to you to check out his story about hiring out the video from Blockbusters.'

'Will do.'

McKay produced a list of names and addresses of the Leisure Centre staff from his briefcase and found where Lopez lived. Soon they were heading west towards Harrow and into a very upmarket area. They turned into Lloyd's Avenue which was tree-lined, with most of the properties having long drive-ways with security gates and hi-tech cameras.

'Blimey, look at that' said Charlie, as they identified Lopez's house 'Young certainly wasn't exaggerating when he said that it was over the top for a catering manager.'

'I agree, this needs looking into. But I can't spare you and Steve – I'll get someone from the local CID to keep an eye on the place for a few nights. I'm hungry. Let's get back to the Centre for lunch.'

******

'Charlie' said McKay, after lunch in the Sports Centre bar 'it's been several days since we visited Richard

Williams. If he's as tough as they make out then he should be fit enough to see us by now.'

They were soon climbing the stairs of Brook Mansions and knocking on Williams' door. They waited. One or two heads appeared round neighbouring doors but there was still no answer.

'He's got to be at home' insisted McKay 'I can't imagine him going anywhere, considering the state he was in the last time we saw him.'

'Give it the treatment, Guv' said Charlie and McKay proceeded to hammer on the door to such an extent as to leave anyone inside in no doubt that the person on the outside was no ordinary caller. Also, that there was little chance of them going away before the door was answered.

It had the desired effect. They heard someone making their way slowly up the passageway towards the door, cursing and complaining as they went.

'Go on, break the bloody door down' a voice grumbled, as the door opened four inches on the safety chain.

'Detective Chief Inspector McKay here, open up will you?' demanded McKay, officiously.

The chain was slowly undone and the door opened inwards to reveal a much improved Richard Williams, no longer swathed in bandages but not looking too good either. The bruising around his still half-closed eyes was a mixture of red and black in colour and his swollen nose, complete with stitches, looked broken and most painful. The pattern of stitches on the shaved parts of his head and face looked incongruous and unreal, as if someone had taken a black felt pen and drawn them on. He was still unable to straighten up and was in obvious pain. The effort required to come to the door had been considerable.

'What the hell do you want this time?' he mouthed through swollen lips 'I've already spoken to the Law.'

'I know' replied McKay, tersely 'That was to do with your present state. I want to speak to you about the death of Dave Fisher.'

Williams' defiance left him and his eyes showed resignation as he turned and mumbled 'You'd better come in then.'

McKay and Charlie followed him as he made a slow, painful return to the lounge, where he collapsed into an armchair. Automatically, he reached for comfort in the shape of a cigarette from a packet on a low table beside his chair. Placing it gently between his swollen lips, he applied a light and puffed, exhaling noisily as he relaxed back into the chair. The stubs in the overflowing ashtray on the table, and the stale atmosphere in the room, indicated how he spent most of his day. McKay and Charlie organised chairs for themselves and waited patiently until Williams had composed himself.

McKay spoke 'Mr. Williams, you are alibi-ed for the actual time of Fisher's death, but I'd like you to fill in some background information.'

'Yes, alright. What sort of thing do you want to know?' replied Williams, unconcerned.

'Well, for a start, I understand that you have been at the Centre since it opened. Is that right?'

'Yes, that's right. Bob Forrester and me have been together since the beginning.'

'Do you get on well together?'

'Very well, we're good mates.'

'And Fisher?'

Williams thought for a moment before answering 'When he first came he didn't know much about the pool side of things, but he soon picked it up and we all got on well together. You won't find a better-run swimming pool than that one, you know.' Despite his obvious discomfort Williams still managed to convey a sense of pride in the job that he did at the Centre and McKay warmed slightly towards him.

Having put Williams at his ease, McKay slipped in the sixty-four thousand dollar question 'You obviously enjoy working at the Centre, but how did you manage to get a Council job like that with your previous convictions?'

Williams nearly choked - he was completely taken aback. Forgetting his injuries for the moment, he tried to sit

196

up but with a scream of pain he collapsed back again, red in the face.

'What previous?' he spat out, his eyes narrowing even more.

'Come off it, Williams' said McKay 'We know all about them, including the actual bodily harm.'

Williams, realising that he would get nowhere by bluffing, changed his tone of voice and pleaded 'But that was bloody years ago. Alright, I was a bit of a tearaway once but not any more. Do me a favour will'ya.'

'You still haven't answered my question' insisted McKay.

'Listen, I worked bloody hard to pass my exams at night school. It wasn't easy I can tell'ya. So, when it came to getting a job at one of the old swimming baths, I leaned on someone who owed me a favour. But I've never been in trouble since - honest - you can ask anyone at the Centre.' There was no hostility at all in his eyes as he pleaded with McKay and then a thought suddenly occurred to him 'Who else knows about this?'

'Only the Manager.'

'Christ - what did he say?' asked Williams, anxiously.

'Look, we're getting away from the point - it's Dave Fisher that we're here to talk about' insisted McKay, pointedly 'Did you ever have a disagreement with him at any time?'

'No, definitely not. I liked him. I told you, we got on well together. He used to go over the top with his drinking but that was up to him - it never bothered me.'

'And can you think of anyone who would want to see Fisher dead?'

'No, nobody' came the immediate reply.

McKay realised that he was wasting his time. He stood up, nodded to Charlie and departed, saying 'Thanks for your help Mr. Williams, we'll see ourselves out.'

As they left the building, McKay said 'Tomorrow, Charlie, you'd better go and find out what you can from the sister, we've only got allegations that she was connected to drugs – but no proof. Also, find where she might have got the drugs from? Something else we haven't given enough thought to, is the possibility that Fisher himself supplied her.'

'That's right, his bank balance was always in the red according to the Manager and maybe he needed the money.'

'Fisher might have got himself mixed up with a supplier in the area and maybe - just maybe - he couldn't settle up and on the night of the Caribbean Evening someone paid him a call. A call that went wrong – stranger things have happened at sea.'

'It wouldn't have been too difficult for someone to find out his movements, everyone seems to know that he was in the habit of staying to the end of a function and having a drink before taking a cab home. OK, Guv. When I catch up with her, I'll put the pressure on and maybe get the truth from her.'

CHAPTER THIRTEEN

Next morning, Charlie and Steve made their way towards Willesden and the address of Fisher's sister, Anne.

The terraced street was pleasant enough, tree-lined, but spoilt as usual by the conglomeration of cars parked day and night, because of the lack of garages. The houses in the street resembled countless others in the semi-outer fringe of London, three-storeyed with a basement and converted into flats, all within easy reach of town. The latter being the most important feature for the occupants who had seen the fares on London Transport rocket over the past few years.

Charlie parked the car in the nearest vacant spot to the address that they were looking for. As they went up the steps to the front door the curtains of the room to their right moved slightly - their arrival had been noticed by someone.

They were two men of above average height, both wearing suits, and were out of place - they had to be officials of some sort. Charlie selected a ground-floor bell from the half-dozen small, black, plastic name holders, pressed the bell three times and waited. Nothing happened. He pressed again and this time the curtains of the room to the right were pulled back and a large woman appeared. She had huge overflowing breasts which seemed to be struggling to escape from an equally huge bra.

'Wat you want?' she boomed, in a flat staccato voice.

'Flat six' replied Charlie, showing his warrant card. The woman recognised it instantly and said 'Wait dere. I let you in.' Seconds later the door opened and the woman's frame filled the doorway, then she stood back and invited them into the hall 'Flat six you say. Who you want?'

'We want to see Anne Fisher' said Charlie.

'You wanna see Anne Fisher' the woman boomed 'I wanna see her too.' She dabbed a huge right index finger on her chest before announcing 'She left owin' rent.'

'Are you the landlady, then?' asked Charlie.

'No. Ma husban'. He's landlord.'

'When did Anne Fisher leave?'

Her hand cupped her chin and her large eyebrows came together, as she thought for a moment before answering 'Was one mornin' at beginin' of lass week. I wen' out shoppin'. A neighbour tole me she left 'fore I come back.'

'You say she left owing you rent?'

'Dat's right. What you wan' her for?'

Charlie answered the question with another 'You have no idea where she went?'

'No. I ask other girls but they say they don' know. They come home 'bout six from work' she volunteered, helpfully.

'OK, thanks very much for your help. We'll come back after six.' They turned and walked back down the steps to the car, watched by the woman from the doorway.

'Not much joy there, Charlie. Looks like our bird has flown. What are we going to do till six o'clock?'

'You know, Steve, right from the beginning something has bugged me about this girl. I think we'll call at the local nick and run a check on her.'

Charlie pointed the car in the direction of Harrow Road Station and it wasn't long before they were turning into the station yard. After making themselves known to the Station Officer, they carried out the check through the computer at Hendon. In no time they had a print out. 'Not like the old days' thought Charlie 'when you had to wait for someone to go and physically search through index cards. Steve wouldn't know anything about that.' Charlie studied the printout. There it was in black and white:

'ANNE FISHER, born 1.6.1960, two convictions for possession of drugs.'

'I knew it. I knew there was something odd about that girl' said Charlie, angrily 'We should have noticed it the first time at Dave Fisher's flat the morning he was murdered. She was a poor scrap of a thing but there was no reason at that stage to connect her with drugs. Wait till Mac hears about this' he continued, enthusiastically.

They had a bite to eat in the canteen, which was average, no better or worse than usual; like any other police catering establishment. Charlie took the opportunity to look up some old CID colleagues and managed to pass the time till just after six o'clock when they went back to the house, again pressing the bell for number six.

This time the door was answered by a tall, pleasant, good-looking girl with long blonde hair, aged about 21. The landlady had obviously told her of their previous visit, as they seemed to be expected. The tall girl, who had a north-country accent, led them upstairs to the small flat which led off the landing of the top floor. It was very sparsely furnished, with just the bare essentials. The girls had attempted to brighten the place up with a variety of posters, everything from their favourite pop stars to copies of the original Moulin Rouge posters.

Charlie and Steve were introduced to a second girl who was also from the north and about the same age, but she was dark, slim and very quiet. The tall blonde was the one that did all the talking. After the usual preliminary chat to put them at their ease, it transpired that both girls worked for one of the big Oxford Street stores and thought that London was marvellous, far better than what they had left up north. London was much more exciting and here was living proof, as they were being interviewed by two CID men, one of whom was tall, young and very handsome. They both fancied him and made it very obvious. Steve, for his part, played them along and, at the right time, Charlie turned the conversation to Anne Fisher.

'How did you come to meet Anne?' he asked, casually. The blonde answered 'Well, we came down from the north together and got this job in Oxford Street and we were living in the store's hostel. Then we saw this advert in the evening paper for two girls to share with one other. We answered the advert and the other girl turned out to be Anne Fisher - so that's how we met her.'

'Did you all get on well together?' asked Charlie.

'I suppose so, considering we didn't know her. But she could be a bit moody at times and secretive. Up north we are always very open and straightforward, you know.'

'Yes' thought Charlie 'I've heard that before.' It had been his experience that, whenever he met people from 'oop north', invariably within five minutes they had told you how open and straightforward they were. He found this irritating; after all he didn't go around telling everyone how quick and clever he was, and how early they would have to get up in the morning to put one over a cockney.

The dark girl was talking solemnly 'She didn't always pull her weight with keeping the flat clean either and was very often short of money for her share of the rent.'

'Did she have a regular job?'

'Not really. She preferred to work as a temp, but she got well paid when the agency found her work. Anne was funny, though; when she had money she used to be quite happy staying in the flat. When the money ran out she would just contact the agency again.'

Remembering the previous convictions, Charlie pressed 'Come on now, there was another reason why she was always short of money, wasn't there?'

The two girls looked at one another, wondering what to say.

'Look, we know that she was into drugs' continued Charlie 'so you can tell us about it.'

'Oh well, if you know about it already' said the blonde, thankfully 'But we never had anything to do with the drugs' she added, quickly 'It was something we hadn't come across before. So, when she was a bit funny or off-colour, we just thought that she was moody and miserable. She never looked very healthy anyway.'

'So how did you find out she was a user?'

'A few weeks ago we went to work at the usual time, about 8 o'clock, but when we got to the bus stop I realised that I had left my purse in the bedroom, so I went back for it.' She paused.

'Go on' urged Charlie.

'Well, I let myself into the flat quietly, because I knew Anne wasn't working and when we left she was still in bed. As I passed her room the door was slightly open and I saw her injecting herself in the arm. I couldn't believe my eyes. I thought at first that she must have diabetes or something like that, I never thought about drugs. Anyway I must have made a noise because she looked up and saw me.'

'What happened next then?'

'Very calmly she told me all about it - as if she was pleased that it was out in the open. About the fact that she had got in with a bad crowd when she first came down to London and got the habit. First it was just soft drugs but after a while these didn't do anything for her anymore and then she had started mainlining - I think that's what she called it. I was horrified, I'd never come up against anything like it before. I told her that she should see a doctor or go to hospital but she just laughed at me. I asked her if her brother couldn't help her, because she was very close to her brother, you know, she often used to visit him and stay the night at his flat.'

'Did you think that was strange?'

'Not really' her blonde hair cascaded around her shoulders, as she shook her head 'She didn't seem to have any other friends.'

'Did her brother give her money?'

'I think he must have done' she continued, pensively 'because several times when she was short she was able to pay her share of the rent after going to see him.'

'Tell me about how she came to leave last week' Charlie asked, keeping the conversation going.

The dark-haired girl took up the story, which was developing into a double act.

'She lost her job. We both offered to take her out to try and cheer her up, but she wouldn't go. She did borrow some money though, from both of us. We didn't like to refuse at the time but now we realise that it must have been used to buy drugs. Anyway, one evening we came home as usual and she had gone, taking most of her things with her - which didn't amount to much' she added.

'Did she leave a note or anything?'

'Yes' said the blonde 'There was a note which just said that she was leaving and that she would let us have the money back as soon as possible and 'goodbye!'.'

'Did she say where she was going?' asked Charlie, hopefully.

'No, not a thing.'

'Do either of you have any idea where she might have gone?'

They both shook their heads in unison.

'Great' thought Charlie 'Just when we think we are getting somewhere, she disappears.'

'Well girls, thanks very much, you've been very helpful. If by any chance she does get in touch with you, will you please ring this number' Charlie handed the blonde his card.

'That's alright, anytime' the girls answered, talking to Charlie but looking admiringly at Steve, who had been confined to note taking.

As the two men made their way down the stairs and quickly into the street, the downstairs curtains moved slightly. Their departure had been noted and no doubt in about two minutes flat the girls would be getting the third degree from the landlady.

Charlie broke the silence 'I think I just got you out of there in time Steve, those two would have eaten you.'

Steve Wade's handsome face broke into a smile, showing his near perfect teeth.

'Well Charlie' he replied 'You know what it's like, either you've got it, or you haven't.'

'You modest young sod' said Charlie, jokingly 'One thing's for sure, Steve, if they ever send you back to uniform branch, you'll need a new helmet, 'cos the old one will be too small.'

Steve, being quite used to this type of banter, laughed and said 'Okay, but where do we go from here?'

'I've got an idea – it's a long shot but we might get something out of it. Back to Harrow Road nick.'

This time they went straight to the front office where the Station Officer, by pure chance, happened to be an old colleague well-known to Charlie. After the usual greeting and inevitable banter which takes place between old friends, Charlie explained the reason for his visit.

'She's just disappeared. As far as we know she hasn't got any money. We thought she might have got herself into a squat. Have you got many on the ground at the moment?'

The Station Officer replied without hesitation 'Yes, as a matter of fact there are three. Two fairly well established, and a new one which only came to our notice yesterday. Do you want the addresses?'

'Yes please' said Charlie, and, after thanking his old friend, they parted with a promise to meet sometime and sink a few pints for old times' sake.

CHAPTER FOURTEEN

Steve Wade turned the CID car into the street where the
new squat had been set up, while Charlie strained forward
to pick out the number they had been given. They had both
agreed that this was the place where Anne Fisher was most
likely to be, if she hadn't left the area altogether.

Peering out of the side window, Charlie remarked
impatiently 'Nobody ever puts numbers on their houses
these days - I pity the poor bloody postman.'

They drove slowly past the house that they were looking
for. The cars that were parked on either side of the road, the
paint peeling from the windows and doors and the tatty
curtains gave the whole street a run-down look. The street
lights came on suddenly, as if on cue to set the scene. It was
that time of day when the fading natural light blends with

the artificial, creating an atmosphere of mystery. However, they had no time to notice such subtleties, as they were too busy concentrating on the house.

'Ground floor and basement look deserted' commented Steve.

'Right, but I can see a light on the first floor, so somebody must be there' replied Charlie, craning his neck to look upwards.

The street was quiet, with the only real signs of life coming from a pub on the corner, whose welcoming lights shone into the road some fifty yards past the house. At this time the occupants of the houses were either eating their dinner after the day's work, settling down in front of the television, or getting ready to go out to the pub.

Steve pulled in at the corner by the pub, reversed, and drove towards the house again. This time he eased gently to a halt between two parked cars on the opposite side of the road. Charlie got out and crossed the road, searching both ways for people as much as for vehicles. He mounted the steps leading up to the front door and gently tried the handle - it was locked. He looked casually in both directions, but nobody seemed concerned about his presence. Descending the steps, he paused on the pavement and then disappeared into the darkness of the basement. He remained still, until his eyes became accustomed to the gloom. In front of him, he could see a door and one casement window. He waited, feeling much more secure now that he was hidden from the street. About a minute later he was joined quickly by Steve, who had remained in the car to see if Charlie's presence had attracted any attention. Charlie turned his attention to the door, but it too was locked.

'Looks pretty frail' he whispered.

'Want me to shoulder it?' volunteered Steve quietly, always ready to show off his physical prowess.

'Make too much noise' said Charlie, shaking his head 'That window looks much easier' and, producing an ordinary penknife, he opened the small blade, Fortunately, the street lighting did not reach into the basement and within seconds Charlie had slipped the catch and was carefully easing the lower window up. Quickly and quietly they ducked through the opening into the pitch-dark room where they remained motionless, the only sound being their breathing. Charlie's was much louder than Steve's.

The air in the room was damp and there was a strong smell of stale urine and rotting vegetation. Suddenly there was a noise in one corner of the room. Charlie flashed a pencil of light in that direction and heaved a sigh of relief when he saw, staring at him from the rotten end of an old mattress, a mangy-looking rat, its beady eyes shining brightly in the torchlight.

He moved the light quickly round the room to get his bearings and, followed by Steve, crossed to an interior door which stood ajar.

They paused at the entrance, before slowly easing the door open. Somewhere, high above them, they could hear the sounds of a radio, probably coming from the room where they had seen the light. The door led up some stairs to the hallway, on which the stair carpet had long since rotted away. Each stair creaked, especially under Steve's weight, and they listened anxiously for signs from above that their presence had been discovered.

Reaching the hallway, with its stained wallpaper hanging in tattered strips, they paused again to listen; no sound came from any of the rooms leading off and enough light filtered through the mottled glass panels in the top half of the front door to show a wide staircase leading to the first floor. Charlie risked the torch again, which showed that the stairs were littered with rubbish, including the odd beer can. 'Sod it' he thought to himself 'I'll have to use the torch all the way up or they are bound to hear us.'

There was no alternative, they had to use the stairs. Steve followed closely, shielding his torch. It would only take one beer can to go tumbling down the stairs and they would be discovered, their element of surprise gone. Keeping close to the wall, because the banisters looked decidedly dodgy, they picked their way to the top of the stairs as carefully as possible. The music was much louder now and appeared to be coming from a room at the end of the landing where a strip of light could be seen at the bottom of the door.

They paused on reaching the landing, adrenalin flowing. Sweat had broken out on Charlie's brow, and he brushed it aside angrily with the back of his hand before moving forward again, always shielding the torch to allow only a minimum of light to escape through his fingers. Just as they were passing the open doorway of a room leading off the landing, Charlie sensed there was someone near, whether it was by smell or sound he never knew. He half turned, there was a swishing sound, his body tensed automatically and something hard struck him between the stomach and the rib cage. An involuntary yell came from his mouth as the air from his lungs was forcibly expelled. He fell, as if poleaxed, on the spot where he had been standing. The torch, uncovered now, clattered along the landing, spinning crazily round and round, the light casting fleeting shadows through the banisters.

Steve, following closely behind, saw Charlie go down in front of him. Before he could do anything there was a movement in the doorway, but thankfully not towards him.

Almost immediately the landing light clicked on and there, confronting him, were two men. One, who was white, short and stocky and about 30 yrs old and wearing a scruffy jersey and jeans, was holding a short thick stick in a threatening manner, his eyes wild and blazing. He was obviously the one that had felled Charlie. The other was black and taller, with hair that hung in dreadlocks, sporting a wispy moustache and small black beard. He presented an ominous sight and Steve's blood chilled when he saw, glistening in his hand, a long-bladed knife which he moved slowly from side to side.

'We're police' yelled Steve hopefully, as he heard Charlie moan, the first sound he had made since hitting the floor.

'Pigs' sneered the black man, spitting on Charlie.

'Put the knife down, you're nicked' said Steve, as officiously as possible, his brain working desperately to think of his next move.

The white man spoke next, his eyes narrowed, mouth curved downwards and in a thick Scottish accent said contemptuously 'Come creepin intae oor hoose like that an' ye can expect tae get fuckin done.' As he spat the words out, he smacked the stick into the palm of his hand menacingly.

Charlie groaned again and Steve sensed him move but he dare not take his eyes off the two men. His heart was thumping so loudly that he felt that they must be able to hear it. Then he decided that the best plan of defence is always attack. He took two big steps forward, the first over the recumbent Charlie and on the second he launched himself into the air towards the two men. He drew both legs up towards his body and kicked out viciously, a heavy foot smashed into the chest of each man and sent them flying. The black man with the knife, whom Steve had singled out for special attention, received the full force of the attack and flew backwards. There was a sickening crunch as the back of his head struck the wall at the end of the landing. His body remained upright, as if glued to the wall, for what seemed ages. Then, with eyes full of pain and disbelief, he slid slowly down the wall into a crumpled heap.

'Right' thought Steve 'one down, one to go.' He turned his attention to the Scotsman, whose body had spun around with the force of nearly thirteen stones hitting him. His battered lungs issued a terrible oath as he hit the floor and the stick with which he had struck Charlie rolled loose. He made a quick move to recover it, but Steve, who had landed on his feet like a cat, was quicker. Launching himself into the air again he landed on the Scot, this time the instep of his shoe crunched down on his wrist, pinning the man's outstretched hand to the floor. He screamed with pain and screamed even louder as Steve forced his arm up his back in a hammer lock and applied pressure. He was now lying face downwards with Steve's left knee grinding into the middle of his back.

'Whit the fuckin hell dae you bastarts want, onyway' he yelled in great pain, hoping that Steve would ease off. His right ear was uppermost and Steve, breathing heavily and sweating buckets from his exertions, gasped 'A young girl...called Anne Fisher...is she here?'

'Whit dae you want her fer?'

Steve applied more pressure and the Scot yelled, cursed and then, banging his hand on the floor urgently as if submitting in a judo hold, gasped painfully 'She wis here but noo she's awaw.'

'Where did she go?' pressed Steve.

'She went awa in a ambulance - she took tae much, the stupit bitch.' Again he spat the last words out with contempt.   Suddenly the end door, from which they had seen the light coming, flew open and music from a transistor blared out. In the doorway stood a scruffy-looking girl. Her hair stood on end and had that effect which hairdressers work for hours to achieve, She was wide-eyed and scantily dressed but Steve was more concerned with the stiletto-heeled shoe which she held aloft in a threatening manner. A scream issued from her painted mouth when she saw the black man lying motionless on the floor, blood oozing from the back of his head. Her misbelieving eyes swivelled towards Steve, who was still pinning the Scot down.

'Let him go you bastard' she screamed, moving towards him, the stiletto heel held menacingly high.

Steve, with visions of that heel embedding itself in his head, reacted quickly. He grabbed the hair at the back of the Scot's head and at the same time jerked the arm further up his back.

'On your feet' he yelled in his ear. The Scot had no option but to obey, as his arm felt as if it were about to leave its shoulder socket. With a sickening scream of pain, he leapt to his feet swearing profusely. Steve forced the body of the Scot between himself and the girl just as she struck out with the shoe, narrowly missing his head.

The girl moved sideways and lashed out wildly again, her face white with anger and frustration, as Steve moved his human shield round to protect himself. Eventually the Scot, who had narrowly escaped injury himself, yelled 'Pack it up ye daft bitch, you'll hae ma ee oot.' In sheer desperation, she hurled the shoe at Steve's head but it missed, hit the top of the stairs and went clattering down to the bottom.

The girl turned in frustration and sank down moaning beside the black man who was still unconscious. She cradled his head tenderly and urged him to speak to her.

Charlie, meantime, was still bent double on the floor nursing his lower ribs. He felt as if a horse had kicked him. With the aid of the banisters, he struggled to get to his feet.

Still unable to think clearly, he had a vague recollection of a figure flying over his head followed by a crunch as the black man hit the wall. Then Steve had pounced on the Scot. He had been powerless to move or speak. 'Christ' he thought, 'I'm getting too old for this bloody lark.' But what a great job Steve had done, and was still doing. He shook himself, fumbled to get his handcuffs out of his pocket and, joining Steve, he helped to immobilise the Scot by cuffing both hands behind him through the banisters.

Steve could relax at last. He pulled a handkerchief from his pocket and thankfully mopped his brow. With a huge sigh of relief, he panted 'Christ, Charlie - that was a bit hairy' adding 'but it could have been worse I suppose.'

'What do you mean worse?'

'Well, it could have been me leading' Steve grinned.

'You flash bugger' said Charlie with a grimace, nursing his ribs. He crossed gingerly to where the girl was trying desperately to stem the flow of blood from the black man's head.

'Better get this stopped or he's going to bleed to death.'

Steve didn't share his anxiety 'I expect he's got a hard head anyway, it's a wonder he didn't crack the wall' he answered, callously.

He could still picture the Scot and the black man in front of him, the knife glinting menacingly as it moved from side to side. The hair stood up on the back of his neck again as he contemplated what might have happened, if he had been allowed to get close enough with that knife. They tied a makeshift bandage around his head and made him as comfortable as possible. Then, satisfied that it would suffice as a temporary measure, they left him with the girl and quickly checked that there was no one else in the house.

The situation was now pretty much under control. The tough Scot continued to curse and bring into question the legitimacy of policemen in general and Steve in particular. His feelings, which he vented loudly in a strong Glaswegian accent, were mainly due to his helplessness, the indignity of being handcuffed to the banisters and, for the moment, being ignored. Added to this was the fact that he had ended a fight on the losing side for a change - something he found difficult to bear.

Steve nipped downstairs to the car, quickly and noisily this time, and radioed for assistance and an ambulance.

Meantime, Charlie knew that the condition of the black man was unlikely to improve until painkillers were administered, so he turned his attention to the girl who had calmed down considerably by now. She was another who looked dirty, ill and obviously into drugs. He had heard Steve obtain some information about Anne Fisher from the Scot under pressure, so he continued 'Anne Fisher. How did she come to be here?'

'I don't know' snapped the girl 'She was the one who found us. But none of us was on the hard stuff. The silly bitch had started mainlining and didn't seem to know much about it.' Her thin colourless lips pouted as she voiced her contempt for Anne Fisher, the girl who had caused them all this trouble.

'So what happened, then?'

'Like I said, she just didn't seem to care about anything and in the end she shot too much into herself.'

'Go on' urged Charlie.

'Well, she went into a coma. We didn't know what to do and, after all, she wasn't really one of us.'

'So what did you do?'

The girl drew a deep breath and burst out 'We carried her downstairs and along to the phone box at the end of the road. We rang for an ambulance and watched them take her away. So we knew she would be alright' she added, as if trying to justify their actions.

'So you've no idea where they took her?'

'No. That was the last we saw of her, and bloody good riddance too' she snarled, turning her attention once again to the black man who had started moaning quietly.

'Well, it shouldn't be too difficult to trace which hospital they took her to' thought Charlie 'and maybe with a bit of luck this time we really will find her.'

The peace of the quiet street was suddenly shattered as assistance arrived in response to Steve's radio call. The first to appear on the scene was the local area car, siren screaming and lights flashing. They had been cruising in the area and had picked up the call for assistance. Two officers jumped from the car to report their arrival. After a brief discussion, one of them accompanied Steve back into the house, through the front door which he had managed to open, leaving the other to control things in the street.

Another car from the local station arrived next, followed by the slower Black Maria out of which spilled several uniformed PC's. The noise of all the police activity had attracted a fair-sized crowd of adults and children from the adjoining houses. Windows were thrown open and neighbours speculated wildly as to the reason for the police presence. Others had ventured from the nearby pub, pints still in fists, and some had even forsaken their beloved tellys for a glimpse of some real live drama.

An ambulance, with its bell ringing shrilly, picked its way down the street and through the crowd, with the help of a couple of the PC's left at the scene. Uniformed men, grey this time with peaked caps, jumped out and opened the huge back doors of the ambulance. Adroitly, they pulled out a stretcher, and, directed by one of the PC's, entered the house.

The crowd, chatting and gesticulating, waited anxiously. Those living nearest to the house, who had seen the squatters going in and out, knowledgeably passed on information, which became more exaggerated at each telling.

The ambulance men reappeared within minutes, carrying the motionless figure of the black man on a stretcher, his body covered with a blanket. His head was now swathed in bandages, the whiteness of which contrasted vividly with his dark face and seemed to have an almost luminous glow under the street lighting.

Surging forward, the crowd fought for a better view and the PC's struggled to hold them back.

The ambulance men carefully slotted the stretcher into the yawning opening. One of them remained with the stretcher, accompanied by a police officer. The driver quickly closed the doors, leapt into the cab and drove off urgently at speed with bell ringing and lights flashing.

Upstairs in the house, a careful search of the main room had revealed a quantity of soft drugs, which would be taken along to the local police station, and later a thorough search of the flat would be made.

The waiting crowd was not disappointed and a mixture of jeers and boos, mainly directed against the police, greeted the handcuffed and still-complaining Scot, followed closely by the girl. Together they were helped into the back of the Black Maria.

Finally, Charlie and Steve appeared carrying two large clear plastic bags which contained the club, the knife and the drugs, which would be needed for evidence. Re-entering their car, with Steve driving, they joined the procession towards the main road.

The crowd slowly drifted away, chatting and speculating as to what had really happened in the empty house in their street. They would have to wait some time before the newspaper reports told the full story. If it was sensational enough, their street might even make the 'People' or the 'News of the World'.

At the local station, Charlie was feeling bushed, even after a huge mug of coffee, and the whole of his midriff felt as if a herd of elephants had trampled over it.

However, the Divisional Surgeon had examined him and informed him that he was lucky and there were no bones broken.

'Lucky be buggered' muttered Charlie, as he had other words for it.

The Divisional Surgeon offered to place Charlie on the sick list, but he promptly declined as he was determined to soldier on. He knew that McKay would take the mickey out of him for allowing himself to get injured and he wasn't looking forward to that confrontation.

They tied up the ends as quickly as possible. The local CID could deal with the drugs side, but it was Steve who would have to bring charges against the Scot and the black man, when he had recovered.

Having left the Station Officer with the job of tracing which hospital Anne Fisher had been taken to, Charlie headed for home. It had been a long and eventful day and he wasn't sorry to see the end of it.

In the privacy of the car, he took the opportunity to thank Steve for coming to the rescue back at the squat when things had gone against them 'I still don't know how you managed to knock both of them over at the same time' persisted Charlie.

'Well' replied Steve 'As you know, judo is my main sport but I've also dabbled in all kinds of martial arts. Getting one of them with each foot was just a bit of improvisation - it was the only thing that came to mind.'

'All I can say is that I'm bloody glad it did, otherwise we could have been in queer street.'

'Anyway, we got away with it without too much damage. That's the main thing' said Steve, modestly.

'I'll be putting you up for a Commissioner's Commendation on the strength of it, anyway' said Charlie 'I'm sure that Mac will agree.'

Charlie had warmed to his young colleague. There was no sign of cockiness now, when it could have been justified.

His action back at the squat had been incredible - like something out of a Bruce Lee movie. He smiled and congratulated himself on his wise choice of companion for the day; a day he certainly wouldn't forget in a hurry.

Steve dropped Charlie off at his house and, as the light was on in the lounge, he declined the offer to come in for a drink. Charlie's wife was obviously waiting up for him.

He entered the lounge. 'Oh Charlie!' exclaimed his wife anxiously. 'You look terrible. What on earth's happened this time?'

Charlie tried hard to straighten up fully, but couldn't 'It's nothing, luv' he replied, as cheerfully as possible 'I've just had a dig in the middle. That's all.' He patted his stomach muscles 'I've had plenty of those before, nothing to worry about.'

'Yes, Charles Herbert Bennett' she replied, angrily 'But you weren't pushing fifty then, were you?'

'Look I'm OK' insisted Charlie 'Don't make a fuss.'

'Oh luv, when are you going to pack this job in?' she pleaded 'You've got more than twenty-five years in, can't you find something easier?'

Like most police wives, she hated having to live with the fear of her husband being injured, maimed or possibly killed. She had put up with it for years now, but it never got any easier to bear.

Charlie tried to pacify her by saying 'Alright, luv. I'll keep an eye out for a quiet security job - don't worry' knowing full well that he would carry on until he had completed his thirty years unless something very good came along. They had had this conversation many times during his police career, so he changed the subject as quickly as possible. Sinking gingerly into his favourite armchair he said 'A large scotch would go down well, luv - and a sandwich if you could manage it.'

'That will give her something to do' he thought, as she put the bottle and the glass down beside him and hurried into the kitchen.

Later, when they were both in bed, sleep eluded him. He was still wound up and the scotch hadn't relaxed him enough. Besides, every time he closed his eyes he could hear a sickening crunch, followed by a vision, through pain-racked eyes, of a black man flattened on a wall, arms and legs splayed out, with his eyes rolling heavenwards.

The vision seemed to remain suspended, as if on wires, until with a terrible groan it collapsed into a jumbled heap.

CHAPTER FIFTEEN

Detective Constable Steven Wade drew the car up outside Charlie's house the following morning and pressed the horn. Charlie appeared after a few seconds and began walking painfully down the path. He was trying desperately to maintain a normal upright position, but failing miserably.

Steve leaned across the passenger seat, pushed the door open and greeted him cheerfully 'Morning, Sarge, how do you feel?'

Charlie, who looked like death warmed up, grunted 'Bloody awful, you chirpy bugger' as he eased himself gently into the car beside Steve.

Once he had settled back in the seat, he continued 'I'm not too bad really - I just couldn't get comfortable last night. In the end I had to take some more pain killers and they've left me feeling dozy' He paused, before asking politely 'How about you?' knowing fine what the answer would be.

'I'm OK, Charlie, just a bit stiff that's all' he replied in an off-hand manner.

The journey was made mostly in silence and they were most surprised to find, on their arrival at the Sports Centre, that McKay's car was already there. Charlie was not looking forward to meeting his Guvnor one bit. They hadn't disturbed him the night before, as it had been such a late finish, but Charlie knew that McKay would not be amused when he heard what had happened. He wasn't disappointed.

'What the hell have you been up to, Charlie. You look terrible?' he exploded 'Why can't you stand up straight?'

'Don't you start, Guvnor' moaned Charlie 'I've had enough stick already from my missus.'

They sat down and between them related the events of the previous day.

McKay listened with interest as the story unfolded, envious at having missed the action himself but pleased that they had come out of the situation reasonably well. In a better humour now, he began to rag Charlie, shaking his head and saying 'I don't know, Charlie. I let you out of my sight for five minutes and look what happens' Charlie opened his mouth to reply, but McKay carried on and, addressing himself to Steve, said 'Thanks, Steve for looking after him yesterday. You did a good job and I'll certainly put you up for a Commissioner's Commendation on the strength of it.'

'Thank you, Sir. I'd appreciate that' replied Steve, formally.

'Now I suppose you're both off to Court, so I've lost the pair of you again.'

''Fraid so, Guvnor, but it shouldn't take too long. Also the Station Officer at the local nick is checking the hospitals for Anne Fisher' Charlie reminded him.

'Alright then. You might as well finish the job now you've started. But don't be too long.'

'Get the car round, Steve, will you?' said Charlie and Steve disappeared quickly.

'Guvnor' said Charlie, once Steve had gone 'I don't want him to get a bigger head than he's got already, but what he did yesterday was out of this world. I was down and almost out, when all of a sudden he jumps over me as if he's got bleedin' wings and hits these two blokes. Flattens one of them against the wall and then handcuffs the other to the banister. I think he'd be a real asset to us.'

Charlie was not one to give praise when it wasn't deserved and McKay knew this. He valued his sergeant's professional opinion and he had already been impressed by Steve's actions on a previous occasion.

McKay replied 'OK Charlie, I'll keep him in mind but you'll have to get him to study for promotion. I can only do so much.'

'Thanks Guv, I just thought you should know.'

Charlie closed the door and made his way to the Centre car park. Heading towards the Marylebone Court, Charlie was the first one to speak 'You did yourself a bit of good yesterday, Steve, and the Guvnor's very impressed.'

'Thanks, Charlie, for putting in a good word for me' He was well aware that his early dismissal to bring the car round was just an excuse for Charlie to do this.

'But' continued Charlie, seriously 'you won't get anywhere unless you get down to the studying.'

'I know that, Charlie - but I never seem to have the time.'

'That's the old excuse. You'll just have to bloody well make time' and he added, pointedly 'Don't forget I had to do it.'

'Yes I know, Charlie, but it was easier in those days.'

'What do you mean?' queried Charlie.

'Well, the study book was only half as thick then.'

'You cheeky bugger' said Charlie, laughing painfully and holding his midriff as they both enjoyed the joke 'Seriously though, Steve, I know that you are busy with your work, the judo training and competitions, not to

231

mention the women, but, if you don't get down to studying, the others will pass you by.'

'I know that' replied Steve, seriously 'and thanks very much for your interest. I really will make an effort this winter for next year's exam.'

They arrived at the back of the Marylebone Court just before 10 am and had the usual trouble parking. The tiny car park had to be left clear for vehicles arriving and departing with prisoners appearing at the Court, so it was difficult to find a space.

Inside they met up with the CID officers from the local station who would deal with the drugs side of the case. They had some good news for Charlie - Anne Fisher had been traced to Paddington General Hospital. She was very ill and on the critical list and it was obvious that Charlie and Steve had to get down there quickly to get some kind of statement from her. They pulled a few strings with the Court Inspector and managed to get their case on early; it was really only a matter of asking for a remand, as they were in no position to proceed with the case. Besides, the injured man was likely to be detained in hospital for quite some time, whatever happened, and the local CID could deal with the rest.

They were soon on their way to the hospital, via various back streets to avoid the inevitable mid-morning traffic congestion on the Edgware Road. On arrival at the hospital they stated their business and headed for the intensive care unit where Anne Fisher was confined. Their footsteps echoed loudly as they made their way briskly through the long high corridors, passing smart young nurses who always seemed to be bustling somewhere urgently. This contrasted with the young white-coated doctors, with stethoscopes hanging from, and bleepers attached to, their top pockets, who seemed to stroll along at a leisurely pace, deep in conversation with a colleague. The usual hospital smells prevailed.

'I hate these places' remarked Steve.

'I don't exactly go a bundle on them myself' replied Charlie 'I've had to put too much time in, guarding injured prisoners and victims alike and there's nothing more boring.'

'Some of the nurses are nice though' said Steve, with a smile 'I've been invited to quite a few nurses' parties.'

'I'll bet you have, you lucky young devil' said Charlie and continued 'Funny how they always team nurses and policemen together. I can remember when I was a young blood and living in an old police section house at Aldgate. The local hospital Social Secretary had forgotten to send out the invitations for one of their dances. Anyway, the phone rang and I answered it and she pleaded desperately for me to send round immediately as many males as I could muster, as the girls were sitting there all togged up and no

233

one to dance with. Well, you've never seen blokes get ponced up so quickly in all your life. We had a great time, though, and I've never been so popular - we were out numbered by at least four to one.' Charlie allowed himself a smug grin of satisfaction as he recalled the incident.

'I'd love to have seen you all dressed up in those days, Charlie. I'll bet you were a bit of a lad. We'd better not spend too long in here' he added, with a grin.

They arrived at the intensive care unit and again stated their business. A very smart, efficient-looking Sister appeared and after a brief exchange of words said 'I think you had better speak to the duty doctor, he's just finishing his rounds.'

A young Indian doctor arrived within minutes, they all went into his office and the Sister explained the reason for their visit. 'I'm afraid you have come too late' said the doctor in soft lilting tones 'Miss Fisher came out of the coma only briefly and it was impossible to save her - she died only a few hours ago.'

Charlie's heart sank. The doctor continued 'She had injected herself with a massive quantity of drugs, you know.'

'Do you think she intended to kill herself and not just have a fix?' asked Charlie.

'I can't say for certain at this stage, but it would appear that way. The post mortem will no doubt give an indication of just how much she had in her body.'

'Thank you very much, doctor' said Charlie.

'Not at all' replied the doctor, and, giving a slight bow, he left the room.

Turning to the Sister, Charlie asked 'Can we see her belongings, please?'

'Certainly, although from what I remember they amounted to very little. The Almoner has been trying to trace her next of kin - perhaps you can help us there?'

'Yes, Sister, we can give you her mother's name and address, but that's all I'm afraid' replied Charlie and then went on to explain briefly the reason for their visit and the death of Anne Fisher's brother.

The Sister was right. The dead girl's property consisted of the bare essentials of some well-worn clothes, a pair of scruffy shoes and a small tatty purse. No jewellery and not even a watch.

'Not much to show for a life' remarked Charlie, continuing 'After her brother's death she probably had to sell her jewellery and anything of value to raise money for drugs.'

'It certainly looks as if she decided to end it all with whatever the last of her money could buy' replied Steve, pensively, adding 'What a waste.'

There was nothing of significance in the front section of the tatty purse and the other half contained only one thing, which was a creased dog-eared photograph of the only person who seemed to have brought any joy to her short miserable life - her dead brother Dave Fisher.

Some Manchester police officer was going to have the onerous task of informing Mrs. Fisher that her worst fears concerning her daughter had been realised.

'McKay's not going to be too pleased' remarked Charlie in the car heading for the Centre 'His idea that Dave Fisher might have had a visit from a drug dealer as he sat finishing his drink at the poolside may have to be ruled out, because the two people who could have proved it are both now dead.'

CHAPTER SIXTEEN

McKay arrived at the Leisure Centre the next day to find two young CID officers waiting for him. They had just completed the observation on Lopez's house and were looking very smug.

'You two look very pleased with yourselves. What have you found out?' asked McKay.

'We managed to find quite a good spot to hide in to do the 'obbo', which wasn't easy, because we didn't want to attract the attention of Neighbourhood Watch and they all had the stickers up.'

'Go on.'

'Well, this morning at one o'clock, a white van pulled into the side of the house and, after meeting Lopez, two men from the van unloaded a quantity of boxes into the garage – the boxes looked as if they might contain wines and spirits. It was all done very quietly and Lopez and his wife supervised the whole thing.'

'What happened then?'

'The van pulled away quietly – we thought the load in the garage wouldn't be going anywhere, so we followed the van. When it reached a small house in Willesden we tackled the two blokes before they could go in, told them what we had just seen, and demanded an explanation. They said that they were just doing a favour for a friend – Mr Lopez.'

'Did they say what was in the boxes?'

'Yes, it was wines and spirits for his business.'

'I asked if they meant the Leisure Centre and they said no, it was for the private catering business that he runs with his wife.'

'Our Mr. Lopez gets more interesting by the minute' quipped McKay.

'The two guys were scared shitless and swore that they only delivered the stuff for someone who gets it from across the Channel, but we'll have to get them in and get proper statements.'

'What about the stuff in the garage?'

'We got one of our lads to keep watch to make sure that none of it disappears. So at the moment we don't know whether it's been nicked or it's just a tax fraud.'

'Well done, you've done a good job – I always thought that Lopez was too clever for his own good and it will give me great pleasure to have another interview with him.'

'These two blokes have been warned not to contact Lopez and they were anxious not to get involved any further with him – so you might catch him unawares when he comes in.'

'Yes, thanks. Lopez should be in his office soon and I want you two to sit in on the interview.'

They waited till Lopez was in his office and knocked on his door. McKay was still turning over in his mind the fact that this man was one of the last persons to see Fisher alive at the end of the Caribbean Evening.

Lopez was not pleased to see them, as they entered 'What the hell is it this time - I've told you all that I know' he fumed.

'Mr Lopez, why is it that the more we dig into things, the more your name comes to the surface?'

'You've got me this time. I haven't got a clue what you are talking about' he insisted.

McKay produced a tape recorder, saying 'We can do this interview here or down at the Station, which would you prefer?'

Lopez was visibly shaken and said' Last time it was all about Young, and I answered all your questions – what on earth is it about this time? And do I need a solicitor?'

'It depends on whether you've got anything more to hide' said McKay, sternly.

'More to hide? I told you everything the last time.'

'Alright' said McKay quietly, switching on the tape recorder 'just tell me why one of your garages is, at this very moment, half-full of boxes of wines and spirits which were delivered in the small hours of this morning.'

Lopez nearly fell out of his chair and fought to gain control 'You've been watching my house' he gasped angrily.

'And not without reason by the look of it, unless you can come up with a good explanation. You could start by telling us about this outside catering business which you run' McKay suggested, forcefully.

Lopez had recovered by this time but still mumbled over his words as he said 'It's - it's my wife's business actually, she runs a small catering business – out of the Borough, naturally' he added.

'Oh yeah' said McKay 'and how many catering qualifications does she have? And before you answer that, we will be speaking to her later, if necessary.'

'She has the cooking experience and I taught her the rest.'

'So it's your business really, is it?'

'Yes I suppose so' he said, putting his hands up in resignation 'but I do pay the correct income tax on it. So what happens next?'

'Mr Lopez, as you well know we are in the middle of a murder enquiry and I haven't got time to deal with you and your business. I'll hand this part of it over to the local CID and they will investigate your garage full of wines and spirits, where it came from and interview the two men who delivered it.'

'Will my Manager get to hear about this?' he asked anxiously.

'That I can't say' replied McKay, officiously 'What I am concerned with is whether Fisher was involved in any way with you or your business' he reached into his brief case and produced a single sheet of paper. Running his finger down Lopez's original statement he stopped at an item 'You said that he fancied himself as a bit of a chef and an expert on drink. Was he involved in your business in any way? And don't make me interview every person who ever worked for you in your catering business.'

Lopez by this time had produced a coloured handkerchief and was mopping his brow furiously 'Alright …alright' he sighed 'He stood in for me several times when I was on duty at the Centre and couldn't make it myself. He did a good job actually.'

'Mr. Lopez, do you realise that this is the second time that you have failed to tell us of dealings that you had with Fisher? If there's a third time, you could find yourself down at the station and on a charge sheet.'

'I know …I know, but honestly I had nothing to do with his death.'

'Honestly is a word which doesn't seem to mean much to you – does it? Now think carefully, is there anything else that we should know about, because my patience is running out fast?'

'Well…er. We did fall out a bit towards the end'.

'In what way?'

'Just because he had done so well standing in for me, he wanted to come into the business with me – that was a cheek. It had taken me years to build it up and he thought he could step right in.'

'Now we are getting somewhere!' said McKay, enthusiastically 'This falling out with Fisher - exactly what was said?'

'It was heated, but never came to blows. He knew about my promotion prospects and he threatened to tell the Manager about my business unless I let him join me.'

'Are you saying that he was blackmailing you?'

'Call it that if you like.'

'So you decided to have it out with him when you left the Leisure Centre at the end of the Caribbean Evening?'

'No…no, that's not true' insisted Lopez.

'You were the last one to see Fisher alive – and there were no witnesses' pressed McKay.

'That may be so, but I left him drinking by the poolside. He was doing quite a lot of that on duty and it was only a matter of time before things caught up with him – he was on a self-destruct course.'

'Mr. Lopez, as I said before, this is your last chance. I hope that you've told me everything and that I don't have to interview you again.'

'I can assure you that I have told you everything and that I did not murder Fisher.'

'We'll leave things there' said McKay, getting to his feet and putting the statement in his briefcase. He switched off the recorder and, with a meaningful look at a much deflated Lopez, left the room.

When McKay and the CID officers were outside and making their way to the cafeteria, McKay said 'That's the third time I've interviewed him and each time he gets deeper and deeper into the mire. The jury is definitely still out on this one.'

CHAPTER SEVENTEEN

It was the tenth birthday of McKay's youngest son, Ian, and on his two previous birthdays McKay had been missing - duty had prevented him from attending the parties, much to his young son's chagrin. This year, however, he had high hopes of being able to atone for this, provided that the plan he had in mind was successful. He had, in fact, seized the opportunity to mix business with pleasure on noticing a poster in the Sports Centre advertising what appeared to be the complete answer.

It was a 'Sporting Birthday Party' deal, offered by the Centre, in which youngsters took part in several different sports under supervision. This was followed by a special birthday meal in the cafeteria, complete with cake and candles, if required. As far as McKay was concerned it was a heaven-sent opportunity, as he could not imagine a finer way of burning up the energy of youngsters of his son's age.

Margaret McKay, who usually found herself burdened with the party, was delighted with the arrangements. She arrived at the Centre, accompanied by another mother and friend. They had, between them, ferried ten very excited boys straight from school. McKay had arranged, all being well, to be at the Centre for the two hours that coincided with the party, leaving Charlie once more looking after the shop.

The birthday deal consisted first of a table tennis knockout tournament for approximately thirty minutes and secondly basketball, for the same length of time, with two teams of five. Then, thirdly, five-a-side football for half an hour and finally a plunge in the leisure pool to cool off. The culmination being a race across the pool. Later, prizes donated by the parents would be presented to the winners of the various events. The competitions would be taken very seriously, as only ten-year olds can, and had to be strictly refereed.

Finally there would be a meal, a special offer designed to satisfy the hunger of the youngsters, who would be starving after all the activity.

The Centre supervisors were at hand to referee and generally supervise, under the guidance of Mark Tyndall, for whom, as an ex-PE teacher and well used to handling large classes of boys, the prospect of dealing with only ten would be a pleasure.

The sports were well underway. McKay and his wife were more than pleased, the occasion was going smoothly and he was just congratulating himself on the brilliant idea when Charlie appeared, looking very serious. He smiled half-heartedly at Margaret and turning to McKay said 'Excuse me, Guvnor. Can I have a word?'

'Certainly, Charlie' replied McKay, sensing trouble from his demeanour.

McKay rose, turned to his wife and said 'Excuse me, dear, I shan't be long.'

Out of earshot of his wife and her friend, McKay asked anxiously 'What's up, Charlie?'

'Trouble I'm afraid, Guv. A report has just come through of a suspicious death at Brookdown Mansions.'

'Brookdown Mansions? That's where we went to see Dick Williams.'

'Yes, Guv, and wait for it…it's the same address, but we don't know who has died, only that it is a man.'

A hundred thoughts raced through McKay's mind. Finally he said ruefully 'If it is Dick Williams, I suppose that he could have died from those injuries. He was half dead the last time we saw him.'

'I've got a funny feeling about this one' said Charlie.

'So have I. We'd better get round there quickly. If it is him, it's just too much of a coincidence.'

'Good luck with the Missus, Guv' smiled Charlie, looking past McKay to where Margaret was sitting, pretending to look uninterested in their conversation.

McKay turned and approached his wife. How the hell could he do this tactfully? Before he could speak she looked up at him and, in a resigned voice, said 'Don't tell me. Something's come up and you've got to leave.' She hadn't been married to him all these years without being able to recognise the signs.

'Sorry love, it's very important. I've got to go.'

'I had hoped that, just for once, you would be able to see this party through. The lad will be so disappointed.'

'Tell him I'm sorry and I'll make it up to him. Now I must fly.'

McKay and Charlie made a hurried exit, leaving his wife to cope once more with the party. McKay felt angry. It was at times like these, when his family was affected, that he had misgivings about his chosen career. No matter how many times it happened, how many times his personal arrangements had to be cancelled and friends disappointed, it never made it any easier to bear.

Being tactful, Charlie kept quiet during the car journey, leaving McKay with his own thoughts. He knew what was going through his Guvnor's mind, as it had happened to him enough times. He also knew that very shortly McKay would shake the mood off and bounce back with one hundred percent concentration on the job.

They arrived at Brookdown Mansions, where the presence of two police vehicles, one a CID car and the other a Scene of Crimes van, had attracted a fair-sized crowd.

'Bad news always travels fast' commented Charlie, breaking the silence.

'I don't know where they all come from' answered McKay.

Quickly climbing the stairs, they pushed their way through a group of people talking in hushed tones. They were probably the other tenants, no doubt speculating wildly as to what had happened to attract so much police attention. Passing the uniformed PC on duty at the end of the landing, McKay entered the open door and, followed by Charlie, went down the now familiar corridor. He stopped automatically and looked into the bedroom where, on their previous visit, they had seen Dick Williams in such a terrible state. The room was now neat and tidy, all evidence of the previous mayhem removed. Despite this, McKay's glance moved from the neatly-made bed to the wall above it where the bloodstains had been. The wall was relatively clean, all that remained was a stubborn pink tinge. Without a word they headed for the sitting-room, where they could hear voices and the sounds of movement.

They were greeted at the entrance by an old colleague of McKay's in the shape of Detective Inspector Albert Robinson, known as Big Bert. His huge frame seemed to fill the doorway. Older than McKay and bigger, he was wearing a crumpled medium-grey, lack-lustre suit. The trousers had more sideways creases than up and down and the waistband seemed to be fighting a losing battle with the overhang of flesh from his hairy paunch, which was just visible where a button was missing and the shirt gaped open. A miserable looking tie, loosely-knotted, almost kept his off-white shirt closed at the neck. Its colour, nevertheless, still contrasted with his reddish-purple complexion. He broke into a smile and beamed at McKay.

Bert Robinson had long since given up trying to be the smartest DI at the station; his basic shape made this a virtual impossibility. His jovial face and outgoing personality reminded one of the landlord of the local, which is where Albert spent a great deal of his time both on and off duty. He was, without doubt, one of the old school, renowned for his humorous expressions such as 'Just going round the corner to see one of my informants.' The informant was usually made of glass, pint-sized and full of a yellow liquid with froth on top.

'Hello Mac' he boomed cheerfully, on recognising McKay 'I understand that you've got some interest in this one already.' He waved a large podgy hand in the direction of a body which could be seen laying half-on and half-off a leather settee on the other side of the room.

McKay, who was trying with difficulty to see past the huge frame of Albert, replied 'If it's Dick Williams who works at the Parkdale Leisure Centre then I am interested.'

'It's okay, take a closer look. They've taken pictures and have almost finished' Bert said, moving aside.

McKay approached the body, which was male and fully clothed. The head and shoulders hung back over one arm of the settee.

It was Williams alright.

Charlie, who as usual was about two paces behind McKay and always ready with a quip, said 'Blimey, Guvnor, this bloke's not havin' much luck at all, each time we see him he gets worse.'

'Well, we're not likely to see him much worse than he is now, that's for sure' commented McKay, looking down at the body.

Williams had been strangled, there was no doubt about that. In fact, it looked as if his neck was probably broken. His adam's apple stuck out prominently, the skin stretched white over it. There were red marks on the neck, some of which had already turned black. The eyes seemed almost to bulge out of their sockets. McKay noticed, particularly, the awful scars and stitch marks from the beating he had suffered previously. They were still very red and prominent, as they healed. Only now it didn't matter how they looked, the healing process had stopped.

'What do you think, Mac?' boomed the voice of Bert Robinson.

'I think that if that damage was done by a pair of hands, then they were bloody strong hands' replied McKay, turning to face his colleague.

'I quite agree' said Robinson, nodding his large head 'and there don't appear to be any other marks on him to suggest a fight - no marks on his hands or knuckles.'

'That was one of the first things I noticed when I came in - how tidy the room is' interrupted McKay.

'I suppose we'll have to wait till the pathologist has a go at him, before we can really find out if there's any other damage' suggested Robinson.

McKay thought for a moment before saying 'Bert, I believe you took over the case after he was beaten up before. What stage are you at?'

'As a matter of fact, it was only on Monday that chummy - he pointed to the body - was fit enough to appear in Court for the first time.'

'What happened at Court?' asked McKay.

'The usual' replied Bert 'The three villains that caused the damage were all remanded in custody again.'

'What I am trying to fathom out' said McKay, slowly 'is whether this job is a continuation of his beating up, or is connected in any way with my Leisure Centre murder.'

Bert's round face broke into a huge smile displaying a full, but unattractive, set of teeth. Somehow they had survived the attack of pub food, cheroots and bitter. As quick as a flash he replied slyly 'In other words, Robert McKay, whether this murder is down to you or me.' His fat index finger pointed first at McKay and then tapped his own expansive chest.

McKay also smiled and retorted 'It looks very much as if we are both going to have a hand in this one.'

'Don't forget my villains are safely locked up' interrupted Robinson.

McKay stroked his chin thoughtfully, before suggesting 'True, but they could easily have got someone to finish the job off.'

'Oh, come off it, Mac. My job was purely a domestic one, you know that. They were only small time villains, murder's a bit out of their league.'

'Yes, you're right, I suppose' replied McKay, reluctantly 'Whichever way you look at it two people from the Leisure Centre have been murdered now. The answer has got to be back there.'

'Certainly looks that way, Mac' boomed Robinson, cheerfully.

'What did the Doctor say when he came?'

'It was old Watson the Divisional Surgeon. He didn't say much, you know him - only that Williams had probably been dead about five hours.'

'Um...about five hours' mused McKay 'That makes it about lunch time. I'll be very interested to see if the pathologist makes it the same.'

'Well, Mac, we're nearly finished here. The Coroner's Officer has been sent for and when he gets here he can make the necessary arrangements.'

'Right. Oh, by the way, who discovered the body?' queried McKay, suddenly.

'The woman he lives with - calls herself Mrs. Williams. She took it all very badly - immediately blamed her ex-husband' he added.

McKay ignored the last remark and asked 'Where is she now?'

'Next door, being looked after by neighbours. Look Mac, I know you've got a lot on your plate, so if you want to get back to the Centre I'll cop a statement from her and tidy up things here - it looks as if I'm lumbered anyway' he added, reluctantly.

'Thanks, Bert' said McKay, gratefully 'I do want to get back to the Centre and it looks as if I'll have to check everyone out again, as to their movements during the past five hours. See you later then.'

'Not if I see you first' quipped Robinson.

McKay and Charlie retraced their steps down the stairs. An even larger crowd had gathered by this time and the uniformed PC struggled to clear a path for them to their car. The Press, as usual, were on to it by now, anxious for information. Cameras clicked and reporters clamoured for a statement. McKay recognised, in particular, the local newshound, a young man in his twenties keen to get something extra with which to please his editor or even pass on to the dailies. It was he who pursued them closely right to the car, bombarding them with questions, most of which elicited 'No comment' from McKay. This young man had been following the Centre murder closely and had attended every press conference conscientiously. His questioning of neighbours while McKay had been inside the flat prompted his final question, which reached their ears as they were actually getting into the car 'Give me a break, Chief Inspector' he pleaded 'I know that Dick Williams, from that flat, works at the Leisure Centre. Has something happened to him?'

'Drive on Charlie!' said McKay abruptly, looking straight ahead.

'Has the murderer struck again?' the reporter pleaded dramatically, to no avail.

Charlie put his foot down and the car sped away with the question ringing in McKay's ears, so much so that he repeated the question to himself 'Has the murderer of Dave Fisher struck again?' He hoped not 'But it's beginning to look bloody like it.'

******

Back in the Murder Room, McKay called a conference for everyone attached to the Murder Squad. He informed them of the death of Dick Williams and set the wheels in motion for every member of the Leisure Centre staff, whether on or off duty, to be interviewed again and their movements checked.

Until he received confirmation of the time of death, he could only concentrate on the lunch time theory. 'Mind you' he thought to himself 'Old Watson had been called to enough dead bodies in his time and he was usually pretty accurate when it came to judging the time of death.'

McKay, at this moment, was feeling very low. A second murder is what every investigating officer dreads, not least because it implies failure on his part. He could picture the headlines now 'A life that could have been saved.' The press would have a field day. However, what was done was done and he tried to look objectively at the situation. The second murder presented a different set of circumstances. The further information gained would have to be checked against that of the first murder and hopefully some small factor would fit, or fail to fit, into place.

He threw himself into the task with renewed effort and headed for the manager's office. Most of the early shift had gone home by now and would have to be brought back. He knocked on the door and entered.

Mike Weston looked up from his endless paper work and said 'What's gone wrong now?'

'I'm sorry, but something else has come up.'

'Go on then, shoot. After what's happened already, it can't be that bad.'

'I'm afraid it is' said McKay, quietly 'Dick Williams has just been found dead in his flat.'

Mike Weston looked at him in total disbelief, mouth open, speechless. 'I don't believe it' he said eventually 'What happened? Was it as a result of his injuries?'

McKay ignored the question.

'I can't believe it' Weston continued, his voice rising 'He was in here earlier this week and I spoke to him - he was alright then.'

'Did you speak to him for any particular reason?'

'No, he just came in to see everybody and said he hoped to be back at work soon.'

'You say he seemed okay.'

'Yes, he was fine. He had just come from the Court and seemed relieved to get the first appearance over and done with - and now you say he's dead.'

'Did he seem to have anything worrying him at all?' persisted McKay.

Weston thought for a moment before answering 'He was a little concerned that his undeclared previous convictions were now known and he wondered how the Council would react.' He paused, before saying thoughtfully 'Now it doesn't matter.'

'What did you tell him about his previous convictions?'

'I assured him that, as far as I was concerned, his work record at the Centre was more than satisfactory and that I would report to the Council accordingly.'

'Do you know who else he spoke to when he came in?'

'As far as I know, he did the rounds and spoke to most people at the Centre.'

'Thanks, Mike. Just to keep you in the picture, we are about to go through the whole procedure of checking the movements of every member of staff all over again.'

'Why? What do you mean? What happened to Dick Williams?' Weston insisted, his face flushed and showing anger.

'It looks very much as if he was strangled' replied McKay, flatly.

'My God' Weston blurted out 'What the hell is going on? First Dave Fisher and now Dick Williams' his voice rose hysterically as he pleaded with McKay 'Christ, it could be me next at this rate.' He grabbed for his pipe and, with trembling hands, sucked hard for comfort.

'Now don't get carried away, Mike' insisted McKay, trying to calm him down 'We don't know yet if the two deaths are connected. So, as I said before, we have to interview all the staff again.'

'That will please them' blurted out Weston, still trying desperately to regain his composure 'Yes...sorry...of course. Do what you have to do, just get this thing over and done with as quickly as possible, so that we can get back to normal.'

'We'll do our best, you may depend on that' replied McKay and, sensing that now would be a good time to make a strategic withdrawal, he rose and left the room.

Weston, alone in his office, filled his pipe automatically, unable to believe what was happening to him. One minute everything was going smoothly at the Centre, morale high, no real staff problems and now, all of a sudden, two of them were dead. The bottom had certainly fallen out of his small world.

******

Weston tried, whenever possible, to avoid taking his job home with him, despite the considerable problems associated with running a very busy sports centre. However, the death of a second member of his staff had shaken him to the core. He sat, in his favourite armchair, in the lounge of his house. His pipe was clenched tightly between his teeth. The television was on, but he wasn't conscious of which programme was being shown. His mind was elsewhere and he had been this way most of the evening.

Jenny sat cross-legged on the sofa, well aware of what Mike was going through, but unable to help. She had tried several times to engage him in conversation without success. He was miles away.

Suddenly Mike sat bolt upright. 'Blast' he said loudly 'I've got a meeting with the Chief Officer first thing in the morning and what with this Dick Williams business I've left my briefcase at the office, with the papers I need for the meeting.'

'Let's go and get them, then' suggested Jenny, uncrossing her legs quickly. She jumped up, anxious to change what had been a pretty miserable evening so far.

'Sure you don't mind?'

'Not at all, we could do with some fresh air' replied Jenny, already on her way out of the room to fetch a coat.

They drove to the Centre, which had only a short time earlier closed for the night. The Murder Room, which had been set up there, had been transferred to the local police station and all telephone calls had been transferred there. So the Centre was deserted. Entering through the side door of the swimming pool, Mike automatically went through the ritual of silencing the alarms and locking the door behind him. Arm in arm they walked down the corridor which ran parallel to the pool in the direction of Mike's office. They were just passing the sauna and solarium suite when Jenny stopped suddenly, pulling on Mike's arm to prevent him going on.

'I've got a great idea' she said, her eyes sparkling 'I know what you need to relax you.'

Mike looked at her, and they laughingly answered in unison 'A sauna.'

'Will it be alright, as the place is closed?' queried Jenny.

'Of course, there's got to be some perks with this job' he answered, enthusiastically.

Suddenly he was more like his old self. He switched on the lights and they entered the luxurious changing and rest area. Mike was justly proud of the sauna suite and it was a facility that the local people had needed some persuasion to use. At first they had been under the impression that a sauna was something only undertaken by Danes or Swedes, something not quite British. However, once they had been convinced that it wasn't a den of vice, the sauna became so popular that a booking system had to be introduced.

Thursday's mixed session for couples proving to be the highlight of the week for some people.

He was particularly proud of the fact that he had managed to persuade the Council not to skimp on the furnishings. The overall effect was one of warmth and soft colour, from the yellow knotted-pine wall panelling to the luxurious light-coloured carpet with deep red mats.

They quickly stripped off their clothes and entered the sauna cabin.

Mike switched on the stove which was still warm from an earlier session and with the ladle from the sauna pail he allowed a few drops of water to fall on the peridotite rocks. Before long the temperature started to rise, producing a steady dry heat. They stretched out on the aspen benches and relaxed and soon the heat opened their pores and gave the pleasant feeling of massage on tired muscles. For the first time in ages, Mike felt relaxed and calm. He sighed with enjoyment.

'Feeling better, Mike?' enquired Jenny, sitting up with her beautiful body glistening with perspiration. Mike opened his eyes and looked at her. He felt a sudden urge to hold her, but instead kissed her gently on the forehead saying 'That was a great idea of yours, I don't know what I'd do without you.'

They relaxed again, with Jenny inwardly congratulating herself on her brilliant idea. She had been really worried about the extra strain that the two murders had placed on Mike. He was beginning to look his age and she had already determined to persuade him to take a holiday when things returned to normal again.

After about another ten minutes, they left the sauna for a cooling shower and then relaxed in the comfortable armchairs of the rest area. They chatted for a while until Mike had shaken off the sombre mood completely. Impulsively, Jenny jumped up saying 'Let's finish off with some sunshine' and headed for the solarium. Mike followed closely, Jenny's lovely body moving gracefully before him. His eyes traced the gentle slope of her shoulders, down past her trim waist and finishing at her small rounded buttocks. These rose and fell rhythmically at each stride. It was more than flesh and blood could stand.

Mike leapt forward and, with a triumphant cry, swept her up in his arms and carried her protesting loudly, but not convincingly, to the massage table. He eased her slowly down his body, feeling her full breasts pressing into him. Her nipples, already hard, sent shock waves through his skin. The effect on Jenny was to set her writhing in his arms, emitting groans of pleasure. When her toes touched the floor their lips found each other, lingeringly, until he gently lowered her onto the table. By now, Jenny was more than a willing partner and all thoughts of Mike being over-tired were completely forgotten.

'Now, Mike, now' she cried, moving into another world, as she pulled him into her fiercely. They kissed wildly and his lips traced first her mouth and then her eyes, her neck and down to her breasts. His lips dwelt on each nipple in turn as she moved rhythmically beneath him. As always, he had to make the inevitable decision, both equally enjoyable. Whether to continue and end in a frantic climax which he knew would satisfy her or to delay, and savour longer, the pleasure of each other's body.

The sight of her in the sauna, the shower and the rest room had been too much for him - he was halfway there already. Jenny groaned loudly as she recognised the signs and he tried desperately to delay the inevitable in order to continue as long as possible. Eventually they climaxed together.

Mike collapsed, his eyes closed. Jenny continued to move gently, to prolong the pleasure. They lay together for what seemed like ages, murmuring words of satisfaction.

'If only we could remain like this' thought Jenny, as time stood still; but she could feel him going to sleep. Her practical nature told her that the best place for them now was at home in their own bed.

'Mike' she whispered, kissing him gently 'It's been wonderful, but we have to go.'

Reluctantly he agreed, because he knew that he had a particularly heavy day ahead of him tomorrow. They dressed, the sunshine long since forgotten, and after making sure that everything was switched off, they left the sauna. Outside in the corridor they turned to leave and Jenny spoke 'Don't forget what we really came for, Mike.'

'Do you know, I'd completely forgotten about the papers' he replied, grinning with satisfaction.

CHAPTER EIGHTEEN

It was the morning that McKay's elder son Jamie had to report for his interview for the Metropolitan Police Cadet Corps.

He arrived at the breakfast table looking very smart, his hair cut shorter than usual, but little did he know that it would have to be even shorter, if he was accepted.

'So today's the big day, son. How are you feeling?'

'Didn't get much sleep last night, Dad. I was worried about the questions that they might ask me and whether my qualifications are good enough.'

'I can assure you that you've got enough – it's not educational qualifications that they're looking for, it's whether you've got any common sense and have the ability to think on your feet – you'll be alright.'

'Of course he will' chipped in Margaret, proudly, bustling around the table 'You got in, didn't you!'

'More tea, anyone.'

'Your Dad's got an interview this morning too, with his favourite lady boss. Let's hope that goes well, Mac, so that we can all have a family meal tonight. I'll do something special.'

******

Later that morning at the Leisure Centre, McKay said 'Charlie, Herself wants to see me again.'

'I thought that when we had that second murder she'd get twitchy.'

'Yes, it's getting near time for that promotion Board.'

When McKay entered Janet Marshall's office for the second interview the greeting was not so cordial – there were no pleasantries on this occasion.

'What the hell is going on in that Leisure Centre of yours, Mac?' she exploded, her face turning red 'First one member of staff is murdered, then another is badly beaten up and now that person is found murdered.' Her voice rose as she fought to remain calm. It was the first time that McKay had seen his boss rattled.

'I agree, Ma'am, that the situation looks grim, but we are working on several angles at the moment and something will break soon.'

'I wish I could share your optimism, Mac – have you got any real suspects?'

'Yes. I have one particular line that I am following but, as you well know, I have to secure the evidence to convict and that takes time.'

'You've had plenty of time to get somewhere, surely' she spat out, angrily 'And what's this I hear about Bennett getting himself injured. Is he up to it these days? Have you got enough men on the job?' The questions came thick and fast.

McKay thought to himself 'She's really got herself worked up. I wonder if she's sleeping at night?'

'Ma'am, Bennett and Wade did an excellent job following a lead which had come up during the investigation. They tracked down the sister of the murdered man to a squat on Harrow Road's patch. It was during the search that Bennett was attacked and Wade threatened with a knife. They dealt with the situation so well that I will be recommending Wade for a Commendation.'

'I'm glad to hear that some good is coming out of this investigation, but did they find the girl?'

'Yes they did – eventually, in Paddington General Hospital - she had taken an overdose of drugs.'

'And?'

'The next morning they had to attend Court first and unfortunately by the time they got to the hospital she had just died.'

Marshall leapt to her feet, bristling to make herself taller and, with hands on hips, yelled 'Mac, are you on top of this investigation? You've got bodies all over my Division. What about the Manager of this Leisure Centre, there seems to be a hell of a lot going wrong – what's his background?'

'He's ex-Army, Ma'am, a paratrooper and the Army Physical Training Corps. He's absolutely shattered by what has happened.'

'I'm not surprised - it doesn't say much for his style of management. Not one but two of his staff have been murdered - he must wonder if he's next, unless he's a suspect also?'

'No, he seems to run things pretty well.'

'Maybe I should put in an appearance myself at the Centre?' she added, sarcastically.

McKay had taken as much as he could. Firmly but politely he said 'That will not be necessary and your presence would not help. It's a very difficult case, but I can assure you that everyone is working full out for a result. My track record speaks for itself and as you have never doubted my ability before, why do so now?' McKay knew that he wouldn't get an honest answer to his question. He was right.

'Well, just keep me informed' she blustered 'and I look forward to some good news from you soon.'

She suddenly stretched out her hand, but this time the handshake was perfunctory and the eyes unfriendly.

Without another word, McKay rose, turned and left the room.

Back in his car again, McKay drove to a park some way from the Centre. He needed to cool down and consider the situation. It was a beautiful day, cloudless with the sun heading high in the sky. Surrounded by greenery and bathed in sunshine, he slowly relaxed. His thoughts turned naturally to the interview. He had never found himself under such pressure before and not able to express his true feelings. He, too, was ambitious and knew that it would not be in his best interests to make an enemy of Marshall. She had certainly got under his skin. 'Was it just a macho thing or did she have a point?' he asked himself 'I wonder how many murder investigations she has solved on her way up to her present rank – or was most of her time spent in admin?'

He too, had been devastated when the second murder occurred – it was an investigator's worst nightmare. She had queried whether Charlie was up to the job and, come to think of it, he hadn't been his usual cheery self lately, maybe he's got problems and I've been too wrapped up in things to notice. 'I'll have a word with him when I get back.'

He shook himself 'What happened to the positive thinking?' he said out loud 'there's two murders to be solved and I'm sitting here feeling sorry for myself – I just hope the promotion bug doesn't get to me the way it's got to Marshall.'

Feeling in a better frame of mind, he started the engine, found first gear and headed for the Centre.

Back there, he found Charlie waiting for him. 'How did it go, Boss? How was her ladyship? Have we been taken off the case?'

'She wasn't too pleased as you can imagine - got herself really worked up, even suggested that she might come here to present a show of strength, but I managed to talk her out of it.'

'Thank goodness for that' quipped Charlie 'That's the last thing we want.'

'She was, however, concerned about your welfare? And I got to thinking that you haven't been your usual self lately. Is something bothering you?'

Charlie thought for a moment and answered, reluctantly 'Actually, yes… it's the missus – what with the son being in Germany and about to be posted to a war zone, naturally she worries about him. Then there's the daughter, who's getting married soon and she can see herself on her own – what with the hours we work. She's not looking forward to it at all.'

'Sorry, Charlie, I hadn't realised. You always play your cards so close to your chest and I've been wrapped up in this case.'

'Also, my last episode with the bruised ribs didn't help – as you know, she doesn't have the best of health and is worried that something more serious might happen to me and then she'll be completely on her own. She's had to put up with that fear all my service and now that I've got my twenty-five years in, she wants me to look for something less dangerous. I tell her that I'm just as likely to get run down by a bus, but she's not stupid, she doesn't buy that.'

'So how have you left it, Charlie? Is there anything that I can do to ease the situation?'

'I've promised to look around for something with more regular hours, but I love the job I'm doing, as you well know.' He added 'I'm hoping that the wedding coming up will take her mind off things and buy me a bit of time.'

'What about a holiday for her after the wedding?'

'Yes I'd thought about that. She's got a sister who moved to Spain and maybe we could pay her a visit.'

'Look, you work along those lines and, in the meantime, leave it with me - I'm sure that I can come up with something where all your experience in thief-taking isn't wasted.'

'Thanks, Boss, and I'm sorry if I've been a bit of a misery guts lately.'

'No need for that. Now let's get on.'

'Actually, I've been thinking, while you've been away enjoying yourself.'

'Take it easy, Charlie, don't strain yourself' replied McKay, smiling.

'No seriously' persisted Charlie 'One of the alibis that we couldn't prove or disprove was that of the manager, Mike Weston, wasn't it?'

'Yes, that's true.'

'He admitted that his girlfriend Jenny was asleep before him and that she's a very heavy sleeper - you can vouch for that.'

'Go on.'

'Well, they left the Centre early and claim that they went to bed early. Weston could easily have waited till she was asleep, got dressed, and returned after everyone else had gone. Especially if he knew that Fisher was in the habit of relaxing with a drink after a function was over.'

'Yes, that's possible' nodded McKay 'He did say that he had seen Fisher knock back a scotch. Maybe he disapproved and went back to remonstrate with him - he'd had a warning about drinking on duty before, remember.'

Charlie mused 'It's just that during our investigations he has always been so helpful and - well, he appears whiter than white. That always makes me suspicious.'

'Come off it, Charlie. What's really bugging you about Weston? Is it the fact that he's divorced and now living with a very attractive young woman? If it is, you're showing your age you know.'

'Maybe I am a bit old-fashioned, Guvnor, and a bit of a family man, but it doesn't alter the fact that he hasn't got an alibi that can be checked, and neither has she for that matter.' He paused before adding 'Could they even be in it together?'

McKay's eyebrows shot up 'Have you got any reason for thinking that, or any evidence at all?'

'No, but if Fisher put himself about, and we know he did, maybe he made a play for Jenny at some time. She's much nearer his age than Weston's, don't forget, and maybe, just maybe, he found out. That would give him a good reason for sorting out Fisher.'

'Funny you should say this, because her ladyship wondered if the Manager was up to the job, as so many bad things were going on.'

'Well, there you go, Boss - great minds think alike.'

'But do you know the other half of that old adage, Charlie?'

'Fools seldom differ.'

'But you do have a point' said McKay, raising both hands in surrender 'But, short of asking her outright, I don't see how we are going to find out.'

'We could get Jenny on her own and just put it to her.'

'Yes, you're right. What have we got to lose at this stage? Actually it shouldn't be too difficult, she's often in the Centre on her own. We can always say that we are re-interviewing everybody.'

******

It had been quite a day for McKay after his second meeting with his boss, followed by his heart-to-heart with Charlie.

Feeling a bit subdued, he shook himself before opening the door, knowing that his wife had created a special meal for the family and he didn't want to spoil things.

The smell of the roast beef reached him as he entered. He was greeted by Margaret and the boys, who ushered him into the dining room where the table was all laid out and completed with what looked like a good bottle of wine.

'Great' said McKay 'what are we celebrating?'

'Ask Jamie' said Margaret, unable to keep a sense of pride from her voice.

'Why? Did something special happen today?' he teased, looking at his son.

'You know very well that I went for my interview today, Dad.'

'Oh yes, I'd forgotten' continued McKay, teasingly 'How did you get on? I suppose that I'll still have to keep supporting you?'

'No you won't, not for much longer.'

'So the interview went well then?'

'Not too badly' replied Jamie, with a glum face. It was his turn to tease his father.

'What does that mean?'

The other son, Ian, was giggling and looking at his mother unable to contain himself.

'It means that you still have to look after me until I'm sixteen and then they'll call me up for the first course starting after that date.'

McKay stopped teasing his son, hugged him and shook his hand saying 'Well done, Jamie, I never doubted it. Your mother and I are very proud of you.'

'Open the wine then, Robert, and let's toast the lad. Ian can have a little taster.'

They raised their glasses and congratulated Jamie, who by now had coloured up with embarrassment.

Margaret spoke up 'You know what this means?'

'What does this mean, Mum?' chirped up Ian, claiming some attention for himself.

'It means that we'll have two policemen in the family. Your dad and another one with big boots, which will have to be 'spit and polished' - but not in my kitchen, right?'

The meal was a great success and it was a happy family that went to bed that night.

Once in bed, Margaret said 'Sorry, Robert, what with all the excitement downstairs I forgot to ask you how you got on with your lady boss?'

'Not the most pleasant of meetings' he answered 'She really has got her knickers in a twist – it was all I could do to hold my tongue. With the Board getting nearer and the murder enquiry dragging on, she's not a happy bunny.'

'I thought you liked these strong women' kidded Margaret.

'I do, but this one is way over the top.'

'Gave you a hard time, did she? I'll bet you didn't like that.'

'I survived – it was just not being able to express my true feelings that got me. I really do hope that she gets her promotion and moves on.'

'That sounds the best outcome. She's really got under your skin, hasn't she?'

'One thing that she did say though, got me thinking.'

'What was that?'

'She asked me if Charlie was still up to it – him being injured that time. I assured her that he was fine, but it got me thinking and I realised that he had not been his usual cheery self lately.'

'And?'

'I tackled him and it turns out that all is not well at home.'

'Do you mean that Rose isn't well? I would have thought that with the wedding coming up, she would have had her hands full.'

'It's a combination of things really, starting with Charlie getting injured, then their son in Germany, about to be posted to a war zone, and now the daughter getting married. Rose can see herself on her own. She wants him to look for a quieter job with better hours and I've offered to try and find something for him.'

'That's a shame, especially as you two get on so well together. Maybe I could have chat with her and see if there's anything I could do.'

'Would you, love? That would be great.'

CHAPTER NINETEEN

The following evening when McKay and Charlie were at the Centre they came across Jenny Marlowe waiting for Mike Weston to return from a Sports Council meeting. As attractive as ever, she was wearing a chunky-knit sweater and black, close-fitting slacks and carrying a black leather handbag. She smiled as they approached.

McKay came straight to the point 'Sorry to intrude, Miss Marlowe, but if you're free there are one or two points I'd like to go over again. We're re-checking everything in the light of our most recent investigations.'

'I understand, Chief Inspector, but are you getting anywhere with your investigations?'

She smiled at them in such an attractive way that McKay thought to himself 'No wonder Charlie is suspicious - who wouldn't make a play for this girl?'

They moved to a quiet corner of the bar, where they wouldn't be overheard and, producing her original statement, McKay replied 'We haven't got very far yet, I'm afraid, but it's a long painstaking job and I promise I won't keep you any longer than I have to.'

'That's alright, I'm in no hurry. Mike won't be back from the meeting for another half-hour at least.'

'Good, then I'd like to run through your statement again.'

McKay padded out the interview till he thought the time was right and then, leaning forward, said 'Miss Marlowe, a rather personal question. Did Fisher, at any time, make a pass at you?'

She was clearly taken aback 'Whatever gave you that idea?' she gasped.

'Never mind that' pressed McKay 'Did he?'

She looked around, as if to make absolutely sure that they were not being overheard, before answering quietly 'As a matter of fact he did, once.'

'Would you care to tell us about it?'

'It happened at a party that we gave at our house when the staff from the Centre were invited. Towards the end, when most of them had gone home, we had a call from the police to inform us that the burglar alarm was ringing at the Centre. Mike cursed but insisted on going himself to see what was wrong. They'd had break-ins before, you know. Anyway, he left me to look after the party till he got back and we carried on dancing. Soon after that people started to leave and, in the end, the only ones left were Dave Fisher and me. He had come on his own and had had quite a lot to drink during the evening, but he wasn't drunk. He wanted to carry on dancing, so we did. I thought Mike would be back any minute.' She paused, took a long drink from her glass and swallowed hard. 'He started to hold me a bit too close and eventually tried to maul and kiss me. I struggled with him and told him not to be so stupid, but he insisted and turned quite nasty.'

'In what way?' interrupted McKay.

'Well, not so much physically, but he taunted me, saying 'What do you see in these older men? They can't be any good to a young attractive woman like you.'

'He was referring to Mike, of course, and, well, that did it. I threatened to scream the place down if he didn't go and that Mike would kill him if he knew what had happened.'

'I wonder if she realises what she's just said?' mused McKay, saying 'So what happened next?'

'Well, he seemed to sober up a bit and I managed to get him out of the house. Shortly after that Mike came back

280

and he was most surprised to find that all the guests had gone. He even joked about me being a lousy hostess.'

'Did you tell him about Fisher?'

'No, not then. He could see that I was upset about something but I managed to convince him that it was just tiredness with all the preparations leading up to the party.'

'So when did you tell him?'

'It must have been during the following week. He could see that something was bothering me although I didn't think it showed; after all it was no big deal, nothing really happened. But Mike could tell. He kept on and on about it till I told him what had happened. I played it down a bit but he was livid.' She paused before saying 'He's very possessive, you know.'

She continued 'I told him to forget it and just put it down to the drink Fisher had consumed, but Mike wouldn't have it. He said that Fisher's drinking was becoming a problem and that he would have to do something about it.'

'Did he say what he would do about it?'

'No. Take some sort of action, I suppose. Fisher had been warned before, you know?'

'Yes, but do you know if he did tackle him about what happened at the party?'

'No. If he did, he didn't tell me.'

'What was the date of the party?' asked McKay, casually.

Jenny thought for a moment and then rummaged in her handbag. Producing a slim gold-edged diary, she thumbed through the pages and stopped at the entry she was seeking.

'It was Saturday the 15th' she said finally.

'That was the week leading up to the Caribbean Evening, wasn't it?'

She consulted the diary again 'Yes, that's right.'

'And you don't know if Mike tackled Fisher during that week or not?'

Her manner, which had been friendly and helpful till now, changed. A frown appeared, lining her beautiful face. Her eyes hardened 'What are you trying to suggest?'

'Well, maybe' McKay paused for effect 'he did tackle Fisher, on the night of the Caribbean Evening.'

'That's absurd' she exclaimed incredulously 'Anyway, he didn't, because we were together all evening. And I've told you that several times already' she nodded towards the statement spread out in front of McKay.

'Yes, so you have' replied McKay, smiling. Picking up the statements he tapped them neatly into place, saying 'Thank you very much for your assistance, Miss Marlowe. Can I perhaps buy you another drink? Your glass appears to be empty. Gin and tonic isn't it?'

Jenny felt as if she had been left suspended and mumbled 'Er...that would be very nice, thank you.' She was confused, not knowing whether to be angry or just relieved that the interview was over.

******

'A half for you, Charlie?'

'Yes, Guv, thanks.'

McKay made his way to the bar and ordered the drinks. Jenny, still feeling uncomfortable, excused herself from Charlie and made her way to the Ladies' Room. She needed time to think and to collect her thoughts. Looking in the mirror she found herself wondering about what she had just said to McKay. He seemed to be suggesting that Mike had tackled Fisher later that night. She shook her head. It was ridiculous, he would never have killed Fisher, she knew him too well for that. More doubts crept in her mind. He had been a regular soldier and in the front line, before he joined the PT Corps. Maybe he had killed people then, although he never spoke of it. What would Mike say when he found out that she had told McKay that he would kill Fisher, if ever he had found out about the trouble at the party? She shook her head again and confidently freshened up her lips from a gold-coloured lipstick case. 'No' she said out loud 'There's nothing to worry about, they've just managed to get me going, that's all.'

McKay returned to the far end of the bar with the drinks.

'You were right, you old fox' he exclaimed, handing Charlie his half of bitter 'But don't settle in for the night, because now we've got to tackle Mr. Mike Weston as soon as he gets back from the meeting. And before Jenny can say anything to him.'

Charlie lifted his glass saying 'Cheers, Guvnor, at least we've got a motive now that's worth looking at.'

Before McKay could reply, they were joined by a more composed Jenny Marlowe, who sat down gracefully and accepted her gin and tonic with style. The conversation which followed was false and awkward and McKay's eyes kept searching the entrance to the bar, as did Jenny's.

Eventually Weston appeared and, coming straight over to the group, he kissed Jenny affectionately and greeted McKay and Charlie cheerfully 'It can't be a bad life, can it. While you three are knocking them back, I'm stuck at a Sports Council meeting which went on for hours.'

'Charlie, get Mike a pint of bitter will you? He looks as if he needs one.' Charlie rose and headed for the bar.

Weston looked tired; the meeting had drained him. McKay realised that now would be a good time to tackle him with the latest discovery. They made polite conversation until Charlie returned with the pint, which Weston accepted gratefully.

Taking a good long pull, he emptied half the glass and relaxed, saying 'Ah...that feels much better.'

'Good' said McKay 'Because, when you are ready I'd like to have a word.'

Weston looked puzzled and annoyed. He was tired after his long day and all he wanted to do was relax, He looked at Jenny, who avoided his glance. Reluctantly, he replied 'Sure. Why...has something come up?'

'You could say that' replied McKay, giving nothing away.

'Well, what is it?'

'I'd rather we spoke in private, if you don't mind. You could bring your drink' suggested McKay.

'Sounds important. OK, my office?'

'That would be fine. It shouldn't take long. Charlie, would you keep Jenny company while we're gone.'

'Be a pleasure, Guvnor' replied Charlie, with a smile.

Weston led the way down the stairs to his office. He entered first and automatically sat behind his own desk, dropping his briefcase on the floor with a thud. Taking another drink from his glass, he signalled McKay to draw up a chair on the other side of the desk, opposite him. He was still very much the manager and, after all, it was his office. McKay opened his briefcase and thumbed through the statements till he came to Weston's.

Weston watched till he could contain himself no longer.

'This all seems a bit unusual. Has something really interesting cropped up?'

'In a way, yes, but I'm not sure whether you will consider it interesting or not.'

'That sounds ominous. What on earth do you mean?'

McKay cleared his throat before saying 'Earlier this evening we were re-checking some of the alibis of the staff and it occurred to us that your own cannot be verified.'

Weston shot forward in his seat, a look of amazement on his face, the usual calm features disturbed 'What do you mean, cannot be verified? Jenny and I came home early that night and went to bed. I've already told you that several times and you accepted it.'

'Yes, I know, but Jenny is a very heavy sleeper. You know that and so do I. Remember the first time we met, when I woke you up on the morning of the murder?'

'I'm not likely to forget that morning. So, what are you actually saying?' demanded Weston, his voice rising.

'Well it's just possible...and I'm only saying that it's possible...that you could have waited till Jenny dropped off to sleep and then returned to the Centre to take Fisher to task over something.'

Weston's mouth dropped open and his tired eyes widened in amazement 'You are joking' he gasped.

'On the contrary' replied McKay, firmly 'Just being thorough. You wouldn't want it any other way, would you?'

'No, of course not. I expect you to be thorough. But, bloody hell, I am the manager here and Dave Fisher was one of my staff.' He paused and a puzzled look came over his face before he asked 'What on earth has led to this line of thinking?'

'You've brought it on yourself, really' replied McKay, casually.

'Oh...how was that?'

'You weren't completely honest in your original statement regarding your feelings towards Fisher and we have had to find that out for ourselves.'

'What do you mean, not completely honest?' snapped Weston, looking even more puzzled and losing his patience rapidly 'I told you that he was a good member of staff apart from his drinking.'

'That's true, but you didn't tell us that you had another reason for taking Fisher to task.'

Weston looked down at the desk, his thoughts racing, until the realisation came.

'Jenny' he exclaimed, looking straight at McKay 'That's it, isn't it? I thought she was very quiet upstairs just now.

You've interviewed her and she's told you about the night of the party.' His speech quickened 'That's it, isn't it?'

'Yes, that is it, and I imagine that you weren't too pleased when Jenny told you about it.'

'You're damn right I wasn't. He had a bloody nerve.'

'So did you take him to task over it?'

'No.'

'Why not? You intended to, didn't you?'

'Well...yes...but, to tell you the truth, there hadn't been a suitable opportunity. I only found out about it from Jenny a few days before he died.' His voice tailed away. Beads of sweat appeared on his brow. Lifting the glass, he emptied it in one gulp and, looking at McKay in despair, he pleaded 'This is crazy, Mac. What the hell do you think happened?'

McKay leant forward and said 'Let's look at it this way. You told me yourself that at the Caribbean Evening you saw Fisher knock back a scotch whilst on duty. You didn't mind the odd half of lager whilst socialising with the customers - right?'

'Yes, that's right.'

'And you intended speaking to him about his drinking?'

'Yes.'

'So now you had two reasons to speak to him, the business over Jenny and his drinking on duty.'

Weston remained impassive.

'Suppose, just suppose, that after Jenny had gone to sleep the night of the Caribbean Evening, and knowing of Fisher's habit of relaxing with a drink after a function, you decided to return to the Centre to take him to task over both matters.'

'Bloody hell' Weston exploded 'Even if it was true, there's a hell of a difference between taking someone to task and murdering them, which is what you're trying to imply.'

'I know, I know' McKay nodded 'But remember that half of the murders committed are not premeditated. They start with an argument which gets out of hand and before you know it, tempers are lost and someone is dead.'

'And you think that I am capable of killing someone?'

'You've done it before' said McKay, quietly and, after a pause, he continued 'You were trained to do it.'

Weston's face fell as he realised that McKay had delved deep into his army past to come up with this information. 'But that was years ago' he gasped 'in the Parachute Regiment, when I was young, before I went into the Army Physical Training Corps.'

McKay was unmoved 'I wouldn't have thought that it was something you'd forget easily. Anyway in the PT Corps you must have trained soldiers in unarmed combat as part of fitness for war.'

'Yes, that's true' Weston admitted, reluctantly, adding 'So where does that leave me?'

'After all our enquiries, you are the only person in this leisure centre with one, the opportunity, two the capability, and three a reason for remonstrating with Fisher that night.'

'All that may be so, but the idea is ludicrous' insisted Weston 'I could have spoken to him any time about his drinking. I'd warned him officially before, but it's true that this time it would have been more serious.'

'And what about the incident with Jenny, how seriously did you take that?'

'Very seriously, of course. I make no bones about the fact that I consider myself very fortunate indeed to have a young girlfriend like Jenny.'

'So you were really angry when she told you about the incident.'

'Naturally I was, but if you think I'd murder him for those reasons you must be mad.'

'Jenny didn't seem to think so.'

'What on earth do you mean?' exclaimed Weston, incredulously.

'Well I don't know if she meant it, or realised exactly what she was saying at the time, but she admitted saying to Fisher, that you would kill him if you knew about this.'

'She was speaking figuratively, she couldn't have meant it.'

'But you still had two good reasons for speaking to Fisher; the business over Jenny and his drinking on duty' persisted McKay.

Weston opened his mouth to speak.

'No, wait' McKay held up his hand 'Maybe that night you introduced both matters to him and an argument took place. He had been drinking. Maybe the argument got out of hand and somehow Fisher ended up in the water. It's logical, it could have happened.'

'Maybe it could have happened, but it didn't' insisted Weston, his face flushed. He was rapidly losing his temper. 'And I suppose that makes me responsible for those terrible injuries he received. How did they come about? Tell me that.'

'We don't know how he sustained his injuries' admitted McKay.

'Yes, and you don't bloody well know who killed him, either. That's why you are reduced to making these stupid allegations about me creeping back there. Christ, I'm the manager. Haven't I suffered enough since all this business began?' He was on his feet by this time, his knuckles pressed hard on the desk. Towering above McKay, who was sitting calmly, his legs crossed, looking at the papers on his knee. Weston finally lost his temper and, in a voice rising hysterically, he shouted 'Look, I can't prove that I didn't go back there that night, the only person who could is

291

dead, but, by the same token, you can't bloody well prove that I did. So it's stalemate and the idea is too stupid for words.' He collapsed back into his chair, exhausted, and glared at McKay.

'That's true, Mike' said McKay, using his christian name for the first time during the interview 'That's true, but it's produced the kind of reaction from you that I had hoped for.'

McKay rose, stuffing the statements into his briefcase, and with a mischievous smile said 'Come on, I'll buy you another pint, you deserve it.'

CHAPTER TWENTY

A haze of blue smoke filled the Murder Room, which although spacious, was showing definite signs of wear and tear. Mountains of cigarette ends flowed over on to the floor from a variety of improvised ashtrays to mingle with dirty cups and saucers. Tables were covered with sheafs of statements, work dairies, maps and pocket books.

The noisy squad of detectives was mostly young. 'Very young' thought Charlie. Several sported moustaches or beards in an effort to make themselves look older and more mature. Most were in shirt sleeves with the more sartorially inclined wearing smart silk-backed waistcoats. Others, with a beer paunch flowing over the front and sides of their trousers, could never look smart anyway.

It had been a long hard slog from the start of the investigation, the results of which they were presenting to McKay and Rogers. Their lined, unshaven faces and the bags under bloodshot eyes told their own story.

The untimely murder of Dick Williams had thrown an additional strain on the already stretched murder squad. It meant an entirely new set of circumstances at Brookdown Mansions. Exhaustive enquiries had been carried out by the squad, fanning ever outwards, visiting every house or flat to check on the movements of each resident. Appeals were made for anyone in the vicinity at the time of the murder to come forward. The whole procedure was about to start again, as factories and workshops, which had been closed for the weekend, would be systematically checked. In addition, fresh statements had been obtained from every member of the now completely demoralised Leisure Centre staff, covering their movements on the day of the second murder.

McKay and the team had searched painstakingly for the past three hours for some clue, some small similarity or consistency between the two murders, which might give them a lead. They had examined the evidence, checked and cross-checked, without success.

Under the guidance of McKay and Tommy Rogers, two blackboards had been used for comparison; the details of Fisher's murder were on one, and those of Williams on the other. They pooled ideas and each suggestion, no matter how trivial, was evaluated and, if necessary, acted upon.

The pathologist's report had confirmed McKay's opinion, that the marks on Williams' neck were consistent with manual strangulation, probably by someone with exceptionally strong hands.

McKay could not fail to notice the irony of the situation. Here he was looking for areas of similarity between the two murders and all the pathologist could do was to highlight the difference. In Fisher's case he confirmed that he was not strangled, and in Williams' case that he was. Either way it didn't help much. He was still acutely aware that, so far, they had failed miserably to find the weapon that had inflicted the terrible injuries upon Dave Fisher. He wound up the session, thanking his exhausted squad for their efforts over the weekend and calling for even more in the days ahead.

Back in the office, McKay collapsed into a chair and closed his eyes; his head was spinning. Charlie sat quietly. Although not called upon to use his brain to the same extent as his Guvnor, he was older and also feeling the strain. Besides, his ribs still hurt like hell, especially when he was tired.

Suddenly, without warning, McKay leapt to his feet and snapped 'What's your swimming like?'

Charlie, who had nearly fallen off his chair at the outburst, looked at McKay with concern 'Are you alright, Guvnor?' he asked, anxiously.

'Just answer the question, Charlie' persisted McKay.

'I don't swim much these days, now that the kids have grown up. But why do you want to know?' he queried, suspiciously.

'Come on, Charlie, I must clear my head. Anyway I want to try out the leisure pool, especially when the wave-making machine is switched on. It's something I've been meaning to do ever since we started this enquiry.'

'What, you mean swim in the pool where they found Dave Fisher - I don't know about that.' He shook his head slowly and pursed his lips, unable to share his boss's enthusiasm.

'I made enquiries the other day; the machine is switched on from 11 am till 11.10 am, so if we hurry we'll just make it.'

Charlie made one last desperate plea. Holding his ribs, he whined hopefully 'I think I should rest my ribs a bit longer, Guv.'

'Nonsense' replied McKay 'The exercise will do them the world of good. They even exercise injured horses in swimming pools, you know.'

Charlie didn't go much on being compared to an injured horse, but he knew that when McKay was in this mood there was no stopping him.

'I haven't got any trunks' he uttered, in a resigned voice.

'No problem, I haven't either. We can borrow trunks, towels, the lot. Come on.'

They headed for the pool and in no time Charlie found himself changed and standing with his feet in the water. It was the first time they had been in the pool area since the early days of the Fisher murder. This morning, however, things looked quite different. Everything about the pool was so pleasant and inviting; the warmth first of all, which cheered Charlie up, and the attractive blue of the water contrasting with the green of the plants, which were in abundance. The whole scene dominated, as always, by the enormous palm tree which almost touched the roof.

'Quite something, isn't it?' said McKay, looking around the pool.

'The kids of today don't know they're born' replied Charlie, using one of his favourite expressions when making reference to the younger generation 'It's a far cry from the old baths we used to go to when I was at school. A right Victorian dump, all white tiles and chlorine which hurt your eyes so much that you couldn't see the blackboard when you got back to school. I also remember that after about ten minutes we were all blue with the cold and shivering. I never did go much on those swimming lessons' he added, thoughtfully.

'You're still not too keen on it, if today's reluctance is anything to go by' laughed McKay.

'Look at those kids over there' said Charlie, unabashed, pointing to a class from a local school. Half of them were receiving life-saving instruction from a tall, bronzed teacher, whose trunks were covered in swimming badges. Others, who were obviously poor swimmers, received tuition in the shallow part of the pool.

'They don't know they're born' repeated Charlie, shaking his head.

They made their way to the sea-shore part of the pool, the floor of which sloped gradually until the water lapped gently over the edge at poolside level. Mothers and young children sat in the shallow water playing and chatting happily.

The water was warm and pleasant and soon even Charlie had to admit that he was enjoying himself. McKay, a strong swimmer with none of Charlie's reluctance, certainly was. A few minutes before 11 am, one of the three attendants present made an announcement over the tannoy, that the wave-making machine was about to be switched on, in order to warn poor swimmers and mothers with young children to keep to the shore area. The school children's lesson had been timed to finish with this final few minutes and they all gathered, chatting excitedly, at the shore end.

At exactly 11 am, the water at the deep end started to bubble and rise, as air was forced into the pool at regular intervals below the surface. As the pressure built up, waves were created which swept towards the shore.

The children, their teachers and McKay and Charlie faced the waves with arms raised and jumped into them as they crashed on to the shore. Charlie's ribs suffered rather, at first, but he soon forgot this and enjoyed the experience along with the others.

McKay had a twinge of conscience for a fleeting moment, as the thought clouded his mind that the Commissioner was paying him for enjoying himself in this way, but he soon dismissed it. Suddenly, without warning, the machine was switched off. The children voiced their disapproval loudly, because the large clock at the end of the pool showed that there was still four minutes remaining. McKay and Charlie, equally disappointed and baffled, looked around and saw immediately why the machine had stopped. Halfway down the side of the pool one of the attendants was moving swiftly towards the wall, where he wrenched a long pole with a large metal ring at one end from its fixing. Expertly, he plunged it into the water and dragged a half-drowned young lad coughing and spluttering to the side of the pool. By this time he had been joined by one of his colleagues who grabbed the lad and hauled him unceremoniously out of the water to the safety of the poolside.

The second attendant who, like the others, had been keeping a watchful eye on the proceedings, had noticed the lad in trouble and had switched off the machine immediately.

McKay and Charlie joined them quickly. The boy, still coughing and spitting up water, seemed no none the worse for his adventure and, perhaps more frightened than anything else, had been joined by his friend, a lad of the same age. It transpired that they were alone, unconnected with the school group who were well supervised. These two had obviously played hookey from their school and would be dealt with later.

One of the bronzed attendants picked up the safety pole and snapped it back into its place on the side wall and the other attendant took the lads to the main office, thankful that the incident had been dealt with successfully.

McKay and Charlie watched them in silence as they carried out their duties. Then they turned and looked at one another - dripping wet with hair all over the place, realisation and astonishment on both their faces. They had reached the same conclusion simultaneously. McKay hit his head with the flat of his hand, in an upward movement with a whack, and with eyes screwed up with anger and frustration said 'How the bloody hell did we come to miss that, Charlie? If that pole with that metal ring can be used to pull somebody out of the water, then it could be used equally to push someone under.'

Charlie nodded 'Yes, specially if the bloke's had quite a few beers.'

McKay continued angrily 'Charlie, it was under our bloody noses all the time - the trouble is, it was too much part of the scenery, it blended in so well. But we shouldn't have missed it all the same.'

Charlie shook his head in disgust 'The trouble is, Guv, we didn't look for the obvious. That metal ring, used viciously, could easily have caused the injuries to Dave Fisher.'

By now, they had moved to where the pole was fixed to the wall. They examined the ring, which, although covered with plastic, was made of metal.

'I agree, Charlie, brought down from a height, with the ring sideways on in a cutting movement, it could easily slice your ear off.'

McKay's headache had cleared and had been replaced by a mixture of elation and relief as they towelled and dressed. For the first time since the case began, McKay was sure that they had discovered the one thing that every investigating officer aims to identify and secure as soon as possible - the murder weapon.

CHAPTER TWENTY ONE

Marlene and Lorraine Beckett entered the Leisure Centre apprehensively. On the one hand they were full of their Italian holiday adventures, but on the other they were worried about the forthcoming interview. The news of the two deaths, that they had received on their return, had put a damper on what had been a most enjoyable holiday.

The sisters were close. Marlene, the elder, was 23 and Lorraine only just 18. Both were attractive and blondes of a sort, but the pre-holiday rinse was beginning to lose its effect at the roots, despite the additional bleaching by the scorching Italian sun. The combination of the blonde hair and the deep golden tan, along with their vitality and good looks, made a very pleasing scene as Charlie ushered them into McKay's office.

'Good afternoon, ladies' gushed McKay, cheerfully, smiling as he greeted them 'I trust you had a good holiday. I must say you both look exceptionally well.'

The girls, blushing at McKay's old-world charm, accepted gracefully the seats offered to them by Charlie.

'Let's see, which one of you is Marlene?' asked McKay tactfully, although it was quite obvious which one was the elder.

'I am' replied Marlene. 'And I'm Lorraine' chipped in her sister, blushing when she realised that she needn't have said anything.

The girls had relaxed a little, now that they had actually met the Detective Chief Inspector and his Sergeant who seemed nice and friendly, if a bit old-fashioned.

'Rimini, wasn't it?' asked McKay, determined to put them further at ease.

'Yes' replied Marlene 'it was smashing. Everything was great and everyone so friendly.'

'Better than Majorca last year' chipped in Lorraine, not to be outdone by her sister 'I liked the Italians much better.' A far away look came into her eyes as she recalled some particularly pleasant moment of the holiday, which was still fresh in her mind.

'Yes' thought McKay 'and I'll bet they liked you too.'

McKay had decided to interview them separately, starting with Marlene, and Charlie now escorted Lorraine from the room. McKay checked out various details and then came specifically to the night of the Caribbean Evening.

'That night. Did you see Dave Fisher at the bar?'

'Yes' replied Marlene 'He came in two or three times.'

'Did you serve him his drink?'

'No, I don't think I did. We were kept pretty busy that night and it's difficult to remember exactly - also such a lot has happened since then' she added, anxiously.

'Don't worry about it now' reassured McKay 'It may come back to you later.'

McKay could well imagine that the bar work at the Sports Centre would be the last thing that the girls would be thinking about whilst on holiday in Rimini.

'Did you have any dealings with Dave Fisher, other than in a work situation?' posed McKay, hopefully.

'If you mean did I go out with him, the answer is no' she replied sharply. 'Too sharply' thought McKay, but he remained silent.

'But Lorraine did' she almost blurted out. The tone of disapproval in her voice prompted McKay to dig deeper.

'What was it you disliked about him?'

'Well, he was the one who got us the job at the Centre and he suggested that we owed him something because of that.' She paused and then added 'He asked me to go out with him but I refused.'

'So he asked your sister and she accepted' prompted McKay.

'That's right, being younger she was rather flattered and didn't like to refuse.'

'She is nearly nineteen' suggested McKay.

'Yes, but she's always been very young for her age' replied Marlene, protectively.

'So what happened when they went out' said McKay, pushing his luck and not really expecting an answer. He wasn't disappointed.

'You had better ask Lorraine that' replied Marlene, sharply 'All I know is that she came home worse for drink, was violently sick, and I had to look after her. He must have really filled her up. Dad would have gone potty if he had seen her in that state.'

McKay remained silent. He could see Marlene was getting wound up and was about to give vent to her feelings. The change in her was remarkable; her tanned face turned even darker as she coloured up underneath, angry at having to re-live an event which was so obviously distasteful to her. She plainly took the protective role of elder sister very seriously.

After she had finished, McKay let her relax before switching back to the Caribbean Evening and asked quietly 'By the way, how did you get home that night?'

'Bob Forrester took both of us home in his car, as usual. It doesn't take him much out of his way' replied a much more composed Marlene.

McKay thanked her for her help and asked Charlie, pointedly, to take Marlene to the cafeteria and give her a cup of coffee or something while he collected Lorraine from an adjacent room.

Lorraine sat down carefully and smiled nervously at McKay; some of her earlier confidence had eroded during her sister's interview. She fiddled with the strap of a small white handbag which she held in her lap. Again McKay started by checking out details of the evening and generally trying to put her at ease. Charlie returned and resumed his usual position, notepad on knee.

McKay started his questioning 'I understand that you got your job at the Centre through Dave Fisher.' He paused before asking 'How did that come about?'

Lorraine hesitated - a frown disturbed her smooth forehead. She shrugged her tanned shapely shoulders and said calmly 'We had gone to the Sports Centre bar with one of our friends who was playing in a darts match against the Centre team. Dave had organised the match and we were introduced to him. During the conversation that followed, he mentioned that he had been let down by the usual barman. He also said that they were always on the lookout for suitable bar staff for the various functions held at the

Centre. I said that it sounded interesting and Marlene agreed with me. We thought that the extra money would come in handy for our holiday. Anyway, Dave said he would fix it with the Catering Manager and that's how we got the job.'

She sat back and relaxed, obviously relieved after her long explanation.

'So Dave was very good to you?' said McKay.

'Yes...er...well he got us the jobs, didn't he?' replied Lorraine hesitatingly, wondering where the questioning was leading.

'And you were grateful to him' added McKay.

'What's that supposed to mean?' asked Lorraine, querulously.

'Did you go out with Fisher, at all?'

At last it dawned on her and her face reddened, as she replied angrily 'You know bloody well I did. Marlene must have told you. What else did she say?'

McKay took a chance 'She told me everything, but I want to hear it from you.'

'The bitch' she exploded, her eyes blazing 'she promised me she would never tell anyone.'

'It would be better to tell me everything and clear the air' pressed McKay.

Lorraine twisted the strap of the white bag until McKay thought it would snap, as she considered McKay's words carefully.

'Will my parents get to know?' she asked finally.

'No, not unless what you are going to say has any bearing on the murder of Dave Fisher.'

'Marlene and me had a terrible row about it. I only went out with him because – well, he did get us the jobs and I didn't like to refuse. Anyway at the time I quite liked him. Well, we went out for a few drinks and he got me to try some cocktails. And I ended up worse for wear.'

'Go on' encouraged McKay.

'Well, he tried to get me to go back to his flat, but I wasn't having any. He was a bit annoyed at first but if he thought he was going to get me into bed after a few lousy cocktails, he was mistaken. I wasn't that drunk.'

She suddenly seemed much more mature and McKay wondered why sister Marlene found it necessary to be so protective.

'So what happened next?'

'Nothing much, he dropped me off outside our house and Marlene looked after me. I was a bit under the weather, that's all. She got up the pole about it at the time and it wasn't till later that I found out he had asked her first.' She paused, before adding 'Maybe it was sour grapes on her part.'

'Did you go out with him again?' asked McKay, innocently.

Lorraine sat bolt upright, her face flushed as she realised that she had been conned. She snapped back, angrily 'You said that Marlene had told you everything.'

'Well, I thought she had' assured McKay, hastily adding 'but obviously there is something more.'

There was silence in the room as McKay waited patiently, but there was no response from Lorraine, who avoided his searching eyes. Her own were cast downwards to her fingers on the white strap. Eventually McKay leant forward and, in a quiet sympathetic voice, said 'Look Lorraine, this is a murder enquiry and I need to know everything that there is to know about Dave Fisher, if I am to find out who killed him.'

Lorraine considered McKay's reassuring words for a moment and then gave in. Looking up with tear-filled eyes she replied slowly 'Yes. Yes, I did go out with him again a couple of times - we had a good time together - Marlene never knew until…' she paused anxiously.

'Go on' encouraged McKay.

'…till I thought I was pregnant' she blurted out the words, avoiding McKay's eyes.

'Exactly when was this?' demanded McKay.

'The night we were getting ready to come out to the Caribbean Evening. Marlene could see that I was worried about something and she asked me outright what was wrong.'

'I told her that I was three weeks overdue with my period and, of course, I had to tell her about going out again with Dave.'

'So what happened?'

'Marlene went potty. She always feels responsible for me, despite my age. She was all for tackling Fisher about it but I managed to persuade her not to. After all, I wasn't absolutely sure and I hadn't had any tests or anything like that, and in the end it was just as well' she added, casually.

'What do you mean?' he asked, anxiously.

Lorraine's face broke into a contemptuous smile as she sneered 'Obviously Marlene didn't tell you everything, after all. You don't care how you get your questions answered, do you?' McKay ignored the comment, as she continued 'It's all very simple - I started my periods during the holiday, so everything turned out alright, didn't it?' She emphasised the last few words and, bitter now that her ordeal was over, she stopped twisting the white strap, looked defiantly at McKay and said 'So now you know everything and I hope you are bloody well satisfied.'

McKay smiled and answered politely 'Thank you, Miss Beckett, for being so helpful - just one more question. Did you leave your house again on the night of the Caribbean Evening, after you got home?'

'No, of course not' replied Lorraine, looking at McKay as if he was mad.

'And your sister, did she leave the house at all?'

'Of course not. What is all this...?'

'Where is your sister's bedroom situated in relation to your own?' interrupted McKay.

'I sleep at the back of the house and she sleeps at the front. But what are you getting at?' she asked, with a puzzled look. Getting no response, she continued 'We just had coffee and went to bed, as we always do.'

'Thank you, Miss Beckett, and now one final question. Did you notice anything and I mean - anything - unusual about Dave Fisher on the night in question?'

Lorraine replied immediately 'Ever since we heard the news, I've tried to picture him on that night. We were very busy but I did notice one thing that was unusual.'

'What was that?' asked McKay, leaning forward anxiously.

'He didn't pay for his drink.'

'What did he have?'

'His usual lager and I'm almost sure he had a scotch.'

'Who did pay for his drinks then?'

'Well, I can only think that Bob Forrester paid for them. He served him. I don't know if it means anything, he may just have been short of money and Bob treated him.'

'Yes, perhaps you are right' agreed McKay, making a note to check this with Forrester later. He stood up, bringing the interview to an end. He thanked a very relieved Lorraine for her help and politely suggested that she join her waiting sister in the cafeteria. Charlie acted as the escort. He returned a few minutes later carrying two cups of coffee.

McKay accepted his gratefully and, putting his feet up on the desk, relaxed, saying 'This is turning out to be quite a day, Charlie.'

'It certainly is, Guvnor. What about that Marlene, she's a bit of a dark horse. But you don't think that she could have killed Fisher, do you?'

'I'm sure she could have, Charlie, but did she? The state that he was in, she could have easily pushed him into the pool. She had a strong enough motive.' McKay paused, shook his head slowly and said 'I don't think I've ever met anyone so protective towards her sister.'

'Could she have caused the injuries though?' posed Charlie.

'If she had used a sharp weapon, it could be possible, but I must admit I can't picture her wielding that safety pole.' His thoughts were wandering 'How about the pair of them together with that pole?'

'But, Guvnor, you're forgetting one thing.'

'I know...I know. If it was Marlene, what about the second murder? She was in Rimini at the time and we still have to establish if the two murders were connected. One thing's for sure, though, it wasn't a woman who strangled Dick Williams.' In his mind he could still picture the flat in Brookdown Mansions. The body sprawled on the settee with the head back over the arm, eyes bulging and the tortured adam's apple stretching painfully towards the ceiling. The pathologist's report had confirmed manual strangulation, possibly by someone with exceptionally strong hands.

'So we just keep checking, Guvnor?'

'We certainly do, Charlie, but not tonight. I've had enough for one day' said McKay, gathering up the papers on the desk and placing them in his briefcase.

'Come on, I'll buy you a pint on the way home.'

'Cheers, Guvnor' replied Charlie, grinning 'I thought you'd never ask.'

CHAPTER TWENTY TWO

The day started with another interminable meeting of all those connected with the murder hunt, with nothing specific to show at the end of it. In an attempt to lift the gloom, McKay suggested hopefully that the statements made by the Beckett girls might reveal something. They were, after all, present on the night of Fisher's death.

McKay had also been following a certain theory himself and now was the time to put it to the test. He knocked on Mike Weston's door and entered.

Weston was burrowing through the usual pile of papers which never seemed to get smaller. He looked up, smiled, and then relaxed, pleased to have a break from the paper work.

McKay had thought from the beginning that Weston looked too fit to be stuck behind a desk. He could just imagine him leading a line of climbers over some mountainous range or some equally strenuous expedition. However, the events of the past few weeks had left their mark, especially around and under his eyes.

'Any particular reason for the visit?' Weston queried, hopefully, after they had exchanged greetings.

'Yes, as a matter of fact, I'd like you to tell me more about this, if you would.'

McKay spread out on the desk one of the charts that hung above Dick Williams' desk in the plant engineer's room. Weston studied the chart for some moments before answering 'It's to do with the wave-making machine. What's so special about it?'

McKay answered his question with another 'What is the purpose of keeping such a chart? Is it standard council policy?'

'No, it's not' retorted Weston 'It's another typical example of interference from the Town Hall, only this time it was one of the councillors.'

'What do you mean?'

'Well, it goes back a long way to the days when the Parkside Centre was in the planning stage. Certain councillors, particularly those living in the Borough, were against such a large Sports Centre, in view of the extra

315

burden it would throw on the ratepayers. Not only with regard to the actual cost of building the place, but also the repayment of future loan charges and interest. That's before they even started on running costs.'

'Yes, yes, I understand that. Don't forget I'm a ratepayer myself' interrupted McKay 'But it still doesn't explain the reason for the chart.'

'Patience, patience, Mac. I'm just coming to that' replied Weston, smiling 'One very influential councillor, together with a few others, objected to the additional cost of having a leisure pool with a wave-making machine. They wanted a traditional rectangular pool. Fortunately, this outdated view was not supported by the majority and the leisure pool was included.'

'Get to the point, Mike.'

'Well, to appease the objectors, it was agreed to monitor the amount of electricity used to operate the wave-making machine.'

McKay shook his head in disbelief 'Surely the makers could have told them the answer, and wouldn't it be peanuts compared to the total costs involved?'

'I know, I know' expressed Weston, throwing up his hands 'It's mad really, another piece of bureaucratic nonsense. What were they going to do if it proved too expensive? Stop using it?' He continued to shake his head. 'Anyway, far be it for me to try and understand the

316

workings of local government; it was much simpler in the Services. So there you are, that's the reason for the chart. Is it important then, Mac?'

'It could be' nodded McKay, producing another sheet of paper 'This is a graph of the figures on the chart, which I understand were meticulously kept by Dick Williams. If you study it, you will find that on the night of the Caribbean Evening the machine must have been switched on by somebody.'

'I don't believe it' gasped Weston, in amazement 'Are you sure?'

They pored over the figures together. 'Look' said McKay, tracing his index finger along the graph 'All the daytime sessions correspond with the previous week's and I've checked that there were no tests or maintenance carried out on that day.'

An astonished Mike Weston continued to gaze at the graph for some time. Eventually he looked up at McKay and said, incredulously 'Are you implying that the machine could have been switched on at the time of Dave Fisher's murder?'

'All I'm prepared to say at this stage is that it could have happened.'

'But members of the public wouldn't know where the key was kept or how to switch it on' volunteered Weston.

'No, but I imagine that every member of your staff would' countered McKay.

'Have you anyone in mind?'

'As a matter of fact, I have' replied McKay 'But I can't prove it yet.'

Weston reached for his pipe and sat back in his chair. With great feeling he said 'Thank God for that. I was beginning to despair of ever getting the Centre back to normal again.'

******

Charlie entered McKay's office looking very pleased with himself. He was carrying a single statement sheet and pinned to it was a small rectangular receipt. McKay was curious to know what had brought about this sudden change in his Detective Sergeant. He wasn't normally a glum character, but nor was he often as excited as he was at this moment.

'Guess who I've just seen coming out of Tommy Pike's betting shop, Guvnor?'

'You tell me, Charlie, I'm not in the mood for guessing games.'

'Bob Forrester.'

'So? He's entitled to have a bet. Isn't he?'

'True. But I thought I would have a word with Pikey on the off chance.'

Pikey was in fact one George Pike, a well-known betting shop owner, frequently to be seen not only at various race tracks but along with local publicans at police boxing shows and charities. He was always good for at least a dozen tickets.

'So? Does Forrester bet heavily?'

'He certainly does, Guvnor' replied Charlie, relishing the moment 'According to Pikey he'd bet on two flies going up a window.'

'Does he get in deep?'

'Apparently there have been occasions when Pikey has had to refuse requests for a private loan when Forrester wanted to get a bet on.'

'Does he win often?'

'Sometimes he does back the odd winner, but nothing fantastic.'

During the conversation McKay had been watching Charlie, fascinated by the statement and the receipt which he was still holding. He knew that at the appropriate moment Charlie would play his ace, just as he would when playing solo, one of his favourite card games. McKay wasn't disappointed.

Charlie, with a smug look on his face, casually dropped the statement and receipt in front of McKay saying 'Oh, and Guvnor, I thought you might be interested in this.'

Showing great restraint, McKay leisurely picked up both pieces of paper. First, he examined the receipt and then carefully read the statement. He felt the hair on the back of his neck stand up, as emotion took over. He looked up at Charlie, who had remained motionless, waiting for his reaction.

'Bloody well done, Charlie. As I've always said, you're not just a pretty face' and McKay's voice cracked with a mixture of pleasure and relief.

'Thanks very much, Guv, I thought you might be pleased.'

'I think a little visit would be in order, don't you?' said McKay with a smile, placing the receipt and the statement carefully in his briefcase.

******

McKay and Charlie made their way through the now familiar cavern which housed the heating and filtration plant, until they arrived at the office.

Bob Forrester was on the phone.

They knocked and entered and he signalled for them to take a seat. He was ordering materials for his beloved swimming pool. Finishing his conversation, he put the phone down, placed the biro he was using in a holder and closed the file. Automatically he reached into one of his jacket pockets, produced a leather pouch and proceeded to roll a cigarette, saying 'Do you mind if I smoke?' Without waiting for an answer, he continued 'I much prefer these to tailor-mades. Old habits die hard, I suppose.'

He lit the cigarette, which seemed to consist more of paper than tobacco. It flared momentarily and white ash drifted through the air. Finally, he sat back and demanded cheerfully 'To what do I owe the honour of this visit, gentlemen?'

'We would just like you to clear up one or two points, if you don't mind' replied McKay, briskly.

'Certainly, only too pleased. Anything to help get this terrible business cleared up' replied Forrester, puffing hard on the misshapen cigarette, which continued to shed ash in all directions.

McKay produced from the briefcase the graph which he had shown to Mike Weston earlier and, placing it in front of Forrester, he asked 'What do you make of that?'

Forrester studied the graph for a few moments, looked up, and, in a surprised voice, answered 'Why it's a graph of that chart on the wall up there' indicating with his right hand 'It's one that Dick Williams always looked after.'

'That's right.'

'What are you doing with it?' his bushy eyebrows came together and his eyes looked from McKay to Charlie and back again 'It's bad enough us having to keep all these stupid charts; surely they don't expect us to start drawing graphs of them as well, do they?'

'No...no, nothing like that' assured McKay, quickly 'Just study the pattern of the graph and the dates more closely.'

Forrester's face showed slight annoyance and bewilderment, but he complied and studied the graph for much longer this time. There was silence in the room, while McKay and Charlie looked at each other patiently. After what seemed like ages, Forrester looked up from the graph and said slowly 'I see what you are getting at. It looks as if there was an extra session on one of the Fridays.'

'Do you recognise which Friday it was?' asked McKay, softly.

Then it dawned on Forrester. His eyes opened wide and the black bushy eyebrows shot upwards 'Yes...yes, it's the Friday that Fisher was murdered.' His voice was almost a whisper.

'Correct' agreed McKay 'I've checked and, as far as I can tell, there was no reason for an extra session on that day, Mr. Forrester. No testing or maintenance. Can you think of any reason for that extra session?'

Beads of sweat appeared on Forrester's thinning hairline, but he answered calmly enough 'None whatsoever. It's checked regularly, and Dick Williams kept the chart up to date religiously. Why? What are you trying to say?'

'Well, if it wasn't switched on during opening hours for the extra session, and, as it obviously wasn't used during the Caribbean Evening, then it could only have been used after the Caribbean Evening.' McKay paused and then ventured, meaningfully 'Possibly when Dave Fisher was in the water.'

'Why on earth should you think that?' replied Forrester, his face and neck reddening 'And what has all this got to do with me?' he added, angrily.

'Don't worry, Mr. Forrester' reassured McKay 'It's just police routine. We are double checking all those with a cast iron alibi for the night in question.'

'Well, my alibi has already been double checked. Tony Lopez saw me leave with the two Beckett girls and my wife confirmed the time I arrived home' replied Forrester, angrily.

'Yes, that checks out alright, at least the first part does.'

'What do you mean? It was one o'clock when I arrived home. The bar closed at midnight, we dried up the glasses and tidied up. Then I dropped the girls off on the way home.'

'Yes, you may have done all that, Mr. Forrester, but when we checked with your wife again, it appears that she only heard your chiming-clock strike once, as you came in.' McKay paused, before stating officiously 'You told her that it was one o'clock. She had no reason to doubt this but she didn't actually look at a watch to verify it.'

'So, what are you trying to say?' demanded Forrester.

'What I am trying to say, as you put it' replied McKay, calmly 'is that it could have been one o'clock - half past one - or even half past two. The clock would still only chime once.'

'That's only theory' replied Forrester, looking worried 'I'm telling you that it was one o'clock when I got in.'

McKay kept the pressure on, but changed tack, saying 'Alright, if you say so. Do you bet very much, Mr. Forrester?'

Forrester looked surprised, but answered calmly 'A little.'

'Our information is that you bet quite a lot.'

'Who told you that?' demanded Forrester, loosening his tie.

'We got it straight from the horse's mouth' said Charlie, not recognising the terrible pun.

'You mean …'

'Yes, from Pikey himself.'

'OK, so I like a bet. What's wrong with that?' He spread his hands expressively.

'Mr. Forrester, you have a young family and you are buying your own house. I believe that your wife doesn't work, so you must back quite a few winners?'

By now Forrester was very agitated and retorted 'If you've spoken to Pikey then you already know how many winners I back.' He paused and eventually blurted out 'Why the hell do you think I work for peanuts as a barman if it's not to make a little extra?'

McKay seized the opportunity he had been waiting for and came straight back 'Talking of working in the bar. How many times did Fisher come into the bar for a drink on the night he was murdered?'

Forrester thought for a moment before answering 'Three times, as far as I can remember.'

'And what did he drink?'

'His usual lager.'

'Anything else?'

'I think he may have had a whisky' replied Forrester, slowly.

McKay looked straight at him and asked in a very quiet voice 'Why did you pay for Fisher's drink that night?'

Forrester was visibly shaken this time and, with his thoughts racing, stammered 'Who...who said I did?'

'You were seen, that's all you need to know' replied McKay.

Forrester, who was white-faced by now, reached for the old tobacco pouch and with shaking hands tried to roll a cigarette. He raised it to his lips but his fingers were shaking so much that it came apart, spilling tobacco over the desk.

'This is the moment' thought McKay and he repeated, firmly 'Why did you pay for Fisher's drinks?'

'The bastard was blackmailing me' Forrester blurted out.

'Why?' demanded McKay.

'He caught me out one night when I didn't ring up a couple of rounds of drinks...well, everybody does it. I was a bit short that night...they only pay you a pittance, you know, and you have to make the money up somehow.' The words came tumbling out of Forrester, as he tried to justify his actions.

'So what did Fisher say about it?'

'He threatened to report me to the manager, unless I saw him alright for the odd drink.' He shrugged his shoulders and spread his hands out, saying 'Naturally I agreed - what else could I do? But I should have known that he wouldn't be satisfied with the odd drink. He started asking for whisky as well as lager. As you know, he was always short of money. In the end, I had to make the money up myself. I was sure that Tony Lopez was suspicious and watching me.'

'Get to the Caribbean Evening.'

Forrester swallowed hard and said 'By the end of that evening, he'd had a couple of whiskies as well as his usual lager, and I had worked for practically nothing.'

McKay decided to put words in his mouth 'So you decided to come back and have it out with him?'

Forrester remained silent looking down at his desk. He casually reached forward and took a letter opener shaped like a dagger, from a pot containing pencils and pens. It was one of those ornate black and gold-handled souvenirs which tourists bring back from Spain. McKay cursed himself for not noticing it before and looked at Charlie anxiously.

Forrester, gazing into space, proceeded to drum absent-mindedly on the desk top with the letter opener. McKay noticed the strong fingers with black hair growing on their backs and also on his hands. Suddenly one sentence in the pathologist's report on the death of Dick Williams flashed through his mind 'Manual strangulation by someone with exceptionally strong hands.'

McKay stared at the hands 'Could these be the hands?' he wondered.

There was silence in the room, except for the sounds of tapping and Forrester's rapid breathing. He continued to gaze at the paper knife and the marks it was making on the desk top. After what seemed like ages, he stopped drumming, looked up at McKay and answered his question.

'You're right, I did go back that night, but only to plead with Fisher to let me off the hook' he added quickly.

'Go on' pressed McKay.

'What happened was a pure accident' he blurted the words out, as if they had been bottled up for so long that he was glad to release them.

'I think you had better let me be the judge of that. Alright, so it was an accident. What happened next?'

'He was still there drinking, when I returned. I pleaded with him, but he just laughed. Things got a bit heated and he stood up suddenly, overbalanced and fell into the pool.'

'At the deep part, I take it?'

'Yes, but he was a good swimmer and I'm not. I think he must have swallowed quite a lot of water when he fell in. He was floundering around and appeared to be choking.'

'So you decided to help him with the safety pole?'

'How did you know that?' replied Forrester in amazement.

'Never mind, just go on.'

'Well, I tried to help him with the pole but he had taken in so much water in his drunken state that in no time at all he had disappeared under the surface.'

'So what did you do then?'

'I must admit I panicked a bit - I put the pole back on the wall and got out as fast as I could...it was accidental and that's the truth.'

'It's partly the truth' corrected McKay 'But you've conveniently missed out one or two very important details.'

'Such as?' retorted Forrester, confidently.

'He may have fallen in the pool, as you say, but I put it to you' said McKay 'that as he struggled for his life, instead of helping him, you realised that here was a golden opportunity to solve all your problems.'

'No...no...that's not true.'

'So, instead of helping him, you made things worse by switching on the wave-making machine and that would account for the extra session shown on this graph.'

McKay stabbed a finger on the graph which he had earlier placed in front of Forrester.

'No, I tried to help him' insisted Forrester loudly, looking flustered and red- faced, with perspiration dripping off his chin.

'I believe that you used the pole, but not to help him. You used it as a weapon. You smashed the metal ring on the end of the pole down on to his head several times. And then you forced him under the surface with it, as he struggled for his life in the waves. The injuries to his head and the broken finger and thumb which he sustained, whilst trying to protect himself from the blows, prove it.'

'It doesn't prove anything' sneered Forrester, desperately. 'It's all supposition. I didn't kill him.' He paused, his eyes moving quickly from side to side, as if searching for help. McKay and Charlie remained silent, waiting patiently.

Finally, as if striking back, his eyes stopped and fixed on McKay and, with his voice a pitch higher, he shouted 'You should be looking for the person who killed my mate Dick Williams - he's the murderer.'

'I quite agree, Forrester, and I don't have to look very far do I?'

'What do you mean by that?'

McKay nodded to Charlie who placed in front of Forrester a single statement sheet. He picked it up and recognised it immediately saying 'It's my statement about the day Dick Williams died. I didn't leave the Centre all day.'

'That's not what it says here' said Charlie, sliding across the desk the receipt which had so pleased McKay earlier. The colour drained from Forrester's face. He had recognised the receipt before he picked it up. It was a copy of one of Tommy Pike's betting slips.

But it was more than that. It was a copy of a bet Forrester had placed on the day that Dick Williams had been strangled and Forrester realised that, apart from the date on the slip, it contained something more important to bookmaker and punter alike - it showed the exact time that the bet was accepted, because each betting slip is clock-stamped accurately to the second.

Without looking, Forrester knew that the time on the slip was 12.15 pm and he also knew that he had been trapped. Trapped by his one weakness, the obsession that kept him short of money. Betting. The obsession which had led to the death of Dave Fisher and his mate, Dick Williams.

Suddenly, and without warning, he leapt to his feet and raised the paper knife aloft in a threatening position, his eyes blazed wildly and his face was distorted with anger.

'Bloody hell' thought Charlie 'Here we go again.'

McKay didn't stop to think, but he jumped up and swung his chair in front of him for protection, as Forrester hurled the paper knife with all his strength. His aim was good, and with a loud thud the knife pinned the statement and the betting slip to the desk top. Then he collapsed, sobbing with frustration, with his huge hands completely covering his face. McKay heaved a sigh of relief and lowered the chair to the floor.

Charlie's heartbeats continued to pound in his ears as he stared at the paper knife still vibrating on the desk top. 'Christ, I'm getting too old for this lark' he thought, as he moved around behind Forrester.

McKay had one more question 'Why kill your mate Dick Williams?' Forrester looked up through tears streaming down his face and answered contemptuously 'He was the clever one - too bloody clever. On the one day that he came in to see us after his accident, he looked at that chart and it took him about two minutes to realise that the wave machine had been used that night. Two minutes and it took you thick bastards bloody weeks. He said he was going to speak to you about it.' He shook his head 'I just couldn't let that happen.'

McKay smiled, looked at Charlie, and said 'Well, we may not be so clever, but we get there in the end.'

Forrester made one last plea 'Dave Fisher's death - it really was an accident, you know.'

'Save it' said McKay, closing his briefcase with a snap.

'Save it for the judge.'